GRUMP

## READ ALL OF LIESL SHURTLIFF'S (FAIRLY) TRUE TALES

*Rump: The (Fairly) True Tale of Rumpelstiltskin*

*Jack: The (Fairly) True Tale of Jack and the Beanstalk*

*Red: The (Fairly) True Tale of Red Riding Hood*

*Grump: The (Fairly) True Tale of Snow White and the Seven Dwarves*

# THE (FAIRLY) TRUE TALE OF SNOW WHITE AND THE SEVEN DWARVES

LIESL SHURTLIFF

A YEARLING BOOK

This is a work of fiction. Names, characters, places, and incidents either are the product of the author's imagination or are used fictitiously. Any resemblance to actual persons, living or dead, events, or locales is entirely coincidental.

 Published in the United States by Yearling, an imprint of Random House Children's Books, a division of Penguin Random House LLC, New York. Originally published in hardcover in the United States by Alfred A. Knopf, an imprint of Random House Children's Books, New York, in 2018.

Yearling and the jumping horse design are registered trademarks of Penguin Random House LLC.

Visit us on the Web! rhcbooks.com

Educators and librarians, for a variety of teaching tools, visit us at RHTeachersLibrarians.com

Library of Congress Cataloging-in-Publication Data is available upon request.

ISBN 978-1-5247-1704-9 (pbk.)

Printed in the United States of America
10 9 8 7 6 5 4 3 2 1
First Yearling Edition 2019

Random House Children's Books supports the First Amendment and celebrates the right to read.

For my seven siblings. We are a crazy crew and I wouldn't want any other.

# CONTENTS

GRUMP

# CHAPTER ONE

## Odd Little Dwarfling

I was born just feet from the surface of the earth, completely unheard of for a dwarf, but it couldn't be helped. Most dwarves are born deep underground, at least a mile below The Surface, preferably in a cavern filled with crystals and gems: diamonds for strength, emeralds for wisdom, and sapphires for truth.

Mothers and fathers try to feed their dwarflings as many healthy powerful gems as they can within a few hours of birth, to give them the best chance in life. But I was fed none.

My parents had been traveling downward the day I was born. Mother could feel me turning hard inside her belly, a sign that the time was drawing near. She wanted the very best for me. She wanted to be as deep in the earth as possible, in the birthing caverns, with their rich deposits of nutritious crystals and gems. But as my parents traveled downward, before they had even descended below the main cavern, there was a sudden collapse in one of the tunnels. The rocks nearly crushed my mother, and me with her. My father was able to get us out of the way just in time.

Unfortunately, the collapse had blocked the tunnel, so we had to go up to find another way down. The strain of the climb was too much for my poor mother.

"Rubald!" she cried, clutching her belly. "It's time!"

And there was no time to waste. A dwarfling can stay inside its mother's belly for a solid decade or more, but when we're ready to come out, we come fast.

And so I was born in a cavern mere feet below the earth's surface, where roots dangled from the ceiling, water trickled down the walls, and the only available food was a salty gruel called *strolg,* made out of common rocks and minerals. Mother was devastated.

"My poor little dwarfling!" she cooed as she spooned the strolg into my mouth, then fed me a few pebbles to satisfy my need to bite and crunch. "What kind of life will he have, Rubald?"

"A fine life, Rumelda," said my father, ever the optimist. "A happy life."

"And what will we call him?"

My parents both looked at their surroundings. Dwarves are usually named with some regard to the gems and crystals within the cavern in which they are born, but there were no diamonds or sapphires in that cavern. Not even quartz or marble. Just plain rocks and roots.

Father brushed his hands over the rough walls, studying the layers of dirt and minerals. "Borlen," he said with wonder.

Borlen was a mineral found only near The Surface. It was not so common in our colony but useful when it could be found. It was too bitter to eat, but potters liked it because it made their clay more malleable without weakening it. Borlen could also serve as a warning. A mining crew knew by the sight of it that they were digging dangerously close to The Surface. Most dwarves would rather not find any.

"We'll call him Borlen," said Father.

"You don't think that name will make him seem a bit . . . odd?" Mother asked.

"No, it's special," said Father. "He'll be one of a kind, our dwarfling. We'll get him deep into the earth as soon as possible and feed him all the best crystals and gems. But wait!" My father pulled something from his pocket and held it out to my mother. "I almost forgot. I've been saving this from the moment I knew we had a dwarfling on the way."

Mother gasped. "A ruby!"

Rubies were rare and particularly powerful gems. They could ward off evil, enhance powers, and even lengthen lives. Emegert of Tunnel 588 was said to have found a large deposit of rubies, and he lived for ten thousand years. Two thousand years was considered a good long life for a dwarf.

Mother took the ruby from my father and dropped it onto my tongue. I crunched on the gem, gave a little belch, and fell asleep.

The very next day, my parents tried to move me to deeper caverns, but as soon as they started to carry me downward, I began to cry. The deeper we went, the louder I wailed, until my eyes leaked tears of dust, a sign of deep distress and discomfort from any dwarf.

"Oh dear," said Mother. "Rubald, I think our dwarfling is afraid of depths!"

"Nonsense," said Father. "He only needs to adjust."

But I did not adjust. I cried for hours on end. My parents tried everything to console me. They fed me amber, amethyst, and blue-laced agate. They bathed me in crushed rose quartz and hung peridot above my cradle, all to no avail. And so, distraught from my endless wails, and desperate to try anything, my parents took me back to the cavern near The Surface where I was born.

I stopped crying.

"Oh dear," said Mother.

"How odd," said Father.

And after that, my parents were obliged to make my unfortunate birthing cavern our home, hoping my fear of depths would subside eventually. But it didn't. It only got worse.

For years, my parents worked to get me used to depths. Father tried to lead me a little deeper each day, luring me with my favorite gems and the different sights and wonders of the colony—the lava rivers, the blue springs, the dragon hatchery, the potters and glassblowers and goldsmiths. But no matter how interesting the surroundings, no matter how many sapphires and rubies he offered, my depth symptoms would always overpower me. I'd start to get dizzy, then I'd feel like I was shrinking and shriveling, and we'd have to go back home.

It was shameful enough that I was afraid of depths, but that wasn't the worst of it. As much as I hated going downward, I was equally drawn to going upward. My first word was "up," much to my parents' chagrin, and as soon as I understood that there was an actual world above us, I wanted to know everything about it. I pestered my parents with questions. What did The Surface look like? How was it different from our caves? Did any dwarves live up there? Why didn't *we* live up there? Could we go there?

My parents knew next to nothing about The Surface. Neither of them had seen it, nor did they have any desire to. Mother usually sidestepped my questions or changed the subject, but Father indulged my curiosity. He took me to the colony's records room—a vast cavern filled with many millennia of our history and collective knowledge engraved on stone tablets and slates. Normally, I wouldn't have tolerated the depths of the cavern, but my thirst for information overcame my fear. I scoured the records for any facts I could find about The Surface. I learned it was a big, open place with an endless blue ceiling called the *sky*, and a big golden ball suspended in the sky called the *sun*. There were things that grew on The Surface that didn't grow underground. Things called *trees* and *flowers* and *bushes.* There were strange beasts that roamed The Surface—*horses, bears,* and *wolves.* But the most fascinating of all were the *humans.*

According to the records, humans were dwarflike creatures, but not really dwarves at all. They could grow three times the height of a dwarf but no wider. They were born without teeth, and they lived no more than a single century. They couldn't eat gems but, instead, wore them around their necks, on their fingers and wrists, and sometimes even on their heads. I imagined a giant, skinny dwarf with no teeth, wearing my dinner as a hat. I laughed at the thought. I definitely had to see that spectacle!

Because we lived so near The Surface, sometimes gnomes would find their way into our cavern and bring us news from the human world. Gnomes were creatures who lived underground like dwarves but delivered messages for humans on The Surface. They were about the same size as dwarves or a little smaller, but they were extremely stupid, probably because they only ate rubble. Still, I loved it when gnomes appeared, because they always brought some fascinating information from the humans.

"King Gerald has been crowned! Long live the king!"

"Queen Eleanor has borne a daughter. Long live Princess Snow White!"

"Queen Eleanor has died!"

Mother hated the gnomes and always chased them out of our cavern with her iron cooking spoon, but they always came back, and I was always eager to hear their news. With each little nugget of information about The

Surface that I mined and collected, my heart seemed to beat a little louder.

*Up-up, up-up, up-up.*

One day, when I was no more than twenty, Father brought me a *leaf* he'd found on his way home from the mine. He said it must have been carried into our caverns by a bat. The leaf was bright green, like an emerald. Curious, I took a nibble of one of the corners. *Blech.* It tasted as bad as emeralds, too. Like bat droppings.

But I loved the leaf. I kept it for almost a year, watching it turn brown and brittle before it finally crumbled to bits. I begged my parents to let me go to The Surface and find another, but they flatly refused. I could get lost. I could get trampled by a Surface beast. Worst of all, I could run into a human.

"But I *want* to see a human!" I told my parents.

"Really?" said Mother. "And what if the human takes you by the beard, hmmm?"

I gasped and put my hands up to my beard. A male dwarf's beard is very important to him. It's the source of his power, and it grows as his powers grow. But it's also his greatest vulnerability. If anyone grabs him by the beard, he is at the grabber's mercy and obligated to fulfill a request. If he tries to resist, he will experience the severest pain, and possibly death. I've never heard of a dwarf taking another dwarf by the beard. It's an offense worthy of banishment. But there were plenty of stories of humans taking dwarves by the beard, and they weren't the happily-ever-after sort of stories. It was the one thing my parents could mention that gave me pause about going to The Surface.

"But my beard isn't *that* long," I said. At twenty-one, I had only a short, pointy tuft, hardly long enough to grab at all. "It'd be less of a risk now, wouldn't it, than when my beard is longer and easier to grab?"

My parents shared a look, the one that said they didn't know quite what to do with me. "Here, try these on." Mother tossed me a pair of bat-hair trousers she'd been weaving for me. I wiggled into them. "How do they feel?"

The trousers felt a little itchy, but the bat hair would eventually soften and become quite comfortable, and they'd last at least a century, so long as I didn't grow too much. "They're fine. What do you think a human would ask me to do if they *did* take me by the beard?" I asked. I wouldn't be distracted.

"Oh, all sorts of horrible things, I expect," said Mother. "Maybe dance on hot coals for a year."

I winced. "Could be worse," I said.

"Yes," said Father. "They could command you to mine every ruby out of the earth and give them all to the humans. You wouldn't be able to eat a single one."

I gave an audible gasp. To mine all the rubies under the earth but not be able to eat one seemed a torture beyond anyone's capacity to bear.

"That's right," said Mother, smiling. "So you be sure to keep your beard underground, safe and sound with us."

That night, Mother tucked me into my little alcove with a heavy slab of granite over my chest to press me to sleep. She placed purple crystals all around my head to ward off nightmares. "We shouldn't be frightening you with such talk about those vile humans. Try to put it out of your mind."

But I couldn't. I'm sure my parents thought they were doing their job well, but, in truth, their stories and warnings only made me all the more determined.

As I lay in the dark and quiet, I took hold of my beard and promised myself that someday I would escape to The Surface.

I felt a buzzing that tickled my chin and shimmied through my whole being, and I knew I had invoked some kind of magic upon myself. I was going to see all the strange, growing things. I'd gaze at the sky and feel the warmth of the sun. I'd find another leaf, or maybe even two! And I'd spy on the strange humans who wore our food on their heads, and see the ugly human babies born without teeth.

My wish would come true. I knew it. If only I'd known that getting your wish comes with its own load of rubble.

# CHAPTER TWO

## Shattered Hopes

"Come down, Borlen."

"Nnnno!"

"Borlen! You're acting like a spoiled little twenty-year-old! Now come down!"

I was fifty-one now, still considered a dwarfling, yet far too old to be hiding from my mother or throwing tantrums, but I didn't care. "I won't!" I clung to the top of the column. Mother was trying to take me down to the nursery mines again. She said I had to go at least once a month. But she couldn't make me. I'd stay here all day and night if I had to. Even longer. I had stuffed my pockets full of limestone this morning so I wouldn't have to come down for food.

Mother pulled her kitchen ax from her apron. "If you don't come down this instant, I'm going to chop down this column and chain you for six months!"

I gasped. Chaining was reserved for simpletons too

dim-witted to avoid falling into the lava rivers. Or for an odd dwarfling like me who tried to escape to The Surface on a regular basis. Last year, I tried to dig my own tunnel to The Surface right from our cavern, but Mother caught me before I had dug a dwarf-length. After that, Father sealed our cavern with a solid gem plaster, and Mother chained me for a month so I couldn't move five feet from her. I was the laughingstock of the colony. I didn't wish to repeat the experience.

"Fizznugget," I grumbled. Reluctantly I slid down the column.

"That's better. Now come on." Mother snatched my hand and pulled me after her. "You're going to make friends today."

"No, I'm not," I muttered. Despite Mother's considerable efforts, I hadn't made a single friend in my five decades of visits to the nursery mines. I didn't see why today would be any different.

We descended a narrow staircase. Each step increased my dizziness. I tried to keep my mind off the depths by counting all the tunnels and caverns, reviewing where they led, how they connected, which ones went up, which ones went down. Which ones I hadn't yet explored for a possible escape to The Surface.

I probably knew the colony as well as any ancient dwarf—the upper tunnels, at least. I'd memorized every inch of our caverns, which tunnels intersected, which ones led to dead ends or sharp drop-offs. I kept track of the collapses that had blocked old tunnels and of the crews that dug new ones. But I still hadn't found any means of escape.

"Come on." Mother tugged on my arm. "We're almost there." We came to a steep, spiraling descent, at least a hundred feet down, that led to the nursery mines. I immediately grew nauseous. I tried to turn back, but Mother snatched me up and placed me on her lap. We slid down and around, down and around. It was probably no more than five seconds, but it felt like five hours. My head was pounding, my heart racing, my palms sweating. Finally we landed in a pile of fine dust.

"Here we are!" said Mother, standing up and dusting herself off first, then me.

The nursery mines were a network of tunnels and caves, made especially for dwarflings. There were stalactites and stalagmites and sparkling mineral columns for younger dwarflings to climb and teethe upon. Older dwarflings played Dig for Diamonds and Pebble, Pebble, Geode and Spitzeroff, which was my favorite rock-tossing game, but I couldn't play it down here, not with my headaches and dizziness.

I usually stayed huddled in a corner, whimpering. Sometimes Mother forced me to go join a game of Pebble, Pebble, Geode, but I would just sit there the entire time, curled up into myself and completely ignored by the other dwarflings as they ran circles around me. I made a good pebble, I suppose.

This time, instead of joining the others, I veered down the tunnel that led to the dragon hatchery, with my mother close behind. It was the only place in the nursery mines where I felt the slightest bit comfortable.

The dragon eggs were kept in a warm, dark cavern.

The burning coals surrounding the eggs were the only source of light, casting a weak glow. The eggshells were speckled gray, like polished granite. A few newly hatched dragons lay sprawled on the table, their thick eggshells in pieces around them. I scooped up a handful of coal and tossed bits of it to the baby dragons, and they snatched them up deftly with their sharp little teeth. They puffed smoke from their nostrils as the coal fed the tiny flames in their bellies. When the dragons were full grown, their big flames would help turn the rubble into diamonds and other gems, and ward off unwanted creatures from our caverns—Surface beasts and humans who feared the dragons would eat them alive. But, really, dragons weren't dangerous. They'd never eat another living creature. They mostly ate coal, and only grew agitated if they were cold or the light was too bright. Dragons preferred heat and darkness. I used to want one as a pet, but Mother said no. They grew too quickly and ate too much. Besides, dwarves didn't have pets. They had the dwarf colony: their mining crews, their friends, and their families.

"All right, enough dragon time," said Mother. "Let's go play with some real dwarves now."

"I'd rather stay here," I said. I picked up one of the baby dragons. He crawled onto my neck and puffed hot steam, which tickled my face.

"Borlen, you're a big dwarfling now," said Mother. "You need to make some friends."

"What if no one wants to be my friend?" I asked.

She ignored me. "And you must get used to the depths by the time you receive your summons."

"What if I don't want to receive my summons?"

Mother sighed and shook her head. "Don't be ridiculous, Borlen."

My parents tolerated my obsession with The Surface to a point, but the thought that any dwarf might not be thrilled with the idea of mining with a crew was completely beyond their comprehension. Most dwarves couldn't wait to receive their summons. And yet, I felt my chest collapse at the thought.

"Come on." Mother pulled the baby dragon off me and dragged me back into the caverns where all the dwarflings were playing. She pulled out a sack of gems—some pink crystal chips and fingerling sapphires—and offered the sack of treats to any dwarflings who passed by. Bribery.

"My son would just love to play a game of Spitzeroff. Won't you let him join you? He's very good!"

Most everyone ignored Mother. A few accepted the treats and then ran away, giggling. No one asked me to play with them. No one ever did. They didn't want to be associated with the odd dwarfling who was obsessed with The Surface. But Mother kept trying.

"Need another member on your crew?" Mother persisted. "Borlen would make a wonderful Fifth . . . or Sixth! Whatever you need. He's a very agreeable fellow!"

I wrapped my arms around my middle and hung my head. "Mother, please stop," I grumbled.

"He can play with us," someone said. I looked up to see an older dwarfling at the head of a small group. I'd seen him in the nursery mines on occasion, though he'd never paid any attention to me. He was much older than me, nearly a full-wise dwarf, with a thick ginger beard already a few inches long. He must have been close to receiving his summons. "I'm Rudger." He took one of the sapphires and gnawed on it as he spoke. "We're playing Dig for Diamonds, and you can be on our crew."

"There, now. Isn't that nice?" Mother smiled down at me. I didn't move.

"You'll be just right for the job," said Rudger. "Won't he, crew?" The other dwarflings nodded vigorously.

I hesitated. I could barely move. My head felt like it was being crushed between two boulders, but I also felt something else—a kind of spark in my chest. Rudger said they needed me. The idea that my presence might have some importance, some essential purpose to others, was like a silver string being threaded through my heart, pulling at me.

I stood up on shaky legs and hobbled toward them.

"Very good," said Rudger. He snatched a few more sapphires and followed behind me.

"I'm the Foredwarf. I'm quite expert-ienced."

I knew he meant *experienced,* but I thought it would be rude to correct him.

"And this is my crew." Rudger gestured to a handful of dwarflings with play axes and shovels. I counted them off. Six. I looked to Rudger, confused. A full crew consisted of six members, including the Foredwarf. Rudger grinned, showing big white teeth with shards of sapphire stuck between them. "You get to be the Seventh," he said.

My heart crumbled like a dry lump of dirt. There were only two reasons a dwarf would be summoned to a crew as a Seventh—because you were a troublemaker or an idiot. Either way, you were treated like rubble. Any member of the crew could give the Seventh orders, and the Seventh was obliged to carry out the most awful and menial tasks.

I looked back at my mother, ready to run into her arms and make her carry me home, but her smile was so big and proud, I didn't have the heart to go back to her without at least trying.

"Okay," I said. "I'll be the Seventh."

"Excellent," said Rudger.

For the next hour, I was ordered about by six dwarflings, half of them younger than me.

"Here, Seventh, take out the rubble."

"Seventh, polish my ax."

"You're not digging fast enough, Seventh!"

Play felt an awful lot like work.

Finally, Rudger tired of Dig for Diamonds, and we played Pebble, Pebble, Geode. I was always a pebble and never a geode.

Then we moved on to Spitzeroff. Surely I'd gain their respect now, especially when they saw how good my aim was. I could knock over two towers at once from fifty feet away. But Rudger and the others never even let me toss the rocks.

"Someone has to pick them up," said Rudger. "That's your duty, Seventh. It's very impertinent."

"You mean *important*," I grumbled.

The others tossed their rocks, dancing a jig each time they knocked over a tower. I had to rebuild the towers and take the other dwarflings' stones back to them. I bore it all with as much patience as I could, right up until Rudger threw a rock while I was still stacking a tower. It hit me right in the fizzy-bone—that place on the elbow that fizzes and burns when you hit it wrong. I grimaced and hopped around, knocking over the tower.

"Sorry about that," said Rudger. "You blend in with the rubble." The other dwarflings keeled over laughing.

My anger erupted like a volcano. I scooped up the pile of stones and threw them as hard as I could. I hit one dwarfling in the chin, another in the chest. I saved Rudger for last. I hit him right in the forehead.

Rudger grasped his forehead and started rolling on the ground, moaning. I knew he was pretending. Dwarves were so tough, we could get hit with a dozen stones twice as big and hard as the ones I'd thrown and not get a scratch. But that didn't matter—I'd wounded his pride more than his forehead.

"Borlen!" Mother shouted.

"What a temper!" said one of the mothers. "You ought not to bring him here if he can't control himself."

"Borlen, come here this instant!"

My chin trembled, and the cavern blurred. I ran out of the nursery. Mother called after me, but I didn't stop. I ran up the winding tunnels as high as I could go. I crawled in a shallow little cave to sulk while I crushed pebbles in my hands. Mother found me not long after.

"I'm not going back down there," I grumbled.

"You don't have to," she said gently.

"I'm not going to be on a crew, either."

"You don't have to worry about that for a few decades," said Mother.

"And I'm going to live on The Surface," I said. "Away from everyone."

Mother sighed. "Come on out now, Borlen. Let's go home."

I was inching out of my hiding spot when I heard a little squeak. I searched for the source of the sound and discovered a dark little lump that twitched.

It was a bat—a baby, I guessed by his size. I scooped him up in my hands. He squeaked pitifully.

My heart ached for the lonely little creature. There was no one to care for him. I showed him to Mother. He was tiny, no bigger than my palm, with a soft furry head and thin little wings wrapped around his warm body. He kept his eyes squeezed shut, and trembled with fright.

"Can I keep him?" I asked.

"He looks like a runt," said Mother. "He probably won't live long."

"Please?"

If things had gone differently in the nursery mines that day, if I had made any friends, I believe she would have said no, but perhaps she thought my having a pet bat was better than nothing at all.

"You'll have to find food for him," she said. "Bugs, I think. Bats don't eat rocks."

"I'll find some," I said.

We went home, and I felt more content than I had

in a long while. Mother and Father worried that my bat would keep us up all night, seeing as bats were nocturnal, but after I fed him a supper of rock mites and spiders, he crawled inside my shirt and curled up into a ball, a soft warm lump against my chest.

"He's an odd bat," I said. "Just like I'm an odd dwarfling."

Mother gave a sad smile.

I named him Leaf, because his soft webbed wings reminded me of the leaf Father had brought me.

My parents hoped that Leaf would be just the distraction to keep my mind off The Surface, and for a time, he was. In the beginning, he needed a lot of feeding, and I had to search for bugs almost constantly to keep him from crying. As he grew stronger, his company consoled me. I loved how he perched on my shoulder and flapped his leathery wings in my face when he was upset or excited. I taught him how to hang upside down and then to fly. Before long, we were racing each other up and down the tunnels.

But, after a time, my attention was again drawn upward. I went back to my Surface hunts, and Leaf aided me in my quest. I drove my mother to madness, escaping our cavern, searching for a Surface hole, or attempting to dig my own. She chained me regularly. She begged and pleaded for me to stop. I didn't. I couldn't, but I underestimated the pains it gave my mother, the constant watching and worrying. Eventually, it became too much for her to bear.

One day, I woke to find my parents sitting solemnly at the table, cups of steaming strolg and a tablet between them.

"Good morning," I said. I poured my own strolg and popped a few pink crystals into my mouth. I hummed while I crunched, thinking of which tunnels Leaf and I would explore today. We'd found a promising one with a steep-rising shaft that might lead to The Surface, if it wasn't too steep or narrow.

"Borlen, dear," Mother said. "Sit down."

"No thank you," I said politely. They were always telling me to sit down, slide down, go down, down, down. Staying upright was my quiet act of defiance, more difficult to punish than outright disobedience. This morning, however, my parents' patience was thin.

"Sit, Borlen!" Father snapped. "We have news."

My crunching slowed as I noticed their expressions. Mother was fidgety and seemed anxious. Father sat rigid, clutching his cup of strolg so tightly I thought it might break. I sat.

"What's wrong?" I said. "Has something happened?"

Maybe there had been a collapse or someone had died. Maybe both. My grandmother Peridoti and my great-grandfather Nuum still worked in the mines. Both were over a thousand years old. But nothing could have prepared me for what my parents told me.

"Nothing is wrong," said Mother. "You've received your summons. You've been assigned to a crew."

I looked more closely at the tablet on the table. It was a golden tablet. Crew summons were always made on golden tablets.

"But . . . I'm not old enough. Neither of you joined a crew until you were almost a hundred. You said yourself it would be at least two decades, maybe three."

"Exceptions can be made," said Father. "For exceptional circumstances."

I looked between my parents. Understanding suddenly crashed down on me like a boulder. "You did this, didn't you? You *made* them summon me!"

"Borlen, dear," said Mother, "it's time for you to be among other dwarves, working in the mines."

"But I don't want to work in the mines," I said.

"I've already told the First Foredwarf," said Father, ignoring me. "You'll be getting your ax and Fate Stone at the crew ceremony. It's tomorrow."

Tomorrow! The room started to spin.

"What tunnel?" I asked. "What tunnel have I been assigned to?"

Father and Mother glanced at each other before Father finally said, "Tunnel 896."

I opened my mouth but couldn't speak. My airways seemed to be blocked. It felt like my whole chest caved in as my heart shrank to the size of a pebble.

*Eight hundred ninety-six?* That was a base tunnel! In the deepest depths! I wouldn't last a day. I felt dizzy already.

"It's an honor," said Mother. "Many dwarves only dream of working on such a distinguished crew."

My suspicions deepened. "Then why would they choose *me?*" I said. It was well known in the colony that I had a fear of depths. The Foredwarf of this crew must have known I would be utterly useless.

"Well," said Father. "The Foredwarf said he could use a Seventh, so . . ."

I gasped. "A *Seventh?*"

Memories of Rudger and the nursery mines came flooding back. Mother must have read my mind.

"He really seems a kind Foredwarf, Borlen," said Mother. "Very cheerful. I'm sure you'll be quite . . . content on his crew. Let's have a nice celebratory breakfast, shall we? You're a full-wise dwarf now."

I slumped in my chair. My parents crunched their breakfast and chattered on about how proud they were, how wonderful it would be. I couldn't eat. I just sat there, thinking how my life had disintegrated in a matter of moments. The shock of what had just happened started to wear off and anger set in.

"I'm not doing it," I said.

Mother's smiled vanished. "What?"

"I'm not joining a crew. I'm not going to be a Seventh."

"Don't be ridiculous," said Mother. "Of course you will. No dwarf refuses a position on a crew. Have some more sapphires." Mother tried to dish me up some of the roasted sapphires, but I slapped my plate away. It fell to the floor and broke into several pieces.

"You didn't even ask me!" I shouted. "You went behind my back and planned my entire life without even talking to me!"

Mother stared down at my broken plate. Father spoke quietly, but his voice rumbled like a cave before a giant collapse. "And how many times have you gone behind our backs, Borlen? How many times have you tried to go to The Surface? Do you understand the consequences of such a thing? You could be killed. You could be taken by the beard. You could be *banished.*"

"I won't go to The Surface," I said. "I promise I won't try to escape again, just don't send me to the depths! You know how ill it makes me." I was whining now, like a little twenty-year-old dwarfling, but I didn't care. I was desperate.

"That's enough, Borlen," said Father. "You've been spoiled. And it's my fault. I've indulged this nonsense for far too long. I believed you would grow out of it, but now I see I've only encouraged your bad behavior. You're a dwarf. It's high time you started acting like one."

"But–"

"We will not discuss it further," said Father, his usually cheerful face now stony and cold.

I looked to Mother, pleading with my whole soul, but she shook her head. "It's for the best, Borlen." She bent down and began to pick up the pieces of my shattered dish.

I did not have the strength to pick up the pieces of my shattered hopes.

# CHAPTER THREE

## Smoke and Mirror

The crew ceremony took place in the main cavern, the largest cavern in all the colony, hundreds of times larger than our home in both width and height. It was difficult to believe there could be any space in the world bigger than this, though I'd read that The Surface was endless. I couldn't imagine. I wanted to see it with my own eyes.

An enormous copper pendulum hung from the cavern's domed ceiling. It arced gracefully back and forth over our heads, marking the earth's rotation, our days and months and years underground.

Glowing rivers of lava in deep trenches below made the air hot and sulfurous. Above and all around floated hundreds of glimmering, pulsing orbs—glowfish. Glowfish were small fireball creatures who lived in the lava rivers, but when we fished them out, they'd float all over the colony to light our tunnels and caverns. When they started to lose their glow, they'd drift back to the lava river to rekindle their light, and then we'd fish them out again. One glowfish bobbed right in front of my face. The heat tickled my nose. I gave the glowfish a gentle nudge and it drifted away.

My attention was then drawn to the bustling activity around me. It seemed the entire colony had come to witness the ceremony and perhaps show off a few of their tricks. There were knife throwers who could juggle twelve blades at once and catch them in their teeth. A lava drinker downed a cup of lava in one gulp and burped up flames while smoke curled out of his ears.

There were Spitzeroff contests and dragon rides. Dwarflings squealed with delight as they rode around in circles on the backs of gentle dragons puffing smoke through their nostrils, the occasional flame streaming through their mouths.

Leaf poked his head out of my shirt to investigate all the noise and commotion. He squeaked his discontentment at having his peace and quiet interrupted.

"You didn't have to come," I said grumpily.

He squeaked further displeasure and tucked himself back into my shirt.

A puppeteer sat on a high ledge and dangled rock puppets from silver strings, terrorizing her audience with "The Tragedy of Beryl's Beard." It was a story as old as dwarves, one that my parents told me regularly in an effort to deter me from trying to escape to The Surface.

The legend goes that a dwarf named Beryl the Bushy-

Bearded attempted to make friends with the humans back when their existence first became known to us. He believed humans were similar to dwarves, even though they were so tall and strange-looking, and not nearly as intelligent or strong. Humans died very young, many at birth, the rest barely living a few decades before they fell to sickness or were devoured by wild beasts. Beryl attempted to help them—taught them how to light fires, make tools, and find shelter and even showed them a bit of magic for healing and protection. Still, Beryl was convinced that humans would die out within a few centuries.

He was wrong.

The humans survived, weak as they were. They continued to die early, and even began to fight among themselves and kill each other, but they could reproduce quickly, too, much faster than dwarves. Some had a dozen children in two decades or less. Their colonies grew and spread over The Surface. With each new generation of humans, Beryl tried to create good bonds between dwarves and humans. Peace and harmony had always been the way with dwarves.

But humans are not dwarves.

It was not long before a human king sought to take advantage of us. He learned of our mines and determined to get his greedy hands on our gems. At first he suggested trades. Wood, furs, and skins for our gems and stones. The trade agreement seemed strange to our colony. The skins and furs were certainly useful to dwarves, but what did the humans want the gems for if they couldn't eat them? Apparently, they were attracted to their shine and color. They used them for crowns and jewelry. They decorated their homes with crystal and silver. The more gems a human had, the more important they were considered in society. And this was when dwarves first learned about greed. It is not natural for a dwarf to be greedy, but it is very natural for humans. They'll take as much as they can and give as little as they can.

The humans wanted more and more gems, but they did not want to give us more skins or furs. They started to give us less. Not understanding humans' true nature, Beryl assumed they were struggling in their industries, so he was apt to be generous and not demand full payment. But the humans continued to give the dwarves less and less, and still demanded more and more. Then the king decided that the dwarves were taking advantage of *humans,* that the dwarves were living in *his* territory and owed him a tax. Beryl tried to reason with him, but the king only grew angrier, and in a fit of passion, he grabbed Beryl by the beard.

"You will give me all your treasure!" he demanded.

At this point in the story, all the male dwarves in the audience flinched and clutched at their beards. Even the females covered their smooth chins.

And so Beryl was obliged to give the human king all that he had—piles of diamonds and rubies and emeralds. Sapphires, and amethysts, and opals. Overcome with grief and shame, Beryl died on The Surface shortly thereafter, at the young age of two hundred and three.

After the tragic news of Beryl reached the colony, the dwarves retreated deeper into the tunnels and caverns.

And ever since, we have sealed ourselves off from The Surface, away from the treacherous humans, away from their greed and violence.

That was the legend, anyway. I always wondered how much of it was actually true.

The play ended. The audience applauded with sober appreciation. I moved on to the food.

All around the caverns were tables stacked with more food than I'd ever seen all at one time—garnet goulash, deviled devic, silver sandwiches, amber-stuffed agates, roasted sapphires, sliced geodes toasted on hot marble, and, best of all, a tower of ruby-dusted diamonds. I went straight for that table and popped one into my mouth. The flavor was exquisite. Sweet and tangy. I felt a surge of strength from the diamond and a slight buzz from the ruby dust. I ate three more of the ruby-dusted diamonds, and my nerves loosened a bit. Mother looked like she was about to object to my binge, but a look from Father quieted her. I was to be indulged tonight.

A moment later, a gong sounded. The crowd hushed as the First Foredwarf stood up from her stone chair. First Foredwarf Realga. I hadn't noticed her sitting there. She was so wrinkled and gray, she nearly blended in with the stone.

"My fellow dwarves," she said in a voice as deep and smooth as polished marble, which did not seem to fit her age. "Welcome to our celebration! I sense strength in you and much promise, and perhaps a bit of mischief." Her dark eyes twinkled as she looked at two dwarflings no older than thirty shoving agates and sapphires and other foods into their pockets. They froze when they saw Foredwarf Realga's eyes on them, and slowly put the gems back on the table.

The First Foredwarf continued. "Tonight we celebrate those who have been summoned to work on a crew. It is an honor to contribute to our colony, and I hope you will all do your work with pride and joy. Our colony has existed for many thousands of years. Our knowledge is vast, our wisdom is deep, and our power is strong, but we must never take this for granted. Knowledge can be forgotten. Wisdom can be misguided, and power taken away. Remember Beryl's beard!"

"Beryl's beard!" the crowd chorused. There was a moment of silence to reflect on the sad tale of Beryl. Several male dwarves still held their beards protectively. I took it as an opportunity to eat another ruby-crusted diamond. I received several sideways glances as I crunched. Mother hung her head in shame.

"And now it is time for the Bestowal of Axes and Fate Stones!" said Foredwarf Realga.

All the dwarves who were joining a crew for the first time lined up, and their parents and friends gathered on either side of us to watch. Most of the new recruits looked to be older than me by at least two decades. One had a bushy beard streaked with white that touched the middle of his chest. He looked well over a hundred. He must have been waiting till now for a particular mine and position.

The first dwarf stepped up to Foredwarf Realga. She

handed him an ax made of the finest, strongest dwarf steel, and then she gestured to the towering wall behind her, where we would all mine out our Fate Stones.

A Fate Stone is a kind of talisman or charm. It's supposed to be a protection and a guide for miners. It can symbolize both your strengths and your weaknesses. It is the first thing we mine out of the earth with our new axes, and we keep it with us at all times. You never eat it, and you show it only to other dwarves you truly trust. Father's Fate Stone is a pink topaz that he always keeps in his pocket. It's a symbol of everlasting hopefulness and optimism, which is probably why I've always felt like I might someday escape to The Surface. Mother's Fate Stone is an emerald that she carries in a pouch around her neck. It's a symbol of her heightened intuition and awareness, which is probably why I've never escaped to The Surface.

I hadn't dared to say it out loud, but I was hoping my Fate Stone would be a ruby. I couldn't imagine any other stone that would be right for me, though I might be severely tempted to eat it. What would be my fate then? I wondered.

The first dwarf readied his ax and swung at the wall. Rock and dust trickled down. He struck again, and a third time, until something shiny appeared. He chipped and scraped all around it until he was able to loose it from the rock. He held up his Fate Stone for everyone to see.

"Diamond!" he shouted, and everyone cheered. Diamonds were fairly common, but a good Fate Stone, symbolizing strength and clarity.

The second dwarf approached, received her ax, and

struck the wall. She found her Fate Stone on the fifth blow.

"Sapphire!" she called. Sapphires symbolized truth and wisdom.

The third dwarf got a pitifully dull piece of agate (I had no idea what that meant), poor fellow, and another got a hunk of rough-cut marble (creativity and productivity), which was nothing special, but certainly not nearly as bad as the agate. One dwarf struck the wall at least fifty times. The crowd began to mutter and whisper until he held up a polished crystal sphere that swirled with smoke. The crowd let out a collective gasp. A crystal ball! That meant this dwarf was a seer, a skill that was usually seen only once a millennium and was much valued in the colony. The First Foredwarf was a seer. Would this dwarf replace Realga when she died and her body turned into rocks and gems?

Another diamond, topaz, tourmaline, opal, emerald, and . . . ruby! A large, deep crimson ruby went to a female with a long silver braid. She held it proudly in her strong hands.

It seemed five hundred years that I waited in line, and then, when I finally got to the front, it was only seconds before my turn, and I didn't feel ready.

I approached with bated breath. I had never been so close to Foredwarf Realga, had never seen the details of her ancient features. She was very dignified, with hair whiter than bones, and dark, leathery skin. Mother said Foredwarf Realga was over two thousand years old.

The chair she sat upon was even older, as old as time,

carved out of the very first stone the earth formed. But the words carved at the top of the chair were inscribed later, after we closed ourselves off from The Surface and the humans.

WE'LL BEAR NO TYRANT, SUFFER NO FOOL
THE FAIREST OF ALL IS THE ONE WHO WILL RULE

First Foredwarf Realga had demonstrated, through her centuries and millennia of life, that she truly was the wisest and fairest of all. I wondered how she judged me. Could she see inside my mind? Did she know what it was that I wanted? What I needed?

She handed me my ax made of fine steel, sharp and sturdy, forged by the best smiths. I gripped it in both hands, trying to become familiar with the tool that would remain with me at all times, for the rest of my life.

Foredwarf Realga then motioned toward the wall. It was covered with jagged cuts and grooves from all those who had dug before me. How had they known where to dig? I thought I would feel something, a pulse, a pull, a buzz, but there was nothing. Just the solid stone before me. I lifted my ax and swung. Dust and pebbles rained down on me. I swung again and again—ten, twenty, thirty swings. Nothing appeared. I lost count. My arms weakened. My ax grew heavy. People were starting to whisper and mutter. Something had gone wrong. Maybe the wall had run out of Fate Stones. Maybe there wasn't one for me.

And then I felt a tingling in my fingers. It was faint at first, but it grew until both my arms were buzzing. I swung harder.

*Crack!* Nothing.

*Crack!* Something!

*Wham!* The something flashed and glimmered. I scraped and dug around it until it came free. Heart pounding, I held my Fate Stone in my hand. It was flat and round, about the size of my palm, and looked to be polished silver, but I'd never heard of a silver Fate Stone.

"I think there's been a mistake?" I said, holding the thing out to the First Foredwarf. "I don't know what it is." I turned it over and saw a flash of light. I nearly dropped it, but caught it in my fumbling hands.

"Ah. A reflecting stone!" said Foredwarf Realga.

"A what?" I asked. I had never heard of such a thing.

"A reflecting stone. Sometimes they are called *mirrors*, but it's mostly humans who call them that. Humans are quite fond of them."

"My Fate Stone is from humans?"

"Oh no," said the First Foredwarf. "Human mirrors are a poor imitation of the real thing. This is a true reflecting stone, a powerful object, much like a crystal ball."

My heart leapt. "So am I a seer, then?" No one would think me strange or useless if I was a seer. I wouldn't be a Seventh.

"No," said Foredwarf Realga. "Not a seer, but this mirror will show you many mysterious things, things you can never see otherwise."

"Like what?" I tilted the mirror to the left and right, hoping that it would show me The Surface or the future. Maybe both.

Foredwarf Realga tilted my hand so my Fate Stone faced me directly. "It can show you yourself. You can't see yourself with your own eyes, can you? And yet we all need to reflect on ourselves from time to time, because life is one big mirror. That which we put out into the world will always come back to us."

I looked down and stared at my image in the stone. I'd only ever seen my reflection in pools of water or on the back of a polished spoon or ax. It had never been so clear and defined as this. I could see the sharpness of my features, the black point of my beard, the dark shine of my eyes, cunning yet a bit empty, like there was something missing inside me. How was this supposed to guide or protect me? For all I could tell, this reflecting stone was just another slight to my oddities. It didn't even look like a real gem! I wanted to bury it back in the wall, dig for another Fate Stone, a real one, but the dwarf behind me came forward, and I was pushed out of the way. Foredwarf Realga handed her an ax, and then she mined out her Fate Stone, a beautiful amethyst, symbolizing peace and tranquility. I was tempted to snatch it out of her hand and claim it as my own.

I stepped away and walked with slumped shoulders to my parents. Father took my ax eagerly in his hands. "Good steel! Keep it sharp, now. A crew member is only as good as his ax."

"And let's see your Fate Stone!" cried Mother, grabbing the mirror out of my hand. "It's so . . . What is it?"

"It's a reflecting stone," I said.

"A reflecting stone!" exclaimed Father.

"What's a reflecting stone?" asked Mother.

"A mirror," I said.

"Oh . . . and what's a mirror exactly?" Mother asked.

"You can see things in it. Like yourself," I said. "And maybe other things," I added.

Father gazed at his own reflection in the glassy surface. "Amazing!" he said, handing it back to me. "Borlen, do you know what this means?"

"What does it mean?" I asked, hoping that Father would be able to offer a little more clarity than Foredwarf Realga, some indication that a mirror for a Fate Stone was something truly wonderful.

"It means . . . it means . . ." Father grappled for words.

"It means our son is special," said Mother, forcing a smile. "But we always knew that."

I looked around at all the other dwarves showing their new axes to their parents, running their fingers over the Fate Stones that were actually stones and precious gems—diamonds, amethysts, and emeralds. I had set my heart on a ruby, but now I would have settled for almost anything else, even the pitiful piece of agate. A few looked toward me and whispered. I heard the girl who'd gotten the ruby whisper, "He didn't even get a real Fate Stone! Look at it!"

"Well, he's a strange one," her mother replied. "Afraid of depths, they say."

I felt my face heat up. I slipped the Fate Stone into my pocket.

Suddenly music filled the cavern. High on a ledge, a dwarf played a silver lute while another dwarf played percussion with variously shaped stones and a dragon-hide drum. Several dwarves began to dance an ax jig. While they hopped and spun, they tapped their ax handles together, then swung them overhead and tossed them in the air.

"Borlen, why don't you dance?" Mother prodded.

"I don't feel like it," I said.

"I wouldn't mind a jig!" said Father. "Shall we, Rumelda?"

My parents joined the throng of dwarves, and I watched them bounce and tap their axes, their faces bright and joyful. I wondered why I couldn't be like them, content with the things around me.

Leaf poked his head out of my shirt, crawled onto my shoulder, and stretched out his wings. He squeaked, letting me know he was hungry.

"I don't have any food for you," I said grumpily.

Leaf squeaked again and then slapped me with his wings a few times before taking off. He flew to the top of the swinging pendulum to find some rock mites.

"Shall we go home, then?" Father asked, his cheeks blue from all the dancing.

"Yes," I said. It was the best idea of the night.

Once we were home, Mother tucked me into bed with my slab of granite and surrounded me with plenty of crystals—amethysts to bring peace, white quartz for clarity, and black tourmaline to calm anxiety and fear. I needed all the help I could get.

"Would you like me to sing you a song?" Mother asked.

I nodded. I was getting too old for lullabies, but tonight I needed the comfort. Mother started to sing "The Lonely Dwarf." Her voice was low and rough, but its familiarity soothed me more than the crystals surrounding my bed did.

*A thousand years he dug in the earth*
*Gathering crystals and gems of great worth*
*He had diamonds and rubies and emeralds galore*
*But he still felt empty, so he dug ten years more*

The song continued, with the dwarf digging and digging for more gems, searching for something to fill the emptiness inside him. But he never finds it. And though he lives five thousand years and gains much power and knowledge, he dies alone and unhappy.

It was a sad song, a cautionary tale, teaching us that happiness cannot be found with a shovel or an ax. It must be found inside of us. I knew why Mother was singing it to me now. She wanted me to be content, not to search for happiness where it didn't exist. But as I listened to the song, I found I had a deep empathy for the lonely dwarf. Was it his fault he couldn't find happiness? Maybe he didn't have any friends. Maybe everyone had been mean to him. Maybe he searched inside himself and found only sadness, so what could he do?

I held the reflecting stone—my Fate Stone—up to my

face. My reflection stared back, sharp nose and chin, dark, somber eyes. Unhappy. How can we find happiness inside when all we feel inside is a longing for something *more*? Where do we find the *more*?

I slept poorly that night. In the morning, I gathered my ax, my Fate Stone, and some sleeping crystals. Leaf curled himself up inside my shirt. He could tell something was happening and preferred to hide. I wished I could hide as well.

Father would take me to my new crew on the way to his own. Mother stood by the front door, clutching a small leather pouch. "I've been saving this," she said. "It's not much, but I hope it will help you adjust."

I took the pouch and looked inside. It was filled with gems and stones to help my depth symptoms: sapphires, amethysts, yellow jasper, black tourmaline, and—blech!—emeralds. Mother could never believe that emeralds made me *more* sick, not less. I'd try to trade those with someone on the crew. I dug around in search of rubies, but there were none. I tried not to look disappointed. My parents had to have sacrificed a great deal just to get me this much.

"Thank you," I said.

Mother wrapped her arms around me and squeezed tight. "Be strong. Be wise. Work hard with your crew."

I nodded, and she released me. I followed Father out the door, and we began our descent.

# CHAPTER FOUR

## The Lowest of the Low

*The deeper I dig, the bigger I feel*
*Till I burst into song and dance a reel*

I could hear the crew—my crew—singing as they worked, their axes pounding in a steady rhythm to the music. My head pounded right along with it. I was now in the deepest depths of the mines, lower than I'd ever been in my entire life.

Father had already left me. I was a full-wise dwarf now, he had said, and I needed to be strong and brave.

The mine was narrow, with a low ceiling. I could spread my arms in any direction and touch stone. Dozens of glowfish bobbed up and down the tunnel. Their pulsing light made me feel like the tunnel was shrinking, walls closing in, ceiling pressing down. In a moment I would be crushed. I reached inside my pouch and popped a sapphire. I'd already eaten a quarter of the stones in the pouch Mother had given me, but it was the only way I could remain upright. I stumbled down the mine toward the sound of the crew.

*A swing of the shoulders, a tap of the ax*
*Brings me good fortune and helps me relax*

When I finally reached them, I leaned against the wall and tried to catch my breath until someone noticed me.

"Halt!" shouted one of the crew, the Foredwarf, if I had to guess. He was definitely the oldest. His long white beard reached his knees. The singing and pounding of axes stopped, but the pounding in my head continued.

"Crew, we have a new Seventh!" said the Foredwarf. No one said anything. I thought I heard someone snort, but I didn't look up. I was certain if I looked at anyone, my stomach would turn inside out and I'd toss my crystals.

"Well, we'd best make introductions," said the Foredwarf when it was clear no one was going to make any gesture of welcome. "I am Epidot, your Foredwarf, and this is your crew. Sound off, crew!"

One by one, each crew member recited his or her name and position.

"Garnesha, Second."

"Amethina, Third."

"Herkimer, Fourth."

"Rudger, Fifth."

My head snapped up. Rudger! Of all the crews in all

the caverns, how did I manage to wind up on *his* crew? I hoped he wouldn't even remember me. It had been over a year since we'd seen each other in the nursery mines, and anyhow, what was I to him? Nothing and no one. But then Rudger's eyes flashed toward me. He smiled, showing his big teeth in all their familiar meanness. He remembered me perfectly. My headache intensified. I pulled out a chunk of black tourmaline and shoved it into my mouth.

The sixth crewmate stepped forward but said nothing. He was obviously older than me, maybe even older than Rudger, though quite a bit smaller, with the exception of his ears, which were alarmingly large, like floppy plates attached to his head.

"Gilpin, Sixth," said Epidot, who then looked at me and nodded with a gentle smile. It was my turn.

"B-B-Borlen," I stammered. "Seventh."

Rudger snorted again. I was certain it had been him the first time.

"Borlen, eh?" said Epidot. "Never seen that mineral myself, though I hear you've seen your fair share of the stuff. Is that true?"

I nodded.

"Well, Beryl's beard, isn't that something?" said Epidot, smiling around at all the crew. None of them responded. They gazed at the ceiling, their axes, or their dirt-caked fingers. It was just as awkward for them to have a Seventh on the crew as it was embarrassing for me to be a Seventh. I was the lowest of the low.

Finally, the Second, Garnesha, cleared her throat

and spoke in a husky, gravelly voice. "Shall we continue, Epidot?"

"Oh!" said Epidot. His smile faded, and he assumed a more serious expression. "Of course. Let us continue with our work." He pressed his palm against a spot on the wall. "I sense a rich deposit of something, maybe emerald or peridot, perhaps twenty or thirty feet in this direction."

Blech. If we had to be mining so deep, couldn't we at least dig for something that tasted good?

"It will take some time," said Garnesha. She was a stout, strong-looking female, probably five or six hundred years old. Her skin had a slight orange tinge to it, like she ate a lot of orange crystals. Just as I thought this, she took out a square stick of orange citrine and crunched on it as she spoke. "If the rock remains this hard, it will take at least a few weeks, unless the sediment changes. Amethina, can you guess what the sediment will be like farther down this way?"

Amethina, the Third, consulted some stone tablets in her arms. She had smoky brown skin, amethyst-colored eyes, and a nervous kind of energy. She tapped her finger over the tablets as she spoke rapidly in a high-pitched voice. "We've dug to the very outskirts of the main tunnels, and digging in this direction will take us outside of what I have on the maps, so it's impossible to tell for certain, though if I had to guess, I'd say it will be a bit softer than usual, so easy digging, but also a greater risk for collapse."

"We can fortify the tunnels, can't we, Rudger?" said Herkimer, the Fourth.

Rudger puffed out his chest with pride. "Of course. I'm a very strong fortifighter."

*"Fortifier,"* Garnesha corrected.

"And Gilpin can tell us if a cave-in is imminent, can't you, Gil?" asked Herkimer.

Gilpin nodded vigorously and flapped his ears.

"Very good," said Epidot. "Let us dig!"

Everyone moved into place, taking up chisels and hammers and axes to work on the wall. As Epidot lifted his ax and took the first swing, he began to sing, and the rest of the crew joined in.

*A dwarfling ate some diamonds*
*He crunched them all the while*
*Till he grew so strong and mighty*
*He could throw a rock a mile!*

They worked in a cohesive rhythm. No one had a second thought for me. There wasn't any real use for a Seventh, except to do whatever tasks no one else wanted to do. So I just stood there with my ax, dizzy and trembling, wondering why under earth I was here.

Gilpin, the Sixth, finally noticed me. He waved with both hands and ears for me to follow him. He showed me the wall he was working on, lifted his ax, and tapped it into the stone. I tried to follow suit, but as soon as I lifted my ax, the floor seemed to tilt beneath me, and I stumbled. Gilpin raised his eyebrows and ears.

I gritted my teeth, determined not to be worthless. I lifted my ax again and swung into the stone. Immediately

I became woozy. Gilpin held something out to me—a piece of yellow jasper. I crunched down hard, and it eased my dizziness some.

"Thank you," I said.

Gilpin smiled and twitched his ears, then went back to mining.

*A dwarfling ate some emeralds*
*Chomped them day and night*
*She grew so wise and witty*
*She was always in the right!*

"Ho there, Seventh! Why aren't you singing?" asked Herkimer, the Fourth. He had a brown beard, peppered with gray, that he tucked into his belt. He had high, round cheekbones and twinkly eyes that made him look as though he had a permanent smile. For some reason it made me feel all the more surly.

"I don't sing," I said.

"Don't sing?!" said Herkimer. "Impossible! All dwarves sing."

A crew's collective singing was supposed to create a harmonious energy that would lead to the densest deposits of minerals and gems. But it was hard for me to get the notes out when every pound of the ax or chisel made my heart sink a little deeper.

"Didn't you know?" said Rudger gleefully. "Our Seventh is afraid of depths!"

"Afraid of depths?" said Herkimer. Clearly he'd never heard of such a thing.

Rudger nodded. "Useless as rubble, that one, but don't go teasing him about it. He's a bit grumpy." Rudger flashed a smile at me that made me want to slam my ax into his foot.

"Well, perhaps the singing will help him get used to it," said Herkimer. "Come now, Seventh. Sing, or you'll bring bad luck to the crew!"

"*He's* not singing," I said, nodding to Gilpin. I hadn't heard him say a single word since my arrival.

"Oh, but Gilpin *is* singing, aren't you, Gil?" said Herkimer. Gilpin didn't respond except to twitch his ears in the rhythm of the song as he tapped at the wall. "See? He might not be making any sound, but in his heart, Gilpin is singing with the crew."

"Can't he talk?" I asked.

"Nope," said Herkimer. "He hasn't said a word in all his two hundred years!"

"Why not?" I asked.

"Because he was borned in the middle of a tunnel that collapsed," said Rudger. "Didn't get so much as a common crystal at birth. Lived off rubble for months, so now he's got rubble for brains."

I looked over at Gilpin. He was still pounding at the rock, but his ears were no longer flapping with the song. They were pressed down so low they nearly brushed his shoulders.

"He may not talk," I said. "But I think he can hear you just fine."

"'Course he can," said Rudger. "Do you see the size of those ears? Gilpin can hear a pebble drop from a mile away!" And he laughed again as though he thought this was a very good joke.

Gilpin glanced at me, a question in his eyes. He seemed to be asking if I would laugh at him, too. I looked away. I wouldn't laugh at Gilpin. I knew all too well what it felt like to be teased and belittled for being different.

"Here, Seventh," said Rudger. "Take out the rubble."

He dumped a shovelful of rocks and dirt at my feet. Dust billowed up to my face and made me sneeze, which Herkimer mistook for an attempt to sing.

"That's it! Sing, Seventh!" said Herkimer. "Help us to the gems!"

Rudger chuckled gleefully as he walked away. I took out another sapphire from my pouch.

*Dig in the dirt, chip at the rocks*
*Find crystals and diamonds*
*Find rubies*
*Find lots!*

Rubies. What I wouldn't give for one at that very moment.

# CHAPTER FIVE

## Genuine Grump

By the end of the day, I could barely stand. I dragged my ax behind me as I followed the rest of the crew to our sleeping quarters. Deep-mining crews didn't usually return to their homes at the end of the day. It took too much time and energy to go back and forth, so we slept and ate in temporary quarters near the mine, often for months at a time.

The crew quarters were a small cavern, even smaller than my home. There was a rough-cut stone table and stools and a cooking cavern with burning coals beneath an iron pot. A copper pendulum swung in a diagonal path over the table, and glowfish bobbed and drifted around it. A few had nestled themselves in the crevices of the walls and ceiling, as though sleeping. Sleep. Against the wall were six stone beds. I looked at them longingly, my eyelids heavy.

"You'll have to sleep on the floor, I'm afraid," said Epidot. "Until we can cut you a bed."

"I can help you make one tomorrow!" said Herkimer.

"I don't need help," I grumbled.

Herkimer's face fell. He glanced at Rudger.

"Told you," said Rudger. "A real grump."

The crew sat around the table and had a supper of limestone and granite stew, sprinkled with shards of jade and obsidian. I was so tired, I couldn't even muster the strength to eat. I'd eaten plenty that day, anyway. It was only my first day, and nearly half my pouch was gone. How would I work when it was empty?

While the crew ate, I walked around the cavern in search of some bugs for Leaf. He hadn't come out of my shirt all day. Down this deep, there wasn't much for him, only some small rock mites. I pulled him out and pried his wings open.

"Come on," I said. "You have to eat something."

He squeaked softly. He was afraid. I don't think he liked the depths any better than I did.

Suddenly Leaf was snatched out of my hands. "What you got there, Seventh?" said Rudger. "Special snacks? It's not polite to bring your own food and not– What the ruddy rubble!"

Leaf suddenly came alive in Rudger's grasp. He screeched and frantically flapped his wings, but Rudger held on to him.

"Give him back!" I pounced on Rudger. He stumbled backward, right into the table, but still he would not let go. I jumped onto the table, knocking over food and dishes.

He was squeezing Leaf! He was going to kill him! I lunged at Rudger and bit his hand. He yelped, and Leaf fell to the ground, flapping all over the place. I jumped down and scrambled to pick him up. "Leaf!" He was squeaking with so much fright, I could feel his little heart beating furiously in my hands. "It's okay," I said. "You're all right now. I've got you."

I wrapped his wings around his body and tucked him inside my shirt. Finally he calmed down. It was then I noticed how silent the cavern was. I looked up to see the entire crew staring at me. Bowls and dishes were crushed, the dinner spilled and ruined.

"He bit me!" cried Rudger. "The crazy little Seventh just bit me!" He held a fist to his chest. I had bitten him hard enough that beads of bright blue blood were forming on his knuckles. Served him right.

Garnesha looked at me sharply. As Second, she was in charge of discipline, and held the power to dole out punishments. "No supper," she said. "And you'll not have anything but rubble for three days."

"What about him?" I said, nodding to Rudger. "He tried to kill my bat!"

"I did not!" said Rudger. "The little beast attackered me!"

"I'll not tolerate such behavior," said Garnesha. To me. Not to Rudger. "Here, your crew is your family, and we work together, not against."

The rest of the crew stared at me with mixed expressions of shock and anger. Gilpin slowly started to sweep up the mess I'd made.

"And you'll keep that creature hidden," Garnesha added unnecessarily. I doubted Leaf would try to come out anytime soon.

After the mess was cleaned up, the crew readied for sleep, shifting rocks and crystals around in their stone beds. Amethina rammed her head into the wall a few times, a common soothing technique for those with high energy or jittery nerves. Garnesha extinguished the coals in the cooking cavern, and Herkimer shooed all the glow-fish down the corridor, leaving only the faintest light in the cavern.

I fumbled in my pocket and pulled out my Fate Stone. I turned it this way and that, letting it catch the dim light, looking at my reflection. I really did look like a grump. Everything about me—my eyebrows, ears, mouth, cheeks, and even my beard—pressed downward in an expression of hopeless misery. I was filled with a longing for home, and for my parents.

Just then my Fate Stone swirled and misted over. After a moment, it cleared, but my own reflection did not appear. Mother! I could see her! I held on to both sides of the mirror, worried she'd disappear if I let go. She wiped a trickle of dust from her cheek. She was crying! I'd never seen either of my parents cry in my entire life.

Father came to her side. He wrapped his arm around her shoulder.

"He's where he needs to be, Rumelda," said Father.

I could hear him!

"I know," said Mother. "I know we did the right thing, but he's still so young."

"It's for the best."

The image faded, and I was left staring at myself again. I shook the Fate Stone, willing them to reappear, but no amount of shaking would bring them back.

The next day was not any better, nor the next or the next. My head still throbbed, and every limb, muscle, and bone in my body ached. Within a week I had eaten all the gems Mother had given me, except for the emeralds. I grew so desperate, I even ate one of those, but I gagged at the rancid flavor and immediately spit it out.

The crew mined in cheerful harmony, digging to the rhythm of their songs. I soon learned that each crew member had a specific strength and role. Epidot could sense valuable deposits in the rock and would tell us where to dig.

Garnesha could dig twice as fast as anyone else on the crew. All the orange crystals she ate gave her extra digging energy.

Amethina had a strong sense of direction. She recorded our progress on the crew tablets and kept track of where we were in relation to the main tunnels, as well as to other mines. She was in a constant nervous state, frequently checking her maps and charts to make sure we were still miles below The Surface. Her greatest fear was that we'd somehow burst through to The Surface and die from the light and open space and elevation.

Herkimer and Rudger had the power to strengthen

and fortify the tunnels as we dug, to ensure against collapse. Rudger acted like he was the most important member of the crew, like all our lives were in his hands.

But in my opinion, it was Gilpin who had the most valuable skill. He could sense even the tiniest tremor in the earth, or the smallest trickle of water. He would warn Epidot if we needed to stop pounding to allow a tremor to settle, or he'd tell him if we were about to hit water. But the crew didn't always listen to him, which was how we got blasted with a hot geyser one day.

And then there was me. The Seventh.

After I bit Rudger, most of the crew kept their distance and only addressed me when they had a task for me to perform. No one ever called me Borlen. They always called me Seventh, except Rudger, who delighted in calling me Grump. Since he gave me the most orders, I was called Grump more than anything else.

"Grump, come sweep out the rubble!"

"Hold my chisel, Grump!"

"Pound harder."

"Don't pound so hard!"

"Sing, Grump!"

"Quiet, Grump!"

It did not improve my mood.

Gilpin was the only one who didn't give me orders, which was a relief since he worked closest to me. Sometimes he gestured and flapped his ears like he was trying to have a conversation with me in his own particular language, but I couldn't understand what he was saying.

The only comfort I had was my parents. I found that I could see them in my Fate Stone whenever I wished, whenever I thought of them, which was often. And they seemed to think of me often as well, at least during my first months away.

Father brought Mother word that I was still adjusting, but working hard.

"Will we see him soon?" Mother asked.

"Foredwarf Epidot doesn't think it wise," said Father. "He fears it would set him back."

Mother decided to return to the mines herself. Without a dwarfling to look after, she had no reason not to. She got a position on a crew as a Third. On her first day, she came home with dust in her eyes. She told Father that her crew had sung a mining song that she used to sing to me when I was a baby.

"I can hardly think of him without worry!" said Mother.

"He'll be fine, Rumelda. I'll bet he's digging up rubies and having the time of his life!"

If only.

Father turned the conversation to his own mine. He'd been promoted to Second. They found a good deposit of emeralds. Each time I saw my parents, they spoke of me less and less.

In the evenings, the crew gathered around the table for supper. Herkimer would share any news he'd picked up from the main cavern—production reports, collapsed tunnels, plans for new tunnels, and trades with other dwarf colonies. I rarely paid attention, until one evening Herkimer brought news that made my ears perk up.

"Gnomes got into the main cavern today," he said. "Apparently, the human king has died."

"Already?" said Amethina. "I thought that king started to rule only a decade or so ago."

"He did," said Herkimer.

"Such a short time," said Amethina.

"Who will be the human king now?" asked Rudger.

"There will be no king, but a queen," said Herkimer. "The king's wife will now rule."

"Does the First Foredwarf have any concerns?" asked Amethina.

"Not really," said Herkimer. "She's been watching this queen through her crystal balls, and the queen doesn't seem to have any ambitions to raid our mines, though apparently she wears a ridiculous amount of gems on her head and around her neck. That's what Crystemum said, anyway."

The crew laughed, imagining the ridiculous sight and the ridiculous notion that any human could actually invade our caverns. There had been attempts in the past, even after the tragedy of Beryl, but they never got far. We'd learned our lesson. Not only had we sealed off every possible entrance, there were spells that repelled humans, and enchantments that kept them from digging into our mines. They would never be able to find our caverns, not unless a dwarf led them, and no dwarf would ever do that. It was a banishable offense.

"What about the princess?" I asked. Everyone stopped

mid-laugh and stared at me as if I'd said something scandalous. I felt my face warm.

"Pin-chess?" asked Rudger as he bit into some quartz. "What's that?"

"Daughter of a king," said Epidot, and I was grateful I wasn't the only one who had such knowledge—though, of course, Epidot would, being a Foredwarf and over a thousand years old. "She is too young to rule—not even two decades, so I hear—though the queen is not much older, merely four decades, if I remember correctly."

Rudger nearly choked. "Ruling a colony at forty! That's preposter-ish!"

"You know how short their lives are, Rudger," said Garnesha. "I imagine four decades to a human is like four centuries to us!"

"But how can anyone so young possibly rule anything?" asked Rudger. "That's like Grump here being First Foredwarf! Can you imagine if he were in charge? If he didn't collapse the entire colony, he'd probably let the humans right into our caves—or worse, make us live on The Surface."

The crew chuckled. Even Gilpin smiled and wiggled his ears until I glared at him.

"Maybe I should grow you some of those florixes," continued Rudger, "so you can feel more at home here."

"They're called *flowers,*" I said. "And you can't grow them down here. They can't grow without a sun."

Rudger laughed. "Bet you'd make friends with those humans, learn all their customs and nasty habits."

"They'd probably be nicer than you," I grumbled.

"Oh ho! He really is a human lover! Careful, Grump. That kind of talk will get you banished. But maybe that's what you want, eh?"

I stood up from the table, seething, and retreated to the shallow alcove where I'd been sleeping. I couldn't decide what bothered me more: Rudger's taunts or the fact that they were true. Not that I wanted to be banished. I didn't, but I had pictured The Surface so often in my imagination, sometimes it felt more like home to me than home. I imagined smelling flowers, climbing trees, gathering leaves. Sometimes I imagined meeting a human, maybe even making friends with one. Then I'd feel guilty and ashamed for imagining such things, because I knew it wasn't normal or even right. Dwarves couldn't live on The Surface. We couldn't be friends with humans. We weren't even supposed to be seen by humans. It was reckless, foolish.

The crew finished their supper and cleaned up together. Rudger struck up a song.

*Oh, the Seventh's gone batty, he longs to ascend*
*To the world up above us to make some new friends*
*He's a daft little dwarfling, absurd and unsound*
*If he had any sense, he'd like life underground*

I reached inside my shirt and pulled Leaf out of hiding. He was unwilling at first. Since the episode with Rudger that first day, he'd become a hermit bat, but as soon as I fed him some mites, he stretched his wings and perched on my shoulder.

Gilpin appeared in front of me, holding two slabs of

granite. He held them out and gestured to the other beds lined up against the wall. He'd brought me a bed. I hadn't bothered to make one myself, and after I'd refused Herkimer's help, no one else had offered.

Gilpin set them down on the floor, then noticed Leaf in my hand. He leaned forward a little and looked at me, one ear folded down, the other perked up in curiosity.

"This is Leaf. You can pet him, if you want." Gilpin reached a finger out hesitantly. He stroked Leaf on his head. Leaf spread out his wings and squeaked. Gilpin jumped back, flapping his ears in alarm.

"It's okay," I said. "He doesn't bite. He likes to be petted." Gilpin moved cautiously forward and stroked Leaf again. Leaf squeaked with contentment, and Gilpin smiled from ear to flapping ear, until something else caught his attention.

Gilpin bent down and picked it up.

"That's mine!" I said, snatching my Fate Stone from him. I had forgotten to put it back inside my pocket. Gilpin looked at me questioningly.

"It's my Fate Stone," I said.

Gilpin nodded. He pulled out his own Fate Stone from beneath his shirt. It was rose quartz, a common enough stone for eating, but unusual for a Fate Stone. Rose quartz represented kindness and positivity, but it was also supposed to enhance insight and clairvoyance. I wondered if Gilpin had those abilities. He couldn't speak, but his large ears allowed him to hear exceptionally well. What if his sense of hearing was so strong he could listen to my thoughts?

Gilpin gave me a knowing grin. He tucked his Fate Stone back inside his shirt, stroked Leaf one more time, then patted the slabs of granite he'd brought for me, as though wishing me to get some good rest.

"Thank you," I said.

Gilpin smiled. The tips of his ears folded downward, as though saying, *You're welcome.*

# CHAPTER SIX

## A Light at the End of the Tunnel

"Coming up on a deposit, crew!" shouted Epidot. "Let's dig deep!"

I shoveled up another pile of rubble and tossed it into the wheelbarrow. I had felt better the past few days. My headaches and dizziness were less severe. I thought maybe it was because of my new slab of granite. I thanked Gilpin again. He shrugged like it was nothing, but smiled. Gilpin was all right.

Amethina consulted her maps, frantically brushing her fingers all over the tablets. "Epidot, are you *sure* we are not traveling upward? The sediment seems unsafely soft, and I'm feeling very dizzy!" She shoved a handful of amethysts into her mouth.

"No, no," said Epidot. "We've been holding steady. Miles underground!"

But the sediment did seem softer, more crumbly than usual. The crew were using shovels more than their axes and chisels. I hauled another load of rubble out of the tunnel as the crew continued to dig and sing.

"Halt!" Epidot shouted when I returned. The crew's singing faded. Everyone put down their axes. Epidot inspected the wall where we had been digging, pressing his hands on it here and there. He looked perplexed.

"Where are we on the map, Amethina?" asked Epidot.

Amethina shuffled her map tablets around. "I told you, we're not even on the map." Her voice was strained with worry. "We're almost a mile outside the perimeter of the outer tunnels."

"Well, we've got to dig new tunnels," said Herkimer.

"Old tunnels collapse, new tunnels have to be digged," said Rudger.

"*Dug,*" corrected Garnesha.

Epidot stuck his fingers into the wall. The sediment was dark and pliable. He took a pinch between his fingers and sniffed, then took a taste. "Borlen!" he shouted.

"Yes?" I responded, a little surprised to be called by my real name.

"Not you, Seventh. The dirt! This is borlen! This whole area is full of it."

The entire crew gasped. Amethina shrieked and covered her eyes. "No wonder I've been getting such headaches! We're near The Surface!"

"Impossible," said Garnesha. "We're miles below The Surface. You said so yourself, Epidot."

"And yet we must be very close," said Epidot. "Borlen is not found anywhere else." Epidot pinched another chunk of the dark dirt and popped it into his mouth. He swallowed and gave a little belch. "A tad bitter, but nice and creamy."

Amethina began breathing very hard and fast. "How? How did we get here? *How?*"

No one seemed to have an answer. No one except me. "I think I know what happened," I said. Everyone turned to me.

"You, Seventh?" said Epidot as Rudger said, "Pfft! Not the grump!"

I ignored Rudger. "Can I see the maps, Amethina?"

Amethina held them out to me, reluctantly. "We began here?" I said, pointing to a place on the map. Amethina nodded. "And now we are here, outside the tunnels, where we have no record of what is above or below us. We've traveled on an even level underground, but The Surface is not all one level. There are peaks and valleys, extreme variances in the land, so one place down here might be far underground, while another at the exact same level could be near The Surface. We could have been digging beneath a very steep decline on The Surface. A mountain, I'd say."

"Oh, I should have known!" said Amethina. "I *did* know! I told you, Epidot! I knew we were going upward. The signs in the sediment, my headaches, my breathlessness."

And my own depth symptoms had disappeared. . . . My heart did a little skip. *Borlen* . . . we had to be just feet from The Surface.

Amethina was in complete hysterics. She turned in

circles and crashed her head against a wall. "What if a *human* comes? What if they take us all!"

"Well, it's nothing for *us* to worry about, Amethina," said Garnesha. "We don't have beards."

"Exactly!" said Amethina. "We're of no use to them. They'll probably eat us!"

"Humans don't eat dwarves," I said. "We're too tough for their brittle teeth."

"Leave it to the grump to know a thing like that," said Rudger.

"Well, *someone* should know about The Surface!" I was tired of being ridiculed for knowing things they didn't. "What if you *do* end up there? What will you do?"

"Oh! Oh! I should die!" cried Amethina.

"I think we should dug downward," said Rudger.

"*Dig,*" corrected Garnesha. "And I agree. Borlen is not a good sign, Epidot."

"It would be a shame to let all this borlen go to waste," said Epidot. "Our own potters would be overjoyed to have it, and we could make a very good trade with another colony."

"But it would be a terrible risk," said Garnesha.

"And we are not acclimated to the Surface environment!" said Amethina. "I can't work in these conditions!" She set her ax down in defiance.

Herkimer and Rudger stood a good distance away from the borlen. They did not seem any more willing than Amethina to start digging. Epidot glanced at the rich, dark mineral deposit, so rare and valuable to our colony.

He seemed conflicted. He wanted to mine the borlen, but he did not wish to endanger his crew.

I had other ideas, though.

"Pardon me, Epidot, but I think I have a solution," I said. "The rest of the crew could start digging downward while I mine the borlen."

Amethina brightened considerably. "Well, obviously that is the best option, Epidot. Of course the Seventh should be the one to dig out the borlen!"

"It does seem reasonable," said Garnesha.

Everyone nodded their agreement.

"You're sure you're comfortable with this arrangement, Seventh?" Epidot asked. "It's a risky endeavor."

I nodded. "You know I was born and raised very near The Surface. I'm quite used to these conditions."

"Very good!" said Epidot. "We'll leave you to it, then. Come, crew! Let us dig down!"

Most of the crew couldn't leave fast enough. Amethina quickly laid out a new course. Then Garnesha crunched a big orange garnet and swung her ax to break ground.

But Gilpin lagged behind the crew. He held out his ax, asking if I wanted help.

"No thanks, Gil," I said. "You don't want to be so near The Surface, do you? You go with the crew." He sagged a little. He seemed simultaneously relieved and disappointed.

"You could come back every now and then, though," I said, "and take the borlen to the main cavern. Only if you want to."

Gilpin brightened. He nodded, flapping his ears up and down, then turned and left to join the rest of the crew. Soon I heard their rhythmic clinks and pounds as they dug downward.

I faced the borlen. My beard buzzed. *This is it,* I thought. *This is my chance at last.* I took a shovel and dug into the rich dirt. It shifted easily, as though it wanted to make way for me.

The crew started singing again.

*Strike the stone, pound the earth*
*Find gems and crystals of great worth*
*Join the throng, our songs abound*
*Our health and wealth lie underground*

I hummed along, but made up my own words in my head for the last two lines.

*Forget the crew, forgo below*
*Up above is where I'll go!*

I mined the borlen carefully. I didn't want to cause a collapse for fear the crew would find out what I was really doing. And I could feel the pull of The Surface. I was so close! For three days, I dug. I got through most of the borlen on the first day. On the second day, I came to a rocky sediment, which was more difficult to mine. On the third day, I hit solid granite and began to despair. Maybe Epidot had been mistaken. Maybe this wasn't borlen at all, and I really was still miles below The Surface.

And then it happened. I was pounding on the granite, removing it bit by bit, when my ax burst through the rock.

Cool air brushed my face. Then I saw a pinprick of light. Not the golden glow of a glowfish or lava, but bright white light. Brighter than a hot diamond.

My beard buzzed with excitement. This was it!

I scraped and chipped around the opening, widening it until the hole was big enough for me to crawl through. A shaft of white light cut into the darkness of the tunnel. My heart pounded in my chest. Decades of failed escapes, and now here I was, mere feet from The Surface, when I was supposed to be miles below.

I paused on the edge of the divide between underground and The Surface. To cross it would be a crime. If I were caught, I could be banished. There was no greater compromise of our colony's safety than unguarded openings to The Surface. But I would be careful. No one had to know.

I crawled forward. I reached my hand up to the edge, and then something tugged on my foot.

"What the . . . ?" I yanked away, but whatever it was pulled me so hard, I slid down and flopped to the ground.

There was Gilpin, looking down at me with severe judgment showing in his eyes and ears.

"Gilpin!" I whispered. "You scared the rubies out of me! What are you doing?"

His ears waggled. He gestured wildly from me to the hole, the bright light rushing through. He was asking the same question.

"I was just—"

Gilpin held up his hand to quiet me. His ears strained upward and twitched. He was hearing things on The Surface. Perhaps the wind and the birds. I wanted to hear them, too. I moved toward the hole, but Gilpin grabbed me by the arm and pulled me back like I was about to fall into a lava pit.

"I just want to see it, Gilpin," I said, pulling free. "I'll come right back."

Gilpin shook his head even more vigorously. He crossed his arms and sliced them outward as if to say, *No way! Too dangerous.*

"Nothing is going to happen to me," I said. "Besides, who would care if it did? No one cares about the grumpy Seventh."

Gilpin's ears pressed down. He pointed to himself, then pointed to me. He tried to grab my arm, but I shook him off.

"You can't stop me! You think you're in charge just because you're the Sixth and I'm the Seventh?"

Gilpin shook his head and pulled at his ears in frustration. He searched around frantically. He picked up a sharp rock and started to scratch into the wall. He moved aside so I could see his crude carving. Two dwarves stood side by side with axes over their shoulders. They were holding hands and smiling. One was clearly Gilpin, judging by the size of the ears. The other, I guessed, was me, judging by the pointy beard.

I looked at Gilpin. "You're my friend?"

He looked down, then glanced back at me, one ear perked up in question. *Are you my friend, too?* he seemed to be asking. I didn't know what to say. In my half century of life, no one had ever wanted to be friends with me, the grumpy dwarf who loved The Surface. But maybe it was the same with Gilpin, a silent dwarf with large ears. I knew things weren't easy for him.

"I have to see it," I said, gesturing to The Surface. "Just once."

Gilpin stepped back. He looked ready to run.

"You won't tell, will you?" I asked desperately, and Gilpin paused. "I'll cover up the hole. No one has to know."

Gilpin pressed his ears down, along with his eyebrows and mouth and shoulders. He was angry with me. I understood. I had put him in a terrible position. I was taking advantage of his offered friendship, but what else could I do? I had to go, and it had to be a secret.

"You could come with me," I offered. "You could see it, too."

Gilpin grew so alarmed, his ears shot straight up, as though he'd been blasted by a gust of dragon fire breath. He shook his head, but then he waved for me to go. He pressed his lips together with one finger, letting me know that he wouldn't tell.

"Thanks, Gil," I said. I glanced at his drawing of us on the wall. "I like that picture."

I got down on my hands and knees and crawled up the narrow tunnel. When I came to the opening, I took a deep breath and crossed the threshold into the bright open space.

For the first time in my life, at the young age of fifty-three, I was standing on The Surface.

# CHAPTER SEVEN

## The Surface

I struggled to breathe at first. There was so much air, and the air moved! It whipped against my skin and tousled my hair and beard like a teasing playmate. *Wind,* I remembered—that's what moving air was called, but I never imagined it like this, cool and frolicking.

And then there was the brightness. I couldn't open my eyes, it was so blinding, like a million glowfish were floating right in front of my eyeballs. At first I screwed my eyes shut and put my arms over my face, then I opened my eyes just a slit and peeked. Slowly, little by little, I opened them wider and wider until, finally, I could keep them fully open. After I'd adjusted to the brightness, I was able to observe this strange world of The Surface. I had imagined it so many times—seen it in my dreams—but it was nothing like I'd pictured. It was better.

There was so much space! So many things I'd never

seen before. *Trees.* Hundreds of them, all clustered together like an enormous deposit of emeralds, all shapes and shades and sizes. They each grew as a single stalk out of the ground, then split off into many arms and gnarled fingers that swayed in the moving air like they were dancing.

*Flowers.* There were flowers dotting the ground—yellow, white, pink, and red, like someone had taken a variety of gems and sprinkled them everywhere.

The *sun.* It was bigger and brighter than I ever could have imagined—so bright, I couldn't even look at it—and its light was so powerful, it spread over all The Surface. And the *sky* . . . it was a bright blue ceiling that seemed to go on forever.

Leaf poked his head out of my shirt, curious to know what was happening. He squeaked in dismay at the bright light and quickly hid himself again.

I took my first tentative steps. The Surface was strangely soft beneath my feet, which were used to rough stone.

I picked a fresh blade of grass, marveling at the intensity of the green and how it curled around my finger. I pulled up handfuls of grass and threw them into the air so they floated down on top of my head and tickled my nose and cheeks. I touched the leaves and the trees and flowers, memorizing their scents and textures.

I came to a stream of water trickling over roots and rocks. I dipped my hands into it. *Brrrrr!* It was icy cold! But I didn't mind. It woke me up. Everything about The

Surface made me feel awake and alive in a way I'd never felt before. My heart had burst from its dark little cell and now it couldn't be contained. I was overflowing, leaping, spinning in circles until I was dizzy, but not a bad dizzy like I felt in the depths. I was dizzy with happiness.

Finally I took stock of my surroundings. Behind me, the earth inclined at a sharp angle—that was the mountain Amethina had said we'd been mining beneath. I had come out somewhere in the middle of it. Below me, the earth sloped downward and then evened out and spread into a great expanse. The trees thinned, and the land became flat. Squat, square little structures dotted the land in haphazard clusters. Smoke curled out of the tops. A human colony! In the center of the colony, on a mound of earth, was a very tall stone building much grander than all the others, with several towers pointing up toward the sky like a bunch of stalagmites. A *castle*! This must be the place where the human queen and the toothless princess lived. Was she still toothless? I wondered.

The wind picked up and pressed against my back, almost as if it were prodding me to move. I glanced back toward the cavern hole. No one had come. Gilpin would keep his promise. The crew wouldn't look for me for hours. I could explore just a little further.

I took one step, and then another, and then my legs, almost of their own accord, broke into a run. I ran down The Mountain, racing the stream. Faster and faster I went, The Mountain's slope pulling me forward while the wind chased me from behind. I was moving so fast, I almost felt like I was flying. I spread my arms wide like a bat, then tumbled, flipping head over feet twice, then crashed into a tree. The leaves and branches spun above me. A laugh gurgled in my throat, but I quickly cut it off. I heard something. Movement. Voices. Very near.

I got to my feet and peered out from behind a tree. I had landed only a stone's throw from the castle I had just seen from above. In a small clearing, closer by, stood two creatures, dwarflike, but with ridiculously long, skinny limbs, like they'd been stretched. Humans! A boy and a girl. They appeared to be children, judging by their youthful faces, but they were still three or four times my size.

"Now lie down and pretend that you're dead," said the girl in a bossy voice.

"Why?" said the boy.

"So I can rescue you."

"How can you rescue me if I'm dead? It seems a bit late for saving."

"True love's kiss, of course," said the girl. "Love conquers all."

"Oh, blech. You are *not* my true love, Snow!"

Snow . . . I remembered that the human princess was named Snow White. Could this be the princess? I tried to see if she was still toothless, but I couldn't tell from where I stood.

The girl frowned. "Don't be difficult, Florian," she said. "You're not my true love, either. That's why it's a *game.*"

"Well, it's a stupid game, if you ask me," said the boy.

"It should be *me* rescuing you, not the other way around, and with a sword, not a kiss."

The girl huffed with indignation. "Why must it always be the boy rescuing the girl? And why must the rescuing always be with a sword?"

"Because . . . ," said the boy, who seemed to be thinking hard. Finally he straightened up and puffed out his chest. "Because that's how it always is."

The girl sighed. "You have very little imagination, Florian. It's a flaw you might want to mend before you become king."

"Well, you needn't be so bossy," the boy grumbled. "You're not queen yet."

I studied the humans as they spoke. The boy had a head of curly brown hair, tan skin like smoky quartz, and soft brown eyes.

The girl's looks couldn't have been more stark in contrast. She had hair as black as onyx, marble white skin, sapphire blue eyes, and ruby red lips. She looked like she'd been sculpted out of all my favorite foods. Looking at her reminded me how hungry I was. My stomach rumbled so loudly, the girl looked right at me. Her eyes narrowed, then lit up in recognition.

I gasped, stumbled back, and fell into the cold water of the stream, then gasped again in shock.

The human boy laughed. "Stupid gnome," he said.

I wanted to attack the boy for calling me a gnome.

"That's not a gnome!" said the girl. "That's a dwarf!"

"So?"

"Don't you know anything, Florian? Father used to tell me stories about dwarves. They have all kinds of magic!"

"Magic! I'll catch it, then," said the boy.

"No you won't. I saw it first!" The girl shoved the boy aside and ran after me.

I needed no further warning. I hopped out of the stream and ran as fast as I could, though to where I was running, I had no idea. I couldn't go back to my tunnel. If I returned to the crew with two humans in tow, I'd be banished for certain! I had to find a place to hide. But where?

"Go to the other side!" the girl shouted. "We'll corner him!"

"Faster!" said the boy.

They were getting closer. I could feel their footsteps pounding the earth.

My breath grew short, my chest burned. My lungs were not accustomed to the Surface air, and I didn't think I would last much longer.

So this was it: My first time to The Surface, I was going to get caught by two humans. Oh, why didn't I listen to my mother!

Ahead, I saw a gnome emerging from a hole at the base of a tree, just twenty lengths to my right. A hole big enough for a dwarf, but not big enough for the humans.

I pushed my legs as hard as I could. I was almost there. The humans were closing in on me from both sides. The boy's hands were outstretched. I dove. The gnome came fully out of the hole just as I crashed into the tree. I shoved the gnome toward the boy and jumped down the hole.

"I got him!" the boy shouted.

"Message for Lord Wiesel! Message for Lord Wiesel!" said the gnome in a raspy, high-pitched voice.

"That's just a gnome!" said the girl. "You let the dwarf get away!"

"Did not!" said the boy. "He went right to this tree, and I caught him. Besides, I don't think you really saw a dwarf."

"But I *did* see a dwarf!" said the girl.

"Your eyes are playing tricks on you. Dwarves aren't even real." The boy dropped the gnome, who ran off chanting, "Message for Lord Wiesel! Message for Lord Wiesel!"

"They are real!" shouted the girl. She stomped her feet in a rage.

The ground started to shake. There was a great rumbling. The rumbling got louder, and for a moment, I thought the girl's stomping was going to cause a collapse, but then there was a blast of sound, a series of rhythmic notes.

"Oh no . . . ," said the girl. "The queen is coming."

"She won't like that you got all dirty," said the boy.

"I don't care," the girl groaned. "She's not my mother."

"She's as good as."

"She's not *good* at all, Florian."

The boy and girl continued to argue as they hurried away. Their voices faded, but the rumbling got louder. The ground shook. Dirt fell down into my hiding place in clumps. I feared the hole was about to collapse. I pulled myself out of it and promptly jumped back in.

A herd of beasts came charging by, four-legged animals, some of them with humans on their backs. *Horses!* These were horses! They were almost as big as dragons!

The horses without riders pulled a strange contraption, like a giant wheelbarrow but with four wheels and a roof and doors.

"Make way! Make way!" shouted a big, deep voice. "Make way for the queen!"

I scrambled out of the hole again to follow the procession from a distance, ducking behind trees as I ran. The herd of horses slowed as they drew up to the castle, then stopped, and some of the humans hopped down from the horses' backs. I could not get used to the humans' appearance. How could they walk on such spindly limbs?

One of the humans went over to the big contraption and opened a door in the side of it. He held out his hand, and someone inside reached out to take hold of it. My mouth fell open. The hand was covered in gems—crystals and diamonds on the fingers and gold and sapphires draped around the wrist. When the human stepped into the light, my jaw nearly fell to the floor.

This could only be the human queen.

She was dressed in a deep purple gown that brushed the ground. Her neck and shoulders were draped with gold and diamonds and sapphires, and on her head, she wore a gold circlet with more diamonds and sapphires. And, most amazing of all, right in the center of her forehead was a fat, juicy ruby the size of my nose.

My mouth watered. My stomach rumbled with hunger

again, but luckily no humans noticed this time. All attention was on the queen.

"Your Majesty," said a human, bowing low to the queen. "Queen Elfrieda Veronika Ingrid Lenore, you look so beautiful."

"You can save your compliments, Lord Wiesel," said the queen. "They won't do you any good today." She swept past the man, followed by a gaggle of humans. The queen entered the castle, trailing the spicy-sweet scent of ruby. It was driving me out of my mind.

I should have turned tail and run back to the colony—to safety—but the scent of rubies lured me forward, pulled me toward the castle and the human queen.

I hopped through the grass, jumped up the steps, and slipped through the door just before it shut.

# CHAPTER EIGHT

## Court Weasel

The inside of the castle, though still considerably brighter than a dwarf cavern, was much dimmer than outside. My poor eyes needed to adjust again, but as soon as they did, I couldn't take my surroundings in fast enough. They were almost like our caverns, with granite walls and floors, crystal lanterns and marble pillars, but nothing had the rough texture of home. Everything was cut, polished, and stacked like the towers in a game of Spitzeroff. I almost felt like I could toss a stone and knock it all over. How precariously the humans lived!

The furnishings were familiar yet different. There were many chairs and tables, but instead of using metal and stone, the humans had made them of wood and soft fibers and furs, all rare things in our colony. A huge luminous ball hung from the ceiling, festooned with glittering crystals and little sticks topped with flames. They flickered and danced like a flock of glowfish swimming in place. The walls were covered with enormous paintings, most of them of humans draped in as many gems as the queen, or even more. One woman wore so many diamonds around her neck and head, I almost mistook her for a picture of a dwarf feast.

Servants bustled around the queen, taking her cloak and gloves. I hopped among feet and skirts until I found a small table to hide behind. No one noticed me. No one seemed to look down at all. They probably never even thought of the dwarves living beneath their own home.

The man who had greeted the queen outside—Lord Wiesel, as the queen had called him—was standing in the middle of the room, shifting from side to side in agitation. He seemed smaller than the other humans, only twice the size of a dwarf, with patches of gray hair on both sides of his head, a small, ruddy nose, and ears that rivaled Gilpin's in size. "And how did Her Majesty find her kingdom?" said Lord Wiesel in a high, wispy voice.

"Appalling. I was attacked!" The queen held up a red sphere about the size of my fist.

"You were attacked? By an apple?" said Lord Wiesel.

"Don't be an idiot, Wiesel. My subjects threw apples at me as I rode through their filthy villages to greet them!"

"No!" gasped Lord Wiesel.

"Yes!" hissed the queen. "And you know who is behind it all?"

"No, Your Majesty," said Lord Wiesel. "I've no idea."

"Snow White!"

He seemed shocked. "Snow White? The princess? How can that be? She is only a child."

"You underestimate that little troll!" said the queen. "Only last week, I caught her throwing apples at the wall beneath my chamber. I should have known it was target practice! When can we marry her off to that prince visiting from the Northern Kingdom? I can't wait to be rid of her."

The queen brought the apple to her mouth and bit into it with her tiny sharp teeth. Aha! The apple was human *food*! I watched as the queen chewed. It was very quiet eating. None of the grinding gravel-crunching heard during a dwarf meal. The apple was ruby red on the outside but white on the inside, almost like a geode or agate. I wondered what it tasted like. My stomach rumbled a little too loudly. I wrapped my arms around my middle, trying to muffle the sound.

"She's a bit young for marriage, still," said Lord Wiesel. "And it's a little more complicated than that, I'm afraid. The princess is your heir, remember, and—I beg your pardon for causing you pain—with your husband's death, your rule has become precarious. The presence of the princess is necessary at this time."

"Yes," said the queen. "I've heard rumors, plots to seize my crown and my throne. I won't have it! I will root out all traitors and destroy them!" Bits of apple flew out of her mouth. Lord Wiesel flinched as some of it hit him in the face.

"Only rumors," said Lord Wiesel, wiping his face. "But we would be wise to take caution, nonetheless."

The queen took another bite of her apple. "And how would you suggest *we* take caution?"

Lord Wiesel's cheeks blushed pink. He became even more fidgety. "Forgive me, Your Majesty. You are far too stricken with grief to think of it now, but should you consider it in the future, a marriage could secure your rule, undermine the princess, and settle the nobles, especially if you were to bear your own child. . . ."

The queen raised her eyebrows. "And whom do you suggest I marry?"

At these words, Lord Wiesel turned a deep crimson. He rubbed his bald head and laughed nervously. "I'm certain you could have your pick. There are so many who adore you, but . . . if I may . . ." He bent to one knee and took the queen's hand.

"Message for Lord Wiesel! Message for Lord Wiesel!" A grubby gnome came toddling into the room, shouting in a grunty little voice. It was the very gnome that had rescued me from the human boy and girl. He went straight to Lord Wiesel and ran circles around him and the queen.

"Go away, you foolish creature!" Lord Wiesel tried to brush the gnome away, but it continued its relentless pestering. Lord Wiesel seemed more agitated than ever, something that was not lost on the queen.

"Don't be ridiculous, Lord Wiesel," said the queen. "The message is obviously too important to be delayed. Come, gnome! This is Lord Wiesel. Deliver your message."

The gnome stopped mid-step and delivered its message in a gravelly, dispassionate voice.

*My dearest Lord Wiesel,*

*Do not attempt to woo the queen in order to gain power. You're too old, too bald, and your breath stinks. There are more effective, less foolhardy ways to take the crown. Like chopping off her head.*

Lord Wiesel looked up at the queen, pale and trembling. "I didn't . . . I don't . . ." But the message was not finished.

*Continue to advise the queen. Make her feel quite comfortable about your loyalty to her. When the time is right, we can storm the castle!*

The message finished, the gnome toddled out of the room, leaving behind the queen and a stunned Lord Wiesel, who was still on bended knee, holding the queen's hand.

Now the queen was the one to turn pale. She yanked free of Lord Wiesel's grasp and shoved him roughly to the ground. "Traitor!" she shouted.

Lord Wiesel scrambled to his knees and groveled before the queen. "Your Majesty, please! There's been a terrible mistake!"

"Yes, there *has* been a terrible mistake," said the queen. "The mistake was my ever believing I could trust you, you sniveling, conniving . . ." She raised her hands high above her head and started to mutter something beneath her breath.

"No! Your Majesty, I beg of you!" Lord Wiesel stumbled back, but as he did, he began to shrink—to the size of a dwarf, then a gnome, then smaller still. He grew fur on his face. His words turned to desperate squeaks, and finally he was so small, he disappeared inside his clothes. A moment later, a furry, ratlike creature with beady black eyes appeared from beneath the pile of crumpled clothes. He skittered around the queen's skirts, squeaking what must have been pleas to turn him back into a human.

"No, I think you are looking quite yourself, little Lord *Weasel*," said the queen. "And now you are dismissed!" She picked Lord Wiesel up by the tail, crossed the room, opened a window, and flung him out. The weasel Lord Wiesel did cartwheels through the air, squealing madly, until the queen slammed the window shut and there was silence.

I stood stone-still, trying to make sense of what I had just seen. The human queen had performed magic, and not a simple spell or trick. She had turned a human into a weasel. I'd seen some dwarves press common stones between their hands and turn them into crystals, or take a diamond and multiply it into ten, but I'd never seen a transformation of this kind before. Dwarves had always believed that humans were rather poor in magical powers, but clearly this was not the case, at least not with this human queen.

I waited and watched, wondering what would happen next. The queen walked slowly back to the other end of the room, and then, with a guttural growl, hurled the half-eaten apple. The apple hit the door with a squishy thud, then bounced and rolled and came to a stop only a few steps from my foot.

I stared at the apple. My stomach rumbled again. I was desperately hungry, and I was curious to know what the apple tasted like, but the queen looked as if she might breathe fire. I didn't dare move.

"Traitors," she muttered. "I shall behead them all! I'll turn them into weasels and rats!" She paced back and forth. "Who can I trust? Who?"

The queen walked to a flat piece of silver hanging on a wall, and when she stood in front of it, her reflection appeared. A mirror! It was enormous, a hundred times the size of my Fate Stone, but the reflection wasn't as clear. As far as I could tell, it only showed what was directly in front of it. The queen gazed at herself in the mirror and took a deep breath. It seemed to calm her. She turned her head this way and that, observing her eyes, her nose, her lips. She hissed and plucked a hair from her chin, then searched for others.

"The only one I can trust," she said, "is staring back at me in the mirror."

She seemed rather occupied, talking to herself, and with her back to me, I thought it would be safe enough to snatch the bit of apple. I reached out and grasped the core. It was wet and somewhat slimy to the touch. I brought it to my mouth and was about to take a small bite when I heard a gasp.

I looked up. The queen was still visible in the mirror, but she was not looking at her own image. She was staring straight at me.

# CHAPTER NINE

## Queen Elfrieda Veronika Ingrid Lenore

My eyes locked on to the queen's. I was frozen by her ice blue stare until she blinked. Suddenly I awoke to the danger I was in.

I turned and ran. But there was nowhere to run *to*! The doors were closed; the windows were too high. I zigzagged around the room in a mindless frenzy.

"Stop!" commanded the queen.

I stopped. The queen had used some kind of magic to hold me in place. I heard her footsteps click on the marble floor.

Without warning, I was swept up by one foot and hung upside down. "Do you have another message, gnome? Another traitorous correspondence?" The queen shook me vigorously. "Out with it! I command you to tell me!"

"I'm not a gnome!" I burst out.

The queen stopped shaking me. She looked at me

closely, then gasped. "A . . . dwarf?" Her grip seemed to loosen, but then tightened again. "Why have you come? Who sent you?" The shaking began anew, even more violent than before. Maybe I should have pretended to be a gnome.

"Are you spying for my enemies? Or perhaps you dwarves are trying to take my crown for yourselves! Well, go ahead and try! I'll crush you in your little caves if I have to! I'll rip you out of the ground like worms and eat you for breakfast!!" She shook me until my teeth rattled and I could barely utter a word.

"I'm n-not a sssss-spy!" I managed. "J-just hu-un-gry!"

The queen stopped shaking me. "Hungry?" She released me so I fell to the floor. I tried to stand, but the room was spinning. There seemed to be more than one queen. At least four. Maybe six. All upside down. I shook my head until the many queens were right side up and had morphed back into one.

"Well then," said the queen. "Eat."

I looked down at my hand. In the struggle, I had squeezed the apple to mash, and the sticky juice ran down my fingers and arm. I didn't really want to eat it now. Right now I just wanted to get away, but the queen looked so expectant, I feared what would happen if I didn't obey. I didn't want to be turned into a weasel! I brought the apple to my mouth and took a bite.

The apple was without a doubt the most disgusting thing I'd ever eaten. It was mushy, mealy, and sickly sweet. I spit it out. Juice and mashed-up apple slopped all over the polished floor. I dug into my pocket for a piece of rubble, and crunched it quickly, swishing it around with my tongue in an effort to get the terrible taste out of my mouth.

The queen laughed. "It's true, then, that dwarves eat rocks? I'd heard rumors, but I never quite believed them. How interesting. I wonder if the other rumors are true."

I took a step back. I hoped she hadn't heard rumors about our beards.

"Don't worry," said the queen sweetly. "I'm not going to hurt you. Are you still hungry? What kinds of rocks do you like to eat?"

I stared at the giant ruby on the queen's head. I couldn't help but lick my lips.

The queen rolled her eyes upward and touched her crown, as though she'd forgotten she was wearing it. "My, you do have fine taste, don't you? But perhaps as my guest . . ." She fumbled around with all the gems she was wearing until she found a ruby on one of her fingers. She pried it loose and held it out to me. "Here. Have one."

My mouth watered. I stepped forward and reached, then stopped. I shouldn't. It might be a trick. Or a trap. "I can't," I said.

The queen frowned. "It's not poisoned, I promise you. Please. Take it as a token of my welcome and good wishes. I have longed to meet a dwarf for many years." She held the ruby in front of my face. The tangy scent tickled my nose.

I was so hungry. Practically starving. I could hear crashing sounds inside my belly. How could I resist a ruby? It would be wasteful and ungrateful.

"Thank you," I said. I took the ruby and popped it

into my mouth. I let it sit on my tongue for a minute, then crunched down hard and fast so the shards and dust spread all over my mouth with tangy sweet flavor. It tingled my tongue and burned ever so slightly as it went down and settled in my stomach. The effects were quick and powerful. Heat flared in my belly, and energy surged in my limbs. I felt an immediate sense of euphoria. Rubies were potent gems.

"Good?" the queen asked.

"Delicious," I said. "Thank you."

"You're welcome," said the queen. "I'd love to give you more, but first I think we ought to be properly introduced. I am Queen Elfrieda Veronika Ingrid Lenore, but you can call me 'Your Majesty,' like everyone else in my kingdom."

I opened my mouth to tell her my name, but she didn't give me the chance.

"And you, Dwarf, how is it that I have been graced with your presence today? I had always heard that dwarves never show themselves to humans."

I shrugged. "I've always wanted to see The Surface," I said. "I was just curious."

"So you've never been aboveground before?"

I shook my head.

"How interesting. And you live underground, where you dig for rubies to eat?"

I stiffened. Was she going to try to get me to reveal the location of our colony? Steal all our food so she could wear it?

"Don't worry," said the queen. "I have no interest in

stealing your gems. I care nothing for them. Only, my subjects expect me to be draped in diamonds and rubies, to make me appear more royal. I suppose it's a rather odd sight for a dwarf."

"A little," I said.

"Yes, I would certainly think it strange to see creatures wearing mutton and carrots." She laughed, and I laughed, too, even though I hadn't a clue what mutton or carrots were. "And how selfish of me to be wearing such jewels when there are hungry little dwarves about! Would you like a diamond?" She popped a diamond off her necklace and held it out to me.

"Thank you," I said.

"Thank you, *Your Majesty*," said Queen Elfrieda.

"Er, yes. Thank you, Your Majesty." I popped the diamond into my mouth. It wasn't nearly as good as the ruby but had a strengthening effect that made me feel I could lift the entire castle off the ground.

The queen smiled down at me. "You are very welcome, little Dwarf. Won't you come sit by me?" She sat on a large chair with many cushions. She picked me up and sat me next to her. I wiggled around, trying to find a nice, hard spot, but it was all squishy and uncomfortable.

"There's a dear. What do you think of my kingdom?"

"It's very . . . green."

"You probably don't see so much green, do you, living in all that rock and dirt?"

"We have emeralds, but emeralds are my least favorite gem. They smell like bat poop."

The queen gave a snort of laughter—which turned into a surprised squeal when Leaf, at the mention of bats, came bursting out of my shirt. He flew circles around the queen's crown, squeaking madly.

"Oh! Oh! Get it away!" The queen started slapping her arms around her wildly.

"Leaf!" I shouted. "Stop!" I reached for him and finally caught him by a wing. He struggled in my grasp until I forced his wings around him and shoved him down my shirt.

Queen Elfrieda was breathing heavily, her hand clutched at her heart. Tufts of hair stuck out at the sides of her head, and her crown was lopsided.

"Sorry," I said. "He's just a little excited. He's never been to The Surface, either."

"Oh," said the queen, trying to compose herself. "So he's a friend of yours?"

"Yes," I said. "His name is Leaf. He's my pet bat."

"A pet bat!" The queen looked faint. "Do many dwarves keep bats as pets?"

I shook my head. "Just me. Leaf is my only friend, really." And then I felt my cheeks blush blue. I hadn't meant to share something so personal with the queen.

"Well," said the queen, trying to smooth her hair and straighten her crown, "at least you have a friend. I haven't got a single one."

"Not any?"

She shook her head. "There are many who pretend to be my friends. They shower me with praise and gifts, but soon enough I discover their plots of betrayal, as I did Lord Wiesel's. He was the last of my trusted advisers, though I suppose he never was trustworthy, the traitor."

I wondered if all her other advisers had been turned into weasels.

"Now I have no one," said the queen. "I can't trust a single person. There are people in this very court who wish to take my crown right off my head." I glanced at her crown. Right now I wanted to *eat* it right off her head. It looked like a grand cake.

The queen told me how she'd been sent away at the age of eighteen to marry the king. *Eighteen!* I was barely out of a cradle at that age. The king's first wife had died, shortly after giving birth to the princess, Snow White, and Elfrieda was chosen to be the new queen. "No one quite accepted me," she said. "They treat me like an outsider."

"No one accepts me, either," I said. I told the queen of my tragic birth, my fear of depths, how everyone shunned me, and how my parents had forced me to work in a mine in the deepest depths.

"What abuse!" cried the queen. "You poor little dwarf—no wonder you came aboveground. If you were my subject, I would never treat you so abominably. You'd never have to dig at all, and you'd have as many gems as you like!"

My mouth watered as I imagined a cartload of rubies just for me.

"Thank you, Your Majesty," I said. "You're much nicer than I expected. For a human, I mean." The queen raised her eyebrows. I felt my cheeks blush blue again. "Sorry.

It's just that we hear a lot of stories about humans underground."

Queen Elfrieda smiled. "I'm sure we've both heard stories about each other that aren't true. For instance, I've heard many fantastical tales of dwarves—that you're very knowledgeable and you possess all kinds of magic. Is that true?"

"Yes, that's true," I said with an air of pride. "Every dwarf has powerful magic."

"Fascinating," said the queen, her eyes glittering. "And what are your particular powers? Can you see the future? Cast spells? Transform things?"

"I . . ." I tried to think of my powers. All dwarves had them. Some just weren't as visible as others. Mine, however, seemed to be nonexistent. But I couldn't tell that to a human, especially when *she* could do such powerful magic herself. No human, even a royal one, should think of dwarves as anything but superior to them.

"I'm not allowed to tell you," I whispered. "Dwarf magic is supposed to be kept secret."

"Oh," said the queen, looking a little disappointed. "Yes, of course. I understand. I'm a human, after all, your mortal enemy."

We both laughed. I had been frightened of the queen at first, but now, after getting to know her a little, I saw that she was really gentle and kind, and not nearly as funny-looking as I'd thought at first glance. Her eyes were the palest shade of blue tourmaline, her hair like shiny waves of mineral-rich dirt.

"How would you like a tour of my kingdom?" asked

the queen. "I would dearly love to show you around and introduce you to some of my subjects."

I hesitated. How long had I been gone? An hour? Two? What if the crew returned and I wasn't there? Gilpin was probably already worried. I should get back now, but . . .

To see The Surface with a human guide was almost too great an opportunity to pass up. There was so much I wished to learn! Gilpin promised me he wouldn't tell the crew where I'd gone. They'd probably just think I'd gone to deliver the borlen. They'd never suspect.

"I'd love a tour of your kingdom," I said.

"Oh, good! I have so many things to show you!" The queen stood and held out her hand. "Shall we?"

I took her hand, hopped down from the chair, and together we walked out of the castle.

# CHAPTER TEN

## A Stroll with Trolls

Outside, I had to adjust again to the bright light. Four human guards in red tunics accompanied us—two in the front and two behind. One raised an eyebrow at me in curiosity, but said nothing.

Earlier, I had been in a hurry, uncertain where I should go or how safe I was on The Surface. But now, with the queen as my guide and four guards to protect us, I felt quite comfortable and took it all in at my leisure.

At first I was overwhelmed. The light, the space, the jumble of noises and smells, the creatures that ran wild. So many things I had heard stories about and imagined but was now seeing with my own eyes! Other things I had never heard of delighted me all the more.

"What are those?" I asked, pointing to a bunch of strange, fluffy creatures on two legs.

"Why, those are chickens," said the queen. "They give us eggs and meat and feathers."

"And that?"

"That's a cow. Cows give us milk."

"And what are *they* doing?" I pointed to a group of humans digging in the ground with shovels and other tools. For a moment I worried they might be trying to dig to our tunnels! But they weren't digging very deep at all.

"They're planting seeds," said the queen. "The seeds will grow into food we can eat."

"Ooh, neat!" I said. I crouched down and poked my finger in the dirt. I wondered how the growing worked, exactly. If I planted a ruby here, would it grow into more rubies? The queen smiled, pleased with my curiosity for her land.

At the bottom of the hill, human homes were bunched very close together, and the humans milled about on their spindly legs, their long arms swinging at their sides. It still baffled me.

And the little humans . . . how funny they looked! Like disfigured, chubby-cheeked dwarflings. A little boy tripped and began to cry. Wet, glistening tears trickled down his ruddy cheeks until a man picked him up and carried him away, murmuring sweet words of comfort. I felt a slight pang of missing my father. He had always been the one to comfort me.

"Is something wrong?" Queen Elfrieda asked, jolting me out of my thoughts.

"No!" I said, a little too loudly. "Everything is wonderful."

All day long, the queen guided me around her kingdom, and I learned more about The Surface in an afternoon than I had in fifty years underground. I was introduced to more of their foods—pies (disgusting), bread (blech), blueberries (ew), and beans (internal explosion!).

Wherever we went, the humans stopped what they were doing and bowed deeply to Queen Elfrieda. They didn't pay me any mind. They likely mistook me for a gnome, which annoyed me, but I had to remind myself how little humans knew of dwarves. Anyway, it was probably for the best.

We came upon a merchant selling jewels, and the queen offered to buy me some, but I could tell in an instant that the "gems" were nothing more than dyed salt crystals. When I told the queen, she was so angry at the deception, she ordered the guards to carry the woman away.

"See how my subjects try to deceive me!" said Queen Elfrieda, seething. "You are so clever, Dwarf. How can I ever repay you?"

I felt my cheeks blush blue. "It was nothing, really. Any dwarf would have spotted it."

"If only I had a dwarf to advise me always. I am surrounded by liars and fools!"

My sense of worth and purpose bloomed. How wonderful to be appreciated! I walked a little taller.

We came to the fringes of the village and entered a wooded area. A foul smell tickled my nose and intensified as we walked. Queen Elfrieda covered her nose with a bit of frilly cloth. I held my breath, wondering what the smell could possibly be.

We came upon some strange-looking creatures, snorting and sniffing at the air and the ground. They weren't human. They were bigger and hairier. Their eyes were yellow, their teeth mangled, and their arms hung below their knees. The rank odor was emanating from their direction.

"What are those?" I asked, pointing.

"Those? Why, they're trolls. Have you never seen a troll before?"

I shook my head. I knew nothing about trolls. They looked brutish, dangerous even, which was probably why they were chained about their wrists and ankles. They snorted and sniffed at the ground madly.

"What are they doing?"

"They're searching for magic, of course. That's what trolls do. They find magic. They can smell it. Did you know that magic has a smell?"

I shook my head. I wondered how the trolls could smell anything over their own scent. It was like a gaseous, sulfurous pit with fermented bat droppings on top.

A masked human walked behind the trolls. He carried a long, thin cord coiled in his hand. When the trolls moved too far in any direction, he lashed the cord out and it snapped around their limbs and pulled them back. I winced as the trolls roared in pain.

"Humans have some magic, too," said the queen. "It's all around us, but we have to gather it like we do our food, bit by bit, every day, and the trolls help with the gathering. They are my faithful servants and bring me all the magic they find—spells, potions, enchanted objects or creatures. . . . When they find them, they bring them to me. If I am pleased, they are rewarded."

Queen Elfrieda clapped her hands three times. The taskmaster snapped the cord again, and it wrapped around all the trolls together, binding them against each other.

"Well, trolls, have any of you found magic for me today?" asked Queen Elfrieda.

"I have!" said a troll. He struggled against his bindings.

"Loosen the whip, you fool," said the queen.

The taskmaster tugged on the cord, or *whip,* as the queen called it, and it loosened. The largest of the trolls ambled forward, holding a little bottle filled with puce green liquid. "We found a potion that will turn you old and ugly for a whole day!"

"Why on earth would I want such a horrible potion?" snapped the queen, but she took it anyway and slid it into her pocket. "Anything else?"

Another troll hobbled forward and held out his hand. In the center of his palm was a little brown pebble, smooth and pointed at one end. "I found this seed," said the troll. "If you plant it in the sunlight, it will grow regular apples, but if you plant it in the light of a full moon, it will grow poison apples."

"How poisonous?" said the queen.

"One bite and you'll fall down dead," said the troll.

"Well, I shouldn't like that seed to get into anyone else's hands." The queen pocketed it. "Anything else?"

Another troll came forward. "I have a spell that will turn you into a rat! It goes like this:

*"Fur and tail, claws and whiskers–"*

"Don't say it out loud!" the queen cried. "Are you trying to turn *me* into a rat?"

The troll looked confused. "Wouldn't you like that?" he said. "It might be fun. Rats are very intelligent creatures, and they can eat just about anything. Best life next to a troll's, if you ask me."

The queen sighed. "Not today. Write it down, please, and be careful not to get your slobber on it." She held something out to the troll. It looked like one of the stone tablets we kept in the hall of records, except when the troll opened it, there were many thin, flimsy sheets with writing on them. The troll took a thin stick and wrote his spell onto one of the sheets, careful to wipe his slobber away before it dripped onto the page.

While we waited, the troll that had given the queen the potion had gone back to sniffing. He was sniffing and snorting very close to us. A moment later, another troll followed him, clearly picking up on the same scent.

"I smell . . . I smell . . . ," said the first troll.

Soon all the trolls were sniffing in our direction. I backed against the queen as they surrounded us, snorting and grunting like mad. Their yellow eyes rolled, and thick gray saliva dripped from their yellow teeth.

"Shhh," said the queen. "Hold still. They're smelling something."

The largest troll bent down so we were nearly nose to nose. His nostrils widened and he sniffed. Once. Twice. He stuck out his long gray tongue as though tasting whatever he smelled. His yellow eyes rolled back in his head and then narrowed at me. "Him." He pointed a thick, dirty finger at me. "I smell magic on him."

"Of course you smell him, you imbecile," said the queen. "He's a dwarf."

"A dwarf? Haven't seen a dwarf in a long while. Peculiar smell. Earthy. Deep. Very magical, but hard to pinpoint the specific kind . . ." The troll sniffed me all over until he reached my pocket. He snorted wildly as he reached inside and pulled out my Fate Stone.

"What is that?" said the queen eagerly.

The troll sniffed at it. "Magic mirror. Very powerful."

"A magic mirror!" The queen snatched my Fate Stone from the troll and gazed at it longingly. "I've always wanted a magic mirror! What will it do? Will it show me the future? My enemies?"

"It won't show you anything except your own reflection," said the troll. "It belongs to the dwarf. It will only work for him." He nodded to me. "The mirror is bonded to him. I can smell that, too."

The queen looked down at me. At first I thought she was angry, but then her face softened. She smiled sweetly. "Of course. I should not have been so presumptuous." She handed my Fate Stone back to me.

"But you know," said the troll. "You could always *mirror* the magic mirror and create another one."

The queen brightened. "Is it a difficult spell?"

"Simple as sludge," said the troll. "All you have to do is point the magic mirror at the other mirror and chant the words 'Magic mirror, mirror magic' over and over until there's a flash of light and the thing is done."

Queen Elfrieda clapped her hands. "Perfect!"

"But be careful," warned the troll. "Mirroring magic mirrors can be a very tricky business."

"How so?" Queen Elfrieda asked.

"Consider that mirrors are already tricky things," said the troll. "*Magic* mirrors are even trickier. But if you take a magic mirror and magically mirror it onto another mirror, you're mirroring magic that could magically mirror the mirror's magic right back to you, and that's the trickiest of all, do you see?"

I didn't see at all, and the queen looked as though she didn't either, but she smiled anyway and nodded at the troll. "Yes, we'll be very careful with our magic mirrors and mirror magic. Now back to work! Sniff, sniff! I'll return soon to see what else you've found for me. Come, Dwarf, before I faint from this foul smell."

She covered her nose and walked away quickly. I moved to follow, but the troll tapped me on the shoulder. "One more thing," he said.

"Yes?"

He looked in the queen's direction, then leaned in close to me. His rank odor filled my nose. "Don't let her touch your beard," he whispered.

My eyes widened. He knew! He knew about beard magic, and he didn't say anything to the queen. Subconsciously, I took hold of my beard as the troll ambled back toward the other trolls. They went on sniffing and snorting. The troll looked back at me until the taskmaster cracked his whip. I winced at the sound.

The queen was quiet as we walked back to her castle. She looked like she was deep in thought. The sun was sinking in the sky, and shadows were stretching over the ground. I knew this was a sign that day was ending and soon it would be night.

"I had better get back underground now," I said. "Thank you for showing me your kingdom, Your Majesty, and for the gems."

"Oh! Must you go?" Queen Elfrieda cried. "I was hoping you might stay. I rather thought you fancied my kingdom. And me."

"I did—I mean, I do!" I said. "But if I don't get back to the caverns, I could get in a lot of trouble. If they find out where I've been, I could be banished."

"And so what if you are? Why should that bother you?" said the queen. "Why would you *want* to go back? You said yourself how much you hate being underground, and how no one appreciates you and they make you do all sorts of awful tasks. Why don't you stay here, where you're valued?"

I sputtered in disbelief. "Stay? Like, forever? *Live* on The Surface with humans?"

"Oh, I know it sounds ridiculous," said the queen.

Ridiculous, dangerous, impossible, and yet . . .

"But we are so alike, you and I," she continued. "We're both outcasts. We're both alone in the world, misunderstood and ill treated. But if you stay here with me, we'll have each other. You can be my new adviser! You'll never have to work in those awful mines again, and I'll feed you all the diamonds and rubies you could ever wish for!"

I pictured a mound of diamonds, heaps of rubies. The idea suddenly became less ridiculous. I was starting to think all the stories dwarves told about humans were more fairy tale than fact. What did we really know about them, anyway?

The queen hadn't demanded I show her where our colony was so she could steal our gems. Instead, she had given me her own gems! And she hadn't tried to take me by the beard—that was probably just a story, too. All stories and lies! I bet nothing would happen if she took me by the beard!

The idea began to warm and bubble inside me like a sweet ruby stew. Never go back to the depths. Never have to work with the crew in the mines again. No more teasing or ridicule. I could stay on The Surface and eat as many rubies as I liked. With a friend. My eyes grew dusty. My heart beat a little faster.

"I'll stay," I said.

The queen clapped her hands. "You have made me so happy! I just know we will be the best of friends!" She smiled, showing all her little teeth.

I smiled, showing all my big teeth.

# CHAPTER ELEVEN

## Magic Mirror, Mirror Magic

Delighted as I was to be on The Surface as the special guest of Queen Elfrieda, the humans did not know how to host a dwarf comfortably, nor did they have any idea about our customs.

The queen gave me a whole crew of human servants, whose first aim was to give me a bath. I thought it might be very nice indeed to bathe in a relaxing tub of crushed amethysts or blue crystals, but I soon learned that was not the way humans bathe. First they wanted me to remove all my clothes! I told them dwarves always bathe with their clothes on, which they thought was ridiculous, but they respected my wishes. Then, before I knew what was happening, they shoved me into a bucket of water! As if that wasn't bad enough, they lathered some slimy, smelly stuff called soap all over me. Luckily, at that point

Leaf flew out of my shirt and all the servants ran away screaming.

I was left sopping wet and cold, with the soap stinging my eyes. Leaf was so upset, he flew to the top of the ceiling and hung upside down with his wings wrapped around his head. He didn't come down for the rest of the night, which hurt my feelings just a bit, as he always slept inside my shirt.

I pulled out my Fate Stone. I wanted to see Gilpin. Had he told the crew where I'd gone? My own image rippled in the mirror, and Gilpin appeared. He was standing in the place where I'd escaped to The Surface. It was well covered with a pile of rubble, but Gilpin paced back and forth, pulling at his ears until Herkimer and Rudger appeared behind him.

"Gilpin!" said Herkimer. "It's time to go home. Where's the Seventh?"

Gilpin glanced at the pile of rubble. I held my breath, waiting. Finally, Gilpin shrugged.

"Idiot probably got lost on his way to the main cavern," said Rudger.

"Should we go and look for him?" Herkimer asked, looking concerned.

"Nah," said Rudger. "He'll find his way back eventually, or he'll fall into the lava rivers. Who cares! Good riddance to the grump. Come on. I'm hungry."

Herkimer and Rudger turned to go. Gilpin stayed behind a moment. He removed a few pieces of rubble and peeked through the hole.

"Gilpin, what are you doing?" Herkimer asked.

Gilpin stumbled back from the hole and scampered after them, looking over his shoulder one last time before disappearing down the tunnel.

I found it impossible to sleep. Even though the sky had darkened, it was still much brighter than underground, and the bed was terribly uncomfortable. It was so soft and squishy, I felt like I was being eaten. Finally, I wriggled free and flopped onto the stone floor. It was a little too smooth for my liking, but at least it was hard. I would be much more comfortable with a big flat stone to press me to sleep. Perhaps I could find one tomorrow.

I wondered if the crew would worry when I didn't return tonight. How long before they'd begin to search? Probably weeks, maybe months. They might not even notice. They would forget they ever had a Seventh and probably wouldn't even send word to my parents. And if I returned with my pockets full of diamonds and rubies, they'd be so excited, they wouldn't bother to ask where I'd been. I'd share with everyone except Rudger.

I woke the next morning to bright light. It took me a moment to remember where I was: The Surface! The sun was shining through the window and the soft sapphire blue fabric around it billowed in the breeze. Such a marvel.

My stomach crunched with hunger. The gems the

queen had given me yesterday provided a quick surge of energy, but I needed something a little more hearty and filling.

I glanced around the room. There was a copper pot in one corner. Copper was good for coughs and dusty noses, but I didn't love the earthy, rusty flavor. There was some clay pottery, but that wouldn't taste much better than rubble. Finally, my eyes rested on a marble sculpture of a human head. That would do. I hopped over to it and bit off the nose just as the door opened.

"Oh!" Queen Elfrieda exclaimed. I froze with the marble nose clenched between my teeth. I didn't know what to do. I couldn't spit it out or put it back, so I crunched down hard and swallowed as fast as I could. The sharp bits scraped down my throat. The sound from my stomach was like a cave-in as the marble settled.

"I came to see if you'd like to join me for breakfast," said Queen Elfrieda, frowning at the now nose-less statue.

"Sorry," I said, looking down at the floor.

"It's quite all right. I want you to feel welcome here, Dwarf."

I wondered if I should tell her my name, but she'd never asked it, and I couldn't think of a way to let her know without seeming rude, so I let it go. She could call me Dwarf. It's not like there were any other dwarves up here on The Surface, so I supposed it was as good a name as any. It was better than Grump.

"Shall we go to breakfast? I had the cook prepare something special just for you."

"Yes, I'll get Leaf." He was still on the ceiling, wings wrapped around his head. "Come down, Leaf. It's morning. Time to wake up."

He didn't move.

"Leaf, come on. Breakfast!"

He squeaked at me with indignation. He was still angry.

"Leaf, you're being very rude!"

"Perhaps it's best to leave your friend here for the day," said Queen Elfrieda, eyeing Leaf nervously. "Shall we?"

I left Leaf hanging from the ceiling. I'd bring him back some flies or beetles and he'd forgive me, and hopefully warm to the queen.

Human breakfast was a smelly, messy affair. The table was covered in dishes and bowls filled with all sorts of shapes and colors. At first glance, they could have been mistaken for gems and minerals, except for the smell, which was awful, and the textures, all squishy and slimy.

The only thing that looked remotely edible was some runny goop that looked a bit like strolg.

"It's porridge," said the queen. "Would you like to try some?" She fed me a spoonful. My face twisted. It was bland and slimy, nothing like strolg.

"Perhaps your own foods will satisfy." Queen Elfrieda rang a bell. A servant rushed forward and set a silver tray in front of me. He lifted the lid. My mouth fell open.

"I wasn't sure what all you liked," said the queen. "So I told the royal treasurer to bring a variety."

A variety, indeed. There were diamonds, sapphires, amethysts, emeralds, opals, garnets, topaz, obsidian, and jade. And a ruby! A small one, but still . . . I ate one of everything except the jade and emeralds, and I saved the ruby for last. I crunched happily until I saw that the queen was not eating. She sat with her chin rested in her hand, frowning at me.

"Is something wrong, Your Majesty?"

"Wrong? No, there is nothing wrong." And then, all of a sudden, inexplicably, she began to cry. Her eyes welled with water, and little droplets rolled down her cheeks. I rushed to her side. "Your Majesty! Whatever is the matter? Have I offended you?"

"Oh, Dwarf! You are too kind. Truly, you are the only creature in this world whom I can trust. Only, I fear that there are ever so many traitors swarming around my court, ready to steal my throne."

"That's . . . terrible," I said. "Is there anything I can do?"

"No, no. I am sure there is nothing anyone can do. It is all hopeless. I must accept my tragic fate." Streams trailed down her cheeks and dripped from her chin. She took a small cloth and blew her nose into it.

The sight of that poor young human—a decade or more younger than I—with all that weight on her shoulders caused me to forget my own troubles and think only about how I could help. She needed wisdom only a dwarf could provide. And when she said the word "fate," I knew precisely what to do.

"Your Majesty," I said, taking my Fate Stone out of my pocket. "We can use my mirror! As the trolls said, we can mirror its magic onto your mirror so that it might show you how to secure your crown."

Queen Elfrieda stopped crying immediately. "How perfectly ingenious, Dwarf! I wonder why I didn't think of it." She snatched my Fate Stone out of my hands. I stood a little taller, proud that I had thought of such a clever solution. "Now, what was it the trolls said I must do? Yes, I remember." She held my magic mirror up to her own large mirror on the wall and said, "Magic mirror, mirror magic," over and over, but nothing happened.

"It isn't working!" she shouted, and hurled my Fate Stone across the room. It hit the wall and clattered to the floor. Heart racing, I ran to the spot and picked it up, expecting it to be shattered, but it didn't have so much as a scratch upon it.

"The trolls lied to me!" shouted the queen. "Oh, those traitorous beasts, I shall whip them! I can't trust anyone."

"Your Majesty," I said, bringing my Fate Stone back to her mirror. "Why don't you let me try it? Maybe it needs to be me who performs the spell. After all, it is *my* magic mirror—maybe the magic needs to come from me."

"Aah . . . of course," said Queen Elfrieda. "How silly of me." She made way for me to stand in front of the mirror. I held my Fate Stone up to it, and the two reflections bounced back and forth again and again, an infinity of mirrors. It made me feel the significance of what I was about to do. Once it was done, I couldn't take it back.

I glanced at the queen. She smiled at me and nodded. She had been so kind and generous to me. Now she needed my help. My *magical* help. It was the least I could do.

I held the mirror and chanted the words the troll had

told us. "Magic mirror, mirror magic." My Fate Stone seemed to warm in my hands. "Magic mirror, mirror magic." My fingertips tingled. "Magic mirror, mirror magic." It started to vibrate, and then a stream of light burst from my mirror and poured into the queen's. The power of it knocked me off my feet. The queen rushed over. I thought she was coming to help me up, but instead she went to her mirror on the wall.

"Did it work? Will it show me things now? Mirror, mirror, how can I secure my crown? Who would try to take it from me? What . . . Oh!" She took a step back from her mirror. It was swirling, much like mine did when it was about to show me something.

"What is that?" the queen said. "It's a person. No, no, it's some kind of animal. . . . It's a . . ."

"It's me," I said. I watched my face come into the mirror, dark eyes, sharp nose, pointy beard. I looked down at my Fate Stone, and there was the queen staring up at me. Our mirrors were reflecting each other.

"Oh," said the queen, her voice drenched with disappointment. "So that's it then, is it? The mirror is only going to show me a dwarf? Or are *you* the threat to my crown? Or some other dwarf? Were you planning to sabotage my throne all along?"

"No! No!" I protested. "Your Majesty, I would never . . . I am here to help you."

"But how? How can *you* help me?"

I didn't know. I squinted at my Fate Stone, begging it to show something useful. How could the queen secure her rule? I focused on that thought, and my mirror began to swirl. So did the queen's. When the swirling cleared, the image in the mirror was dim and ill defined, but I knew instantly what it was. It showed no person, but ancient words etched in stone. It showed the epitaph carved into the First Foredwarf's chair.

"A prophecy! I think it's showing a prophecy, Dwarf. About me!"

WE'LL BEAR NO TYRANT, SUFFER NO FOOL

THE FAIREST OF ALL IS THE ONE WHO WILL RULE

The mirror swirled again and faded until it showed only my reflection and the queen's. "The fairest of all? That's it?" She looked at me in the mirror.

I shrugged. "That's how it always works with dwarves," I said. "Whoever is the fairest will rule, and none can challenge them. Unless someone fairer comes along, of course."

"The fairest of all . . . Can I look at myself now?"

"Oh, yes, of course." I put my Fate Stone away, and the queen's mirror faded and then showed her own reflection. Queen Elfrieda gazed at herself in the mirror, turning this way and that. "It's not so unfathomable that I should be the fairest of all, is it? It is, in fact, why the king chose me to be his queen."

"Of course," I said. "You're the fairest human of all as far as I'm concerned." What other human would treat a dwarf with such kindness? What other human would give a dwarf so many fine gems! Besides, she was the only human I knew. Of course she was the fairest to me.

The queen smiled fondly at me through her mirror. "You are too good to me, Dwarf," she said, then turned her attention back to herself. "Yes, the fairest of them all. I think that is something I can manage. Thank you, Dwarf. You have been very helpful. I am ever so glad that we are friends."

I smiled. It felt good to be a helpful friend.

"But we mustn't be complacent," said Queen Elfrieda. "Someone fairer than I could come along at any moment and snatch my crown right off my head! Come, Dwarf, we have work to do. We must root out the traitors and make sure that I am always the fairest of all!"

# CHAPTER TWELVE

## The Fairest of All

"Mirror, mirror, on the wall, who's the fairest of them all?"

Queen Elfrieda gazed at my image in her mirror. I gazed at hers in mine.

"You are fairest, of course," I said.

The queen giggled. "Again! Mirror, mirror, on the wall, who is the fairest of them all?"

I decided to wax poetic this time. "Over the land, as far as I've seen, thou art the fairest of all, my queen!"

She squealed with delight. "Oh, you are too much! Have a treat!" She pulled a ruby out of her pocket and tossed it to me so I caught it in my mouth. I crunched and swallowed, then smiled dazedly.

It had been three weeks since I came to The Surface. I'd never been happier in all my life. The queen doted on me and showered me with more delicious crystals and gems than I'd ever enjoyed underground. We were almost always together. When we were apart, we could see each other in our mirrors, so long as we were both looking at them, and we could talk, too. Mostly, she wanted to know who was the fairest of all. I always told her that she was, of course. It was her favorite game. Sometimes, if I gave a particularly good answer, she'd give me a ruby. It was my favorite game, too.

"You know what I think, Dwarf?" said the queen. "I think we should have a ball!"

"What's that?" I asked. "Does it taste good?"

Queen Elfrieda laughed. "No, silly. A ball is a party! A celebration! I want to throw a celebration in your honor, my most trusted adviser."

"That sounds nice," I said. "Are there rubies at a ball?"

"Now, now, Dwarf, don't get greedy. Who's the fairest of them all?"

"You are fairest by far," I said.

"There's a good dwarf." The queen shoved another ruby into my mouth.

But life on The Surface was not all rubies and games. I had work to do, too, for there were traitors everywhere, lying in wait to steal the queen's throne. I aided the queen in rooting them out, though the queen spotted them best. To my surprise, most of the traitors were young females, younger than the queen even. They all cried that they were innocent, but the queen apparently had proof of their guilt, for she threw them in dungeons or towers. We imprisoned a young maiden at least once a day, and I began to regard all the human girls with suspicion. They looked as innocent as baby bats, but the queen had shown me otherwise.

Speaking of bats, Leaf had grown strange since coming to The Surface. His sleeping patterns had shifted. He slept most of the day and hunted for food at night. This shouldn't have worried me—it was normal bat behavior, after all—but I felt like he was doing it to punish me. I thought he was jealous of my friendship with the queen. And he wouldn't touch any of the flies or beetles I brought him as peace offerings. At night, he flew off to hunt his own food. When he came back, he went right to the ceiling and stayed there all day. He never slept in my shirt anymore. It didn't bother me too much. I had obligations to the queen now, and those took up quite a bit of time. But I missed Leaf.

I rarely thought of home, and I certainly didn't miss the mines. But sometimes, if I looked in my mirror when Queen Elfrieda was not looking in hers, I'd get a glimpse of the crew or my parents.

My parents looked older, like they'd aged a century in the time I was gone.

"I've organized a search party, Rumelda," said Father. "We'll find him, if he can be found."

"Do you think . . . ," Mother began, but couldn't finish the sentence.

"We may never know," said Father.

Sometimes I caught a glimpse of Gilpin, waiting for me by the Surface hole, covered with rubble. Sometimes the mirror showed me the pictures he'd drawn of the two of us.

I put my mirror away. The images of home, Gilpin, and my parents, the weight and sadness I'd put upon them, filled me with guilt—but not enough to go back. I couldn't possibly leave Queen Elfrieda now. She relied heavily on my wisdom, my depth of knowledge, my magic. Underground, I was a lowly Seventh, the grump—a nobody. On The Surface, I was valued. I was somebody.

One day, the queen and I were walking together in a village on the outskirts of The Kingdom when I heard a high-pitched wail. I looked around for the source, certain someone was injured or in grave danger. A woman stood at a window, holding a squirming, squealing bundle in her arms. "Hush, baby," she said.

"A human baby!" I said. "I've always wanted to see one of those!" I hopped onto a stone and peered over the window ledge, into the bundle of blankets. The baby was still wailing, its mouth open so wide I could see its toothless gums. I stifled a laugh. It was hideous. Its face was round and red, and it was nearly bald, except for a thatch of blond hair on top of its head.

"Oh, how glad I am I never had one of those vile creatures!" said the queen. "A stepdaughter is bad enough."

"This one doesn't have any teeth," I said. "I heard the princess didn't have teeth, either. Is that true?"

"Perhaps," said the queen. "I rarely see the child, but I hear she's a sickly, pale creature. We don't have to worry about *her* taking my crown."

I was about to ask why being pale and toothless would eliminate the princess as a threat, but I was interrupted by the baby's wails.

"Why are you crying, my pretty one?" The mother rocked her child. "Don't you know that you're the prettiest baby in the land? Yes, you are," she cooed. "And you will grow into the prettiest maiden." The baby calmed a little.

The queen stiffened. A crease formed between her brows.

"Your Majesty? What's wrong?"

The queen shook her head. "Nothing. Only, the cries of infants distress me. I always wish to comfort them but cannot."

"You have a heart of rubies, Your Majesty," I said. "You truly are the fairest in the land."

The queen smiled at me. "And you, my Dwarf, practically *are* a ruby." She took a ruby out of her pocket. I opened my mouth for her to drop it in, but then the baby began to wail again, louder this time. "Oh, what a horrid sound! Let's get away from here." She put the ruby back in her pocket and hurried away.

Night fell as we returned to the castle. "Ah! Look at the moon! It's full!" said the queen.

Indeed, the moon was a full, glowing circle of marble in the onyx sky. "I have been waiting for this." She reached into a pouch at her waist and retrieved the poison-apple seed the trolls had given her. I had almost forgotten about it. I hadn't thought the queen would remember, either, but she planted it carefully just outside the castle, in a spot of dirt in the full light of the moon. No sooner had she patted the seed beneath the earth than a tiny black sprout began to unfurl. The next day it had already grown several inches.

# CHAPTER THIRTEEN

## Fall at the Ball

The day of the ball arrived. I was nervous and excited and extremely uncomfortable as I was being fitted for special clothes. "I want all The Kingdom to see my most trusted friend," said Queen Elfrieda, "and so you must be dressed in The Kingdom's finest."

The Kingdom's finest was far too soft and slippery for my comfort. I would've preferred to wear my everyday bat-hair trousers and spider-silk shirt, but I didn't wish to seem ungrateful, so I endured it as best I could. I was dressed in a purple shirt and emerald green trousers embroidered with purple thread. On my head, I wore a pointy purple hat, which looked completely ridiculous.

As the ball began, I sat on a small throne right next to the queen. The nobility wore extravagant costumes embroidered with silver and gold, studded with gems, and topped with feathers and filigree. When they entered, they bowed deeply to the queen and then turned to me and bowed, though not quite as deeply. Some seemed afraid, unsure what to make of the dwarf sitting next to their queen. I tried to smile extra big, showing all my teeth, but that didn't seem to help.

Most guests brought gifts for the queen—flowers, spices, herbs, potions, and baskets of fruit. One guest brought a silver box encrusted with gems. It looked like a birthday cake.

"And for the queen's most trusted adviser . . . ," said one nobleman, holding out his hand. Cradled in his palm was a ruby. "The queen told us they were your particular favo— Oh!"

"Thank you!" I immediately popped it into my mouth. "They are my favorite food in all under earth!"

The man smiled hesitantly, glancing at the queen. "We are pleased that *you* are so pleased." He and his wife whispered to each other as they moved away.

I was brought rubies by nearly every noble guest. I ate them almost as fast as they were dropped into my hands, until I was feeling quite euphoric.

"It was very thought—*hic*—ful of your noble subjects to bring me such nice—*hic*—gifts," I said to the queen.

"And why shouldn't they?" asked the queen. "You are just as deserving of their praise and adoration as I am."

A group of entertainers took the floor. Four acrobats did cartwheels and fancy flips. They tossed each other high in the air and caught each other on the way down.

The crowd clapped and cheered. I stood on my chair and clapped the loudest.

"When dwarves dance," I said, "they toss—*hic*—their axes into the air and spin around before catch—*hic*—ing them as they come down."

Another entertainer juggled a dozen wine bottles at once, and then another man blew fire out of his mouth. "Oh, very good!" I said as I clapped. "Some dwarves can drink lava—*hic*—and then burp a stream of flames twenty feet long, ha-ha-ha—*hic*!"

A man came forward with a lute. He strummed the instrument and sang, in a high, clear voice, a sad song about the beauty of his true love and how she had died too young.

"Dwarves sing songs, too," I said. "But we never sing songs about death."

"Pray tell me, what do dwarves sing about?" asked the queen.

"Things that last. Wisdom—*hic*—and knowledge, power and magic, stone and gems."

"I should like to hear one."

"I would be honored to sing one for you someday."

The singer finished out the last high, quavering note of his love song. The crowd applauded, and then the queen tapped her royal staff three times. The room quieted. All eyes rested on her.

"My most trusted adviser will now favor us with a dwarf song."

Murmurs rippled through the crowd.

I stared at the queen. "Sing? *Hic.* Now?"

"Of course," she said, smiling. "Delight us with one of your songs about things that last."

The guests moved closer to the dais, forming a tight circle around us. I stood with crumbly legs on top of my chair. The crowd waited expectantly. I decided I would sing the song about the First Foredwarf, which praised her deep wisdom and power, but I would sing it about the queen. I took a deep breath and began.

*Oh, Fairest of the Fair*–hic–
*Her wisdom guides us true*
*Guide us to the depths of earth*
*Where we'll find*–hic–*wisdom, too!*

I sang all seven verses, each one praising the First Foredwarf's wonderful qualities. On the final verse, I turned to the queen and sang directly to her.

*Oh, Fairest of the Fair*
*Her justice brings us*–hic–*peace*
*May she live five thousand years*
*Our health and wealth increase*–hic!

My last hiccup bounced off the marble floors and walls. There was a moment of silence, and then the room burst with applause and cheers.

"Bravo!" shouted a nobleman.

"Brilliant," said one of the musicians. "Long live the fairest of the fair!"

"Hear, hear!" said the other musicians. "Long live the queen!"

I grinned from ear to ear, elated. It was a common

dwarf song, often sung in the mines or at ceremonies, but here it was unusual and therefore more appreciated. *I* was appreciated. Wanted. I ate another ruby, then turned to the queen. My chair tipped beneath me.

"Woops! Careful there, Dwarf!"

"Did you like my—*hic*—song?" I asked, smiling.

"I did indeed! I wish more dwarves would come to The Kingdom. I'd have balls every night."

I disliked the idea. What if she liked other dwarves more than me?

"They'd never come," I said. "Dwarves *hate* humans."

"But why? You like me, don't you?"

"Of course! I like you better than anyone in the whole world, above or below, but—*hic*." I lowered my voice, whispering conspiratorially. "Don't tell anyone else, but dwarves are afraid you might take them by the beard and—*hic*—then they'd have to do whatever you—"

I stopped talking. I stopped breathing, too, and for a moment my heart stopped beating. What was I saying? I had forgotten myself. *I* was a dwarf, and I had possibly revealed our most carefully guarded secret to a human. I glanced furtively at the queen.

"What were you saying?" the queen asked. She was watching one of the entertainers jump through rings of fire. She didn't seem to have heard what I'd just said.

"Nothing important," I said, and breathed again. "Dwarves just don't like The Surface, is all." I popped another ruby into my mouth, this time trying to get rid of the awful sinking feeling I suddenly had in my stomach. I shook myself. She hadn't heard me. Besides, even if she had, the queen and I were friends, and she was a fair human, the fairest. She would never take me by the beard.

A slew of musical chords sounded, and the humans rushed to line up and down the ballroom. Their dance was similar to dwarves', though they didn't throw axes. They circled about each other, then hopped and spun.

"Shall we dance, dear Dwarf?" said the queen.

"Me? Dance?"

"Of course!" said the queen. "Who else would I dance with?"

I had never been a good dancer underground. My headaches and dizzy spells caused by the depths usually prevented me, but here, I felt light as a feather and nimble as a cat. I bowed to the queen, and she curtsied. We circled around each other and then wove in and out of the other guests. I had to be careful of all the hopping feet and flailing limbs, lest I get kicked or squashed. Not all the humans noticed me.

I spotted a young girl and boy dancing raucously together. I recognized them instantly as the young humans who had chased me when I first came to The Surface. "Is that Princess Snow White?" I asked, pointing.

The queen spun around and glared. "What is *she* doing here? I don't recall offering her an invitation."

The princess laughed as she danced with the boy. She *did* have teeth! Quite wonderfully large ones, in fact. And surrounded by those ruby lips . . . "She's very pretty," I said absentmindedly.

"Really?" said the queen, shocked. "Most people think the princess pale and unattractive."

"Oh no," I said. "For a human, she's very—*hic*—beautiful, the prettiest human I've ever seen."

The queen stumbled and stopped dancing. She grimaced with pain.

"Are you all right?"

"Agh! I think I've twisted my ankle." The queen hopped and limped, gasping in pain. I tried to assist her, but of course I was too small, and the queen stepped on my foot with the pointy heel of her shoe. I howled in pain.

"Out of my way!" she snapped.

Two servants came forward and assisted the queen back to her throne. I limped after her, but the queen turned around and said, "Go. Make yourself useful!" She looked to where Snow White was dancing. I wasn't sure what she wanted me to do, but I made my way over to Snow White. She was laughing and bouncing around with the boy. They bumped into several guests, until a woman wearing a bird on her head barked at them to behave or be gone!

"Let's be gone, then, Florian, for I shan't behave!" They bounced their way out of the ballroom and into the hallway. I followed them, keeping myself hidden behind furniture and food.

"Did you see who was sitting on your throne?" said the boy, Florian.

"A dwarf!" said Snow White. "Can you believe it? I've been replaced by a dwarf."

"He looks grumpy," said Florian.

"He does!" said Snow White, laughing. "But who wouldn't be grumpy with only Stepmother for company?

No doubt she's making him do all sorts of awful things for her. Did you hear his singing? *Oh, Fairest of the*—hic!—*Fair!*" She impersonated my rough voice and slurred her speech perhaps a bit more than necessary. I winced. I didn't sound that bad!

"What if she makes him her heir?" said Florian.

"Who? The dwarf?" asked Snow White. "She can't do that! I'm next in line. I should have been first in line. Everyone knows it, but Stepmother has convinced everyone that I'm too young and foolish to rule! Well, I'll show her. . . ."

My ears perked up. Could the princess be plotting against the queen?

"It probably didn't help matters when you threw apples at her carriage," said Florian.

Snow White stifled a laugh. "She deserved it." And then she grew serious. "She wouldn't even let me see Father before he died, Florian. And I know there were things he wanted to tell me, important things, but now I'll never know."

She looked down at her hands, and I couldn't help but feel a little conflicted. Was it really fair for the queen to keep the princess from her father before he died? Perhaps she had her reasons. . . .

"I'm sorry, Snow," said Florian. "I wish I could do something to help."

"Well, there is one thing."

"Name it," said Florian. "You are my dearest friend."

"Okay, dear friend. Race me to the end of the hall?"

Before Florian could respond, Snow White flashed a

grin and took off. Florian ran after her. "No fair! You cheated!"

Troubled and alarmed, I hurried back to the ballroom. The queen looked pale and pained, which was my fault, and I feared that what I had to tell her would give her even more pain.

"And what did you hear from our dear princess?" Queen Elfrieda asked.

"She said I was sitting in her seat."

The queen snorted. "That seat is for the one I trust most, and that is certainly not Snow White."

"No, I wouldn't think so. She seems to think she should've been crowned queen after her father died. But that's ridiculous, isn't it? She's far too young!"

The queen clenched her jaw and dug her fingers into the arms of her throne. Her knuckles turned white.

How I hated to see her in pain! It caused me pain. "Are you well, Your Majesty?"

"I have a headache. Fetch me a glass of wine, Dwarf."

I went straightaway. When I brought the wine back to the queen, I tripped right before I reached her. I dropped the glass, and it shattered. Wine splattered the hem of Queen Elfrieda's gown.

"Oh, what clumsiness! Clean it up!" she ordered.

I gathered the shards with my bare hands, then crunched on one when no one was looking. It was good crystal, but the coating of wine quite ruined the flavor. I spit it out. When I had cleaned it all up, I brought another glass to the queen.

“I think I shall retire now,” said the queen, ignoring the goblet in my outstretched hand. “But before I do, I have an important matter of business to attend to. Come with me, Dwarf.”

I set the goblet down and followed the queen. I had just a tiny tingling in my beard.

# CHAPTER FOURTEEN

## Queen E.V.I.L.

"You!" The queen took a royal guard by the collar in the corridor outside the ballroom. "Fetch me the huntsman. I wish to see him immediately."

"What? Oh. Yes, Your Majesty. The huntsman. Right away!" He hurried off.

"What's a huntsman?" I asked, trying to keep up with the queen. She was walking so fast, I nearly had to run.

"A man who hunts and kills animals," she said. "Or whatever I tell him to hunt and kill." She said the last part more to herself than me.

I gulped, feeling the knot in my stomach expand and tighten at the same time.

The queen and I entered her private chambers, and we were met by one of her servants, who held a squealing bundle in her arms. I recognized the cries at once.

"The baby you requested, Your Highness," said the

servant. "The mother was not happy to part with her. It took a bit of convincing."

"What are you bringing it here for?" said the queen.

"I'm s-sorry," stammered the woman. "What would you have me do with the child?"

"Drown it."

"D-drown?" stammered the woman, horrified.

"Oh, very well," said the queen. "Lock it up, then."

"Lock her up? A child?"

"Yes, lock it up. It may be a child, but it's far from innocent."

The baby cried all the harder. The servant looked down at her with pity. "And who will care for her? She is only a baby. She still needs a mother's care."

"You are a mother, are you not, Gothel? You have children?"

"Y-yes," said the woman.

"Then I will entrust it to your care."

"Oh, but–"

"And you'd better keep it hidden," interrupted the queen. "Do not let *anyone* come within a mile of it. There shall be grave consequences if you do. Now get that squalling creature out of my sight. My ears are about to explode."

The servant did not argue. She bowed, and left quickly with the screaming child.

My brain was spinning. I couldn't make sense of what was happening. "Was that the baby we saw in the village?" I asked. "What's wrong with her? Why did you have her taken away?"

"For the safety of my kingdom and crown," said the

queen. "You heard what the mother said. She was plotting, saying her child would be the prettiest. Who knows if she was spouting prophecies or nonsense? I have to take precautions."

"But—"

There was a knock at the door.

"Enter!" said the queen.

Through the door came a very large man, at least twice the size of the queen in both width and height. He wore furs and animal skins all over his body, and he had a bushy beard that could rival most dwarves'. Over his shoulder he carried a quiver of arrows and a bow, and at his waist he had a long, curved knife that looked extremely sharp. It was also smeared with something dark red. I couldn't fathom what it was until I remembered that human blood was red, not blue. All the rubies I'd just eaten turned to rust in my stomach.

He bowed on one knee to the queen. "You sent for me, Your Majesty?"

"I have a job for you," said the queen. "And it's imperative that you succeed. My very crown is at stake."

"Anything you require, Your Majesty," said the huntsman.

"You are familiar with my stepdaughter, Snow White?"

The huntsman nodded. "I remember the day she was born. I killed a young deer in the princess's honor."

"Very good. Now I need you to kill the princess in *my* honor."

I froze on the spot, staring in disbelief at the queen.

The huntsman shook his head and twisted his fingers

in his ears. "I'm sorry, my hearing often plays tricks on me. You mean you wish me to kill again for the princess, for her birthday, perhaps? It is not until mid-winter, of course. . . ."

"No," said the queen. "I do not wish you to kill *for* the princess. I wish you to *kill* the princess. Immediately. Tomorrow."

The huntsman blanched. "You want me to . . ."

He couldn't seem to finish the sentence.

"Take her for a morning walk," said the queen. "She could use some exercise and sunshine, anyway. Take her deep into the forest. Tell her whatever you want. Tell her you want to pick wildflowers or apples. And then kill her."

"But . . . *why*, Your Majesty?"

"It is not your place to ask why. You are my huntsman. I have ordered you to hunt and kill a creature that is a threat to me."

The huntsman just stared at the queen, unable to speak.

"Oh, and one last thing," said the queen. "I wish to have proof of her death. You will bring me back Snow White's heart in this box."

The queen held out the jewel-encrusted box that had been given to her as a gift at the ball. The huntsman took it in trembling hands.

"And if you fail me, huntsman," said the queen, "then it is *your* life that will be in danger, and I will know if you fail."

The huntsman turned gray as granite, but he nodded and said, "Yes, Your Majesty. I shall not fail you."

The huntsman bowed, and left. The queen immediately went to her mirror and gazed at her reflection. She smoothed her hair, pinched her cheeks, and plucked a hair from her chin.

Finally my senses returned to me enough so I could speak. "What are you doing?" I sputtered. "Why did you take away that baby? Why do you want to kill the princess?"

"I must eliminate the threats to my crown," said the queen. "That baby may or may not be a threat, but I must assume that she will be once she is grown. But Snow White . . . she herself admitted her treachery. She must be disposed of for good."

"Yes," I said, scratching my beard, "but death seems a bit . . . extreme. What if you just locked her in a tower? Or banished her? That's what dwarves would do."

"Do I look like a dwarf?" she spat. "Banishment is not enough. Remember the prophecy?"

"The prophecy . . . ," I mused.

"The prophecy! The mirror! The fairest of all shall rule!" The queen was shouting, shaking with rage.

"But Snow White isn't the fairest," I said. "You are."

"You said Snow White was the prettiest human you'd ever seen!" the queen snarled.

"I did," I said slowly, "but why does that matter? Why would you kill her for being pretty?"

"It all makes sense now," said the queen. "Snow White has been rallying the nobles and peasants, gathering followers to go against me, pelting me with apples. Soon she will proclaim herself the fairest in the land and will come after my crown. Well, I won't have it! Snow White must die, and then I will be fairest." The queen turned back to the mirror and spoke to herself. "I'll never grow old. I'll make potions. I'll keep my youth and beauty through magic, and no one shall ever take my crown from me!"

The fog in my brain suddenly cleared. My jaw dropped. All this time I'd been saying "fairest," she wasn't thinking about being the wisest and most just. She thought I meant *prettiest*! How could the queen have misunderstood my meaning so completely? What did beauty have to do with ruling a kingdom? What did looks have to do with anything? It was ridiculous, preposterous, utterly foolish!

"Your Majesty, I think you've misunderstood—"

But I had no chance to explain. The queen took two long strides, bent down, and snatched me by the beard.

"I misunderstand nothing, *Dwarf*," she said in a low, dangerous voice. "I am queen! And as long as I am queen, you will do as I command."

I felt invisible threads weave their way into my beard, into the center of my brain, binding my will. The queen released me. I stumbled back and fell to the floor. I clutched at my beard and looked at the queen, horror-struck.

"Now go," she said. "I command you to follow the huntsman and see that he kills the princess properly."

# CHAPTER FIFTEEN

## Princess Hunt

It is difficult to find words to describe the sensation of being snatched by the beard, but I will try. First, there is the physical pain of having someone pull your hair. Tears pricked my eyes, and a whirring rushed in my ears, but that wasn't the worst of it. The worst was the feeling of the curse taking hold. It felt like someone had ripped open my stomach and flipped it inside out. Everything that was supposed to be inside had flopped to the outside, and all that was supposed to be on the outside was squished on the inside. It was a sickening, frightening, horrifying feeling, and there was absolutely nothing I could do about it.

The queen shoved me unceremoniously out her door and slammed it shut. I stood there in a numb state of shock. I could not think or feel, except for a slight twitch in my beard.

The guests from the ball were flowing out of the ballroom now, exiting the palace and getting into carriages. Some noticed me.

"There's that adorable dwarf, the one who sang," said a woman. She started to come toward me, arms outstretched. I panicked, and fled to my chamber.

Once I was safe behind the door, I slumped down on the floor and sat in the dark. It was raining outside. I hadn't noticed it at the ball, but now the rain was beating hard upon the roof, and several drips came through the ceiling, splashing onto my forehead, nose, and feet. The cold splashes cleared my ruby-stupid state, and all that had just happened came crashing down like a tunnel caving in.

I had been taken by the beard. By my only friend, the queen. I tried to find some excuse for her. Perhaps she did not know what she had done. Perhaps it had been a mere coincidence that she had taken me by the beard so soon after my slip.

But then I thought of all that had come before the beard-snatching. All those maidens locked away in towers. The baby. Snow White. The queen commanding the huntsman to *kill* Snow White, all because the queen had misinterpreted the message from the mirror. *Fairest.* One word. Two meanings. How did I not see it?

The sky was turning purple. Dawn was approaching. My beard began to pull ever so slightly, reminding me of my task. How could I have been such a fool? I'd been warned all my life of the treachery of humans, but I had thought I knew better.

I *did* know better! *Think, Borlen! You're a dwarf, wise and knowledgeable. Outsmart the pitiful human!*

I'd read tales of dwarves taken by the beard who found ways to elude their masters by obeying their commands to the letter, but managing to bend the meaning and evade their true wishes. But it was a tricky business—and dangerous. To defy such binding magic could bring grave consequences. Agonizing pain, madness, even death. I was barely half a century old—much too young to die! But I didn't want to do the queen's bidding for half a century, either.

I recalled the exact words Queen Elfrieda had said to me: *As long as I am queen, you will do as I command.* I was bound until she died or until she was no longer queen. I could try to help someone else take her crown. She certainly had enough rivals, but the queen had just ordered her greatest rival executed and ordered me to see it done! And why should I help another human to the throne when she might be just as awful as Queen Elfrieda? Or worse.

But . . . Queen Elfrieda had said nothing about my returning to her after I fulfilled her first command. If I never saw her again, never spoke to her, I'd never have to do what she said. Ha! All I had to do was make sure the huntsman killed Snow White, and then I'd be free!

Fizznugget. I didn't want to witness murder! I was going in circles. I bashed my head on the floor a few times to clear my thoughts.

The first rays of sun filtered through the little window, and a flash of light caught the corner of my eye. My Fate

Stone sat next to me on the floor. I snatched it up. My face was splotchy, and my beard was mangled and twisted from the queen's grip.

"How can I be freed?" I asked.

I waited for the mirror to swirl and show me some magical prophecy or something, but there was only my pitiful reflection.

"How can the queen be defeated?" I practically yelled, and shook the mirror. Maddeningly, the queen appeared, preening in her mirror. She powdered her face white and painted her lips red. "Mirror, mirror, on the wall, who's the fairest of them all?" She sucked in her cheeks and batted her eyes.

Disgust and fury exploded inside me. I wanted to hurt the queen the way she'd hurt me. "Snow White is fairest," I snarled.

The queen hissed, "Then you'd best be on your way. Go see that the huntsman kills Snow White!"

Her image faded. My beard tugged for me to go.

Something swooshed through the window and flew straight toward me. "Leaf!" I exclaimed. He landed on my shoulder and emitted a tired little squeak. He was wet and shivering. I wrapped his damp wings tightly around his body and tucked him inside my shirt. My wounded heart was given a pebble of comfort. I was not completely alone.

My beard twitched. The time for planning and subterfuge was up.

I slipped out of the castle, into the brisk morning. Rainwater dripped from the trees. The dew on the grass sparkled in the sunlight like thousands of diamonds strewn all over the ground. It made me hungry. I wished I had saved some of the rubies from the ball.

As I walked, I picked up a few stones and pebbles off the ground and gnawed on them. They were sour and moldy, but they settled my rumbling stomach.

The poison-apple tree had grown magically to full height, and its branches were laden with black blossoms. Some of the apples had begun to form, their tight spheres a deep red on one side and bright white on the other. I could smell the sickly sweet of them, but also a fainter odor, more putrid and acidic. Surely no one would be foolish enough to eat them.

I wasn't sure where to go, but it didn't matter. My beard seemed to know. It tugged me along. If I tried to resist, it twisted and yanked.

I moved as quickly and quietly as possible, keeping watch for any strangers. Now that I had been taken by the beard once, the possibility that it could happen again seemed even greater.

The land sloped upward and the trees grew increasingly taller and closer together. My breath grew short with the effort of climbing. I was headed in the direction of my Surface hole, I was fairly certain, though I couldn't recall the exact spot.

I heard voices nearby and paused.

"Can't we go back now, Horst? I'm tired."

"Her Majesty wishes you to get some exercise. She says you look pale."

"I've always been pale. My name is *Snow White.* I was

born pale. And if anything, I need *rest,* not exercise, after staying up all night at the ball." Snow White trudged behind the huntsman, grumbling her objections. "Stepmother has never cared about my health before. Why should she start now?"

The huntsman ignored her. His expression was as hard as granite.

"I don't know why we couldn't at least wait for Prince Florian," said Snow White. "He'll wonder where I am."

A deer leapt in front of them, and the huntsman instinctively nocked an arrow to his bow.

"Stop!" the princess commanded. She tugged on the huntsman's arm so his bow shifted upward. The arrow shot into a tree, and the deer bounded away.

"What did you do that for?" the huntsman said angrily.

"Why were you going to kill it? We're not on a hunt!"

"I'm always on a hunt. I'm a huntsman. And how do you expect to eat without my killing animals?"

Snow White squared her shoulders and lifted her chin. "I command you not to lift your bow again on our walk. It would be an abomination to kill an innocent creature on such a beautiful day."

The huntsman stared at the princess. His eye twitched a little. "If you wish it, Your Highness." He slung his bow over his shoulder and trudged on.

"I *do* wish it. I also wish to go home. Florian is probably having a panic attack by now. He'll think I'm *dead.*" Snow White turned around, but the huntsman blocked her path. "Get out of my way!" She pushed him, but he didn't budge. Instead, Snow White stumbled back and fell to the ground.

The huntsman pulled his long knife from his belt. Snow White looked up at him. She grew even paler than she already was. "What are you doing?"

The huntsman took a step forward. "I'm sorry, Princess," he said, "but I am at the queen's command."

"What do you mean? What command?"

"She wants you dead."

"Dead? Why? What have I done?" Snow White's bravado was gone. She sounded small and terrified now.

"I don't know why. She only told me to bring back your heart. I'm sorry, but I must." He stepped forward and brought up his knife.

She tried to scramble away from the huntsman, but he closed the distance with just a few steps. My beard buzzed. This was the moment. Snow White was about to die, and I could do nothing but watch.

The princess clutched a rock in her hand and threw it at the huntsman. Her aim was true. It smacked the huntsman square in the jaw, hard enough for him to grunt and stumble backward. The princess stood and ran.

The huntsman recovered quickly. He drew an arrow and pulled back on the bow, aiming toward the fleeing princess, but the trees covered her well and the arrow missed its mark. He cursed and ran after her, and I ran after the huntsman. I couldn't run nearly as fast, what with his long legs, but he was easy enough to follow. Birds and other creatures screeched and fled before him, and my beard practically dragged me in his wake.

Suddenly I was bowled over by something large and heavy. I was trapped in tangles of fabric, hair, and limbs. I struggled to free myself. The huntsman was getting farther away. My beard was twisting painfully. "Get off!" I shouted.

"Please help me!" someone whimpered, and I realized the thing that had knocked me over was Snow White. Her pale little face was tear-streaked, her blue eyes full of panic, and her ruby red mouth stretched wide in horror. "He's trying to kill me! *She's* trying to kill me!" She reached out blindly, as if to grasp me by the shoulders.

Instead, she caught me by my beard.

"Please! Please! Please! Protect me! Don't let anyone kill me!"

The magic of the curse took hold of me, only this time it was worse, deeper and more violent, like a wound barely healed being ripped open again. I'd scarcely had time to catch my breath when I saw the huntsman running through the trees, charging straight toward the princess and me. His knife was outstretched, his teeth bared in a snarl. I was supposed to witness the huntsman kill Snow White. But I could not let him kill Snow White! Obey the queen. Protect the princess. My beard wrenched in pain, lifting me clean off the ground. I had to do something.

"Run!" I shouted.

The princess took my hand, and we ran together through the trees. I feared we wouldn't make it. The princess ran as fast as she could, but in her panic, she was clumsy and tripped over rocks and tree roots. Her blue cloak snagged on the brambles and branches. The huntsman's arrows whirred all around us, sticking into the ground and trees, but I was sure it wouldn't be long before one stuck into me. Or Snow White. I felt my beard wrenching farther, threatening to rip off my face.

The huntsman was gaining on us. Our only hope was to lose him somehow. Find a place to hide.

"We have to hide!" said Snow White.

I nodded. "Yes!"

I scanned the area to see if there was any place we could hide. A hollow log. A gnome hole. Behind some big rocks. Anything.

"There!" I pointed to a small hole in the ground, just big enough for a dwarf and a small human. "He won't be able to follow us in there!"

"Oh, we're saved!"

I pulled the princess toward the hole, but then I stopped short. Snow White almost tripped over me. "What's wrong?"

"We can't go in there," I said.

"Whyever not?" Snow White asked.

That wasn't just any hole. It was my Surface hole, the one that led to the dwarf colony! I scrambled for some excuse. "What if a bear is in there? Or a snake? A poisonous one?"

"I'm not scared of possible snakes!" said Snow White. "I'm scared of the actual huntsman who wants to kill me *right now!*"

I looked around, desperate to find some alternative,

only to see the huntsman coming through the trees. My beard twisted. I had no choice. "All right, get in!"

Snow White got down on her hands and knees and shimmied through the hole. I ducked down and squeezed in behind her, hoping the huntsman wouldn't see. His big leather boots crunched on the gravel. My heart thudded as his footsteps came nearer and nearer, then stopped directly in front of the hole.

He stood, waiting. The world was silent, save for the pounding of my chest, so loud I was certain it would reveal our hiding place.

I could see the glint of his sharp knife. He stood there for the longest time, searching, listening. A wind blew, and then there was a grunting noise. I raised my head just enough to see a boar coming through the trees. With a flash, the huntsman threw his knife. I ducked back down just as the creature let out a high-pitched squeal. I pressed my hands over my ears until it stopped. When it did, the huntsman spoke in a booming voice.

"Princess!" he shouted. "I've decided to spare you. I will take the heart of this boar to the queen in place of yours, but don't ever come back to the castle. If you do, the queen will kill us both." The huntsman went into the trees to retrieve his heart. Or, the boar's heart. I was beginning to think humans didn't have hearts at all.

The huntsman's heavy footfalls gradually faded, and I finally let out my breath.

"He's gone," I whispered. "We'll wait here for a minute, and then we must go. We can't stay in these tunnels."

There was no response. "Princess?" I turned around. "Snow White?"

Snow White was not behind me. I crawled down the narrow tunnel. The rubble at the end had been pushed aside.

Double fizznugget!

Snow White—a human—was inside the dwarf caverns.

# CHAPTER SIXTEEN

## Human Invasion

I slid down the hole. The tunnel was narrow, and my eyes had to adjust to the darkness. Only a few glowfish floated along the ceiling, their light flickering and fading. It didn't seem like anyone had been in this tunnel for a long while.

The rhythmic pings and clinks of hammer on rock echoed in the distance, and I heard the barest hum of a song. The crew. If they were still mining these tunnels, they didn't know about the Surface hole I'd created. Gilpin must have kept my secret all this time, hoping I'd return.

Snow White was just up ahead, walking cautiously through the tunnel, drawn by the crew's song.

"Princess," I whispered. "Come back!"

"Who's down there?"

"Come back!" I said. "We can't stay here. It isn't safe!"

A shadow stretched along the wall. The dull thud of footsteps and the squeak of a rusty wheelbarrow grew louder. Someone was coming!

I caught up to Snow White and snatched her by the hand, pulling her down another tunnel so we were hidden from view.

"What is it?" asked Snow White. "Is it a dragon?"

I pressed my finger to my lips to silence her. She nodded. I peered around the corner. It was Gilpin, rolling a wheelbarrow down the tunnel. He stopped at the site of my escape. He lifted his lantern and looked around, making sure he was alone. He moved a small stone and peeked through the opening, then quickly put the stone back. He then went over to the picture he had drawn of us on the wall. He looked at it for a moment, frowning, then picked up his wheelbarrow and went back down the tunnel, toward the song of the crew and away from us.

"All right," I whispered. "I think it's safe for us to go back now. Princess?"

She didn't answer. I turned around. She wasn't behind me anymore. Down the tunnel, I saw the faintest shadow entering a dim cavern. The crew's quarters.

"Wait!" I called. "Come back!"

I ran after her.

When I entered the quarters, I found Snow White sitting on the row of beds, crying. Tears streamed down her mud-spattered cheeks, but when she saw me, she drew her knees up to her chest for protection. "You're that dwarf," she said accusingly. "You've been plotting with my stepmother. Did she send you to kill me, too?"

"No," I said. "I'm here to protect you."

"Oh," she said. "Why?"

I let out a long breath. I didn't really want to go into the details of my beard. The less Snow White understood about that, the better. "I just didn't think it was right, what the queen was doing."

Snow White nodded. She seemed to accept this, but then she suddenly broke down in tears again, her whole chest heaving so she could barely speak through her sobs. "Father is d-dead. He always said Stepmother would take care of me, and now she wants to k-kill me. Why does she want to kill me? I've done everything I can to please her! I've kept from getting dirty, mostly. I've stopped throwing things, mostly. I've stayed out of her sight, mostly. I even memorized the poem 'A Princess Is Prim, Proper, and Practical' by heart, even though it's the most ridiculous poem in the world!"

I raised one eyebrow. I had to agree, it sounded not only ridiculous but redundant and boring.

Snow White cried until she took a few rattling breaths. "I'm so tired. I've never run that fast in my entire life." She stretched herself out over the stone beds, using her cloak as a pillow.

"You can't stay here," I said. "We have to leave before the other dwarves return. They won't like you being here. Or me."

"Let me rest for just a minute," she said. "I couldn't move right now if my life depended on it. I must rest." She closed her eyes, and a moment later was asleep.

I stared at the spectacle of a human sleeping on all the

dwarf beds. What would the crew make of this? I couldn't let them find her here. Or me. Not after I'd been taken by the beard. Twice.

But where could I go? The huntsman could still be prowling outside the cavern, waiting for us to come out. I searched my pockets and felt for my Fate Stone. It could show me the huntsman. Or it could show me the queen if she was looking in her mirror—which meant she would be able to see me, too. Was it worth the risk? I had to know.

The mirror swirled. The huntsman appeared, but he was no longer in The Woods. He was in the castle. His hands were caked with dirt and blood, clutching the jewel-encrusted silver box. He held it out to Queen Elfrieda, head bowed.

"Her heart, Your Majesty."

Queen Elfrieda opened the box like a greedy dwarfling inspecting a birthday present. "This is the heart of Snow White?"

The huntsman nodded, but he did not look the queen in the eye. The queen did not seem to notice, however. She was focused on the heart in the box. "Very good, huntsman," she said with a smile. "I thank you for your service." She took a sack of coins and held it out to the huntsman, but when he took hold of it, she did not let go.

"There was a little dwarf who was out and about in The Woods this morning. Did you see him, by chance? I am concerned for his safety."

Concerned! I'll bet she was concerned.

The huntsman's eyes showed only a flicker of knowledge. "No, Your Majesty. There was no one else in those woods."

"Very well. You may go." She released the coins and the huntsman hurried away.

The queen began to turn to her mirror, and my own image began to appear, but I quickly put my Fate Stone down. I hoped she hadn't seen me.

One thing was certain—I couldn't go back to the queen. I was lucky she hadn't commanded me to return to her and report on Snow White's death. Otherwise, I would've had to tell her that the huntsman failed. I was still under her command, but as long as I didn't have to see her or talk to her, I was safe, and so was Snow White.

I mused over my new predicament. I'd been taken by the beard twice, and now I was enslaved to two mortal enemies. I could almost feel my beard splitting in opposite directions. What would become of me?

My thoughts went round in circles until I was dizzy, and exhaustion set in. I hadn't slept in almost two days, and between all the rubies and dancing and beard-grabbing and chasing, I was completely exhausted. I sat down on the floor against the wall and leaned my head back. It was still morning. The crew wouldn't be done with work for hours. I closed my eyes. Snow White and I could both rest for just a minute.

# CHAPTER SEVENTEEN

## Collapsing Crew

I woke with a start. How long had I been asleep? I looked over at the beds. Snow White was still fast asleep, breathing heavily, her mouth slightly open.

A song echoed down the tunnels, getting louder. It must have woken me.

*One pebble, two pebbles*
*Three pebbles, four*
*Put 'em in my pocket*
*Roll 'em on the floor*

It was Herkimer. I knew from my days on the crew that he was expecting a dwarfling, so he'd been learning lots of dwarfling rhymes and lullabies. I could hear Gilpin whistling along with him. The crew was returning.

“Hey!” I whispered. “Wake up!” I shook the princess a little, but she didn’t budge.

“Get up! We have to leave.” I poked and prodded. I slapped her cheeks, but she only groaned and turned over.

*Five pebbles, six pebbles*
*Seven pebbles, eight*
*Feed ’em to a dwarfling*
*Grow a crunchy fate!*

Herkimer’s voice was getting louder. There was no way I would be able to get the princess out, not without being seen.

“Never mind!” I said, pulling the cloak from under her head and throwing it over her. “Stay asleep! Don’t make a noise!”

I raced toward the tunnel. I’d have to keep the crew away. Maybe my presence would be enough of a distraction. They would have questions for me. They’d want to know where I’d been all these weeks. What would I tell them? Could I get Snow White out without them noticing?

I stepped into the tunnel just as Herkimer arrived, and when he saw me, his singing trailed off.

Gilpin came tripping behind Herkimer, and turned still as stone mid-whistle, lips still puckered. The rest of the crew was not far behind. Epidot came up the tunnel, followed by Garnesha, Amethina, and Rudger. All of them stopped short when they saw me.

"Hello," I said.

No one spoke for several moments, and then Rudger said, "Well, for depth's sake, it's Grump! We didn't think we'd ever see you again." He didn't sound too happy to see me now.

Epidot pushed through the crew to the front. "You're alive!"

"You thought I was dead?" I asked.

"We thought you'd fallen into a lava river," said Herkimer.

"We thought you'd died and turned to rubble," said Rudger, with the slightest hint of regret.

Gilpin jumped forward and started gesturing madly, his ears flapping in a frenzy.

"Gilpin was convinced you were all right," said Herkimer. "He told us you'd return."

"And he was right!" said Epidot.

Gilpin beamed.

"Yes, it's all fine and well that the Seventh has returned," said Garnesha. "But we don't know where he's been all this time. There have been search crews looking all over the colony for you. Your parents are petrified with worry."

I felt a twinge of guilt at the mention of my parents. I had barely given them a second thought in all this.

"What happened?" asked Epidot. "Did you get lost? Are you hurt?"

"I . . . I . . ." I tried to think of what to say, what story I could tell them that would explain my absence without raising too much suspicion.

Suddenly a high, sleepy sigh echoed from the quarters. All the crew jumped.

"What was that?" asked Herkimer.

"Maybe a bat?" said Amethina.

"We don't have any bat colonies in these parts," said Garnesha. "It's too deep. Unless it's the Seventh's pet."

"What? Oh. Yes. I'm sure it was Leaf you heard." I gave him a poke to make him squeak. The crew almost believed me, until a deeper groan sounded.

"That was definitely not a bat," said Herkimer.

Everyone stood completely still. "Go see what it is, Grump," said Rudger.

"Why me?" I asked.

"Because you're still the Seventh, and you have to do as I say," said Rudger. "Now go." He shoved me forward, but I stepped back. Even though I knew what was there, I had more reason to be afraid than the rest of the crew. Sometimes knowing what's ahead is worse than not knowing.

"We will all investigate together," said Epidot. "As a crew. In order. Seventh to Foredwarf." Everyone lined up behind me. Epidot passed down the lantern. I could feel Gilpin trembling.

We crept to the quarters. I could see the outline of the sleeping princess, her shoulders rising and falling as she breathed, but I walked quickly past the beds, hoping the others wouldn't notice her. But Gilpin noticed. He gestured frantically, pointing at the beds. I tried to shove him behind me and make him be still, but not soon enough.

"Someone is sleeping in our beds!" squealed Amethina.

Everyone gasped. Snow White was mostly covered by her cloak, except for her tangled black hair, which fell down over the edge of the bed and coiled on the floor. With the cloak covering her, she looked like a beast of some kind.

"What is it?" asked Garnesha.

"It looks like it might be a *bear*," said Epidot.

"What's a bear?" asked Herkimer.

"Surface beast, but they like to sleep in caves," said Epidot.

"Are you sure it's a bear?" asked Garnesha. "How many bears have you seen?"

"One. Carved on a rock. It was maybe this big." Epidot held his hands about a foot apart. The crew looked from his hands back to the beds.

"This is a very big bear, then," said Amethina.

"I want to see it!" said Herkimer, edging a little closer. "Can we wake it?"

"I wouldn't do that," I said, feeling that this might be my salvation. "I've read all about bears. They can be very dangerous, especially with their sharp claws. They could tear us all to bits!"

Herkimer scurried backward, knocking into a chair. "Don't wake it! Don't wake it! Let's get out of here!"

But it was too late. Snow White groaned. As she shifted, her cloak slid to the floor.

Epidot and Garnesha lifted their axes over their shoulders, as though they would strike, but paused when they got a better look at the princess, at her pale, dwarflike face and her long, gangly limbs.

"That's a bear?" asked Rudger. "Do bears wear dresses?"

Gilpin inched a little closer and inspected the princess. He reached out with a finger, as though he were about to poke her, when Snow White suddenly flung her hand out and slapped him in the face. Gilpin jumped back, stunned. He gestured to the crew frantically, pointing to the princess and then up.

"It's a . . . It's a . . . ," stuttered Rudger.

"It's a human!" said Herkimer.

Garnesha gasped. "A human! How is that possible?"

"Guard yourselves!" said Epidot. "Don't let it touch your beards!" He backed away, clutching at his long white beard.

"I can't be taken by the beard!" said Herkimer. "I have a dwarfling on the way!"

"Let's chase it out," said Rudger. "We'll go after it with our axes. We'll run it right into the lava rivers." He lifted his ax again.

My beard automatically wrenched. I stumbled in front of the sleeping princess. "No!" I said. "You can't. She's only a child."

Rudger snorted. "That humongous thing? A dwarfling?"

"I'm not sure the humans call their children dwarflings," said Garnesha.

"I don't care if it was born yesteryear," said Rudger. "It can't stay here. I won't allow a long-limbed, rubble-brained human anywhere near my beard!"

"Shhh!" said Herkimer. "I think it's waking!"

Snow White's eyes fluttered open. The whole crew

froze. She sat up and looked around, confused, as though she couldn't remember where she was, or why. Finally she saw all of us huddled around her, seven dwarves looking in wonder at the human in their cavern. Her eyes flicked to the axes they carried, then flooded with panic. She opened her mouth wide and let out a high, ear-piercing, earth-shattering scream.

The crew jumped again and covered their ears. The scream echoed off the walls. It went on and on, and the cavern began to shake. Trickles of dust fell from the ceiling.

I sprang forward. I clamped my hand over the princess's wide-open mouth, and the scream stopped. Her eyes bulged, as though the scream were trying to burst out of some other part of her head.

"Be quiet!" I said. "They're not going to hurt you."

Snow White's frightened eyes suddenly grew wild and fierce. She bit down hard on my hand. I yelped and released her.

"Stay away from me!" she yelled. She grabbed a chair and threw it at the crew, then she grabbed an ax resting against the wall and started to swing. "Think you can hold me captive? Ha!" She swung the ax from side to side. She hit more chairs, the beds, the table.

The crew were too terrified to do anything except protect themselves. Epidot pressed himself against the wall, clutching his ax to his chest. Garnesha and Amethina crouched down together on the floor, covering their heads with their hands, while Herkimer and Rudger crawled beneath the table. Gilpin was trying to crawl inside the strolg pot.

"Stop!" I shouted while dodging bits of flying chair and table.

Snow White continued to swing the ax wildly from side to side, hitting everything in her path. Finally she swung it up over her head, but she was too tall for our caverns, so the ax crashed into the ceiling.

A fissure snaked across the ceiling, then split in many different directions.

"Oh no . . . ," said Snow White. "Did I do that?"

Rock and rubble rained down. A huge stone slab fell on the table, causing it to crack down the middle. Herkimer and Gilpin scrambled out from beneath the table.

"Collapse! Collapse!" shouted Herkimer.

"Take cover, crew!" ordered Epidot. The crew tried to press against the walls, putting their hands flat over their heads, but it was not enough. The very walls were crumbling behind them; the entire ceiling was coming down.

"We have to get out, Epidot!" shouted Garnesha.

"To the tunnel, crew!" The crew ran out of the cavern, into the tunnel. I grabbed Snow White and pulled her after me, but it wasn't any better outside the cavern. Cracks continued to spread over the walls and ceilings. Rocks showered down. The whole tunnel was caving in.

We ran along the tunnel, hoping to find safety down another tunnel, but all the passages were blocked.

Snow White started to scream as rocks pelted her. My beard twitched. The rocks would surely kill the princess.

They might kill all of us if we didn't get out. Ahead, I could see a few specks of light where the rubble had shifted in front of the Surface hole. My beard wrenched in pain.

"This way!" I shouted. "I know a safe place!" I pulled Snow White. The rest of the crew followed me, not knowing where I was leading them. There wasn't time to counsel or consider. Either we went to The Surface or we were all doomed to be crushed.

"Go toward the white!" I shouted. White light was gleaming like a beacon as the tunnel crumbled around us. I grabbed Snow White and pushed her in front of me. She crawled through the hole. I followed after her, and the crew followed after me. I emerged from the ground and immediately turned around to help the others. Gilpin, then Rudger, Herkimer, Amethina, Garnesha, and, finally, Epidot. A moment after we were all out of the tunnel, it imploded. Trees toppled. Boulders sank beneath the ground, and a great cloud of dust billowed up into the air, sprinkling down on all of us like a final farewell.

There was a long silence. Once the dust cleared, the crew stood from their crouched positions and looked around to assess the situation. All of them recoiled at the light.

"Where are we?" Garnesha asked.

"Why is it so bright?" asked Herkimer. "Are we near the lava pits? Did we make it to the main cavern?"

"Something smells funny," said Rudger.

"Oh no," moaned Amethina. "Oh no, oh no, oh no!"

She said it over and over again, her hands covering her eyes. "Please tell me we're not where I think we are. Please, oh please, oh please!"

Epidot shook his head, and bits of rubble flew off him. "Beryl's beard," he muttered. "We're on The Surface."

# CHAPTER EIGHTEEN

## Senseless on The Surface

Chaos erupted like a volcano. The entire crew groaned and writhed on the ground like they were being sprayed with hot lava.

Epidot kept his hands up in the protective position for a collapse. He stuttered nonsensical commands. "T-take cover, crew! Dig deep! D-d-don't be lofty!" I'd never seen Epidot even the least bit nervous before. The Surface seemed to have addled his brain.

Garnesha tried to help, but all she did was tell everyone to calm down, which no one was able to do, including Garnesha. Everyone was in a panic from the bright light, the fresh air, the immense open space—all of it so completely foreign to dwarves.

"Oh, I shall faint!" cried Amethina. "I can't see! I can't breathe! I'm going to die!" She ran around in circles with her arms over her head. Finally she dug a shallow hole in the soft ground and stuck her head into it, her backside sticking up to the sky.

Rudger sniffed at the air, his nose twitching. "The air . . . it tickles!" he said. His eyes grew dusty. He sniffed and sniffed until . . . "ACHOO!" He sneezed. "AAAA-CHOO!" He sneezed again and again, until his bulbous nose was cobalt blue.

Herkimer just closed his eyes, as though this were only a nightmare and when he woke up it would all be gone.

Gilpin walked in circles around Herkimer, pulling at his big ears so hard I feared he would stretch them to his elbows.

I could see it would be up to me to keep everyone from crumbling to dust.

"Listen!" I called, but no one listened. I climbed onto the giant mound of stones and fallen trees from the collapse and whistled. "Quiet!"

The crew stilled. They kept their faces shielded from the sun but turned toward the sound of my voice. "If you want to survive on The Surface, you're going to have to listen to me."

"Why should we listen to you?" said Rudger. "You're supposed to do what *we* say!"

"Because," I said, "I know more about The Surface than you do and . . ." I paused, unsure if I should reveal the next part, but I saw no use in trying to hide it. "And because I've been here before."

The crew stared at me. Amethina spoke from her head-hole. "What do you mean, you've been here before?" she said in a muffled voice.

I took a breath. It was time to come clean . . . mostly. "When I was mining the borlen, I broke through to The Surface." I glanced at Gilpin. "And I couldn't help myself. I decided to go and see it. That's where I've been all this time."

"And you thought we'd all want to come to The Surface with you?" said Rudger testily.

"We would have died if I hadn't brought us here," I said.

"Some of us might have preferred death to coming here!" said Amethina. She emerged from her hole and glared at me. "The light! The height! I can barely breathe!"

"Calm down," I said. "The Surface won't kill you."

"No," squeaked Herkimer. "But the humans might!" He pointed.

Snow White was on her hands and knees, coughing up dust. I'd almost forgotten about her. She stood on wobbly legs and shook her skirt, causing clouds of dust to billow off it. Her dress was torn in several places, and she was so filthy, she was almost unrecognizable. Her black hair was brownish gray from all the dirt and rubble. She looked wild and terrifying.

"N-now, human," stuttered Epidot in a shaky voice, clutching his beard with both hands. "We won't harm you, so long as you t-t-take your leave immediately. You're in dwarf territory now. N-no humans allowed."

"Dwarf territory?" said Snow. "I'm quite sure we're in *my* kingdom."

"*Your* kingdom?" said Garnesha. "What makes you think this is *your* kingdom?"

"Because," said Snow White, standing a little taller. "I am the princess."

The crew gasped.

"You're the human pin-chess?" asked Rudger.

"Well, I was," she said. "I'm not sure *what* I am now."

"You're our prisoner now!" said Rudger. "But don't come anywhere near us." He grabbed his beard and shoved it down his shirt.

"Rudger, you know we can't take a human prisoner," Garnesha said, then turned to Snow White. "But we would like to know how you got into our caves. No human can enter our caverns, not unless a dwarf leads them in."

I tried to hide myself behind Gilpin, but Snow White found me anyway. She said the words I'd been dreading. "But I *was* led by a dwarf. This dwarf here." She pointed to me. "He brought me to your cave to protect me. He saved my life."

The crew turned toward me. I kept my eyes fixed on the ground.

"Is this t-true, Seventh?" asked Epidot.

I let out a long breath and nodded.

"I knew it!" said Rudger triumphantly. "I knew he was a human lover! I told you all!"

"But why?" said Garnesha. "Why under earth would you do such a foolish thing?"

There was no point in hiding it anymore. I was already in deep lava. "Because," I said, "she took me by the beard."

The crew all gasped. Amethina let out a shrill cry, and Gilpin's ears stuck out like two plates glued to his head. Everyone backed away from Snow White and me and put their hands to their chins, whether they had a beard or not.

"I'm sorry," said Snow White. "Did I do something wrong? Did I hurt you?"

No one said anything. It was clear that Snow White—unlike the queen—didn't know what she had done, but no one was about to explain it to her.

Epidot inched closer to me and whispered, "What did she ask you to do?" The rest of the crew leaned in.

"To protect her from the queen," I whispered. "Or anyone who might try to kill her."

"Why did you bring her to the caverns?" Herkimer asked. "Why couldn't you take her somewhere else?"

"She was being chased by a huntsman," I said. "Our cavern was the only place we could hide where he couldn't follow. I didn't have a choice."

"Well, I suppose it could be worse," said Garnesha.

My chest tightened. It *was* worse. So much worse. What would they say if they knew about the queen taking me by the beard? They couldn't find out.

"Ooh, I can't wait to bring the Seventh before the council," said Rudger. "He'll be banished for certain!" He slapped the butt of his ax in his palm. "Achoo!"

"You can't just banish someone for protecting your princess!" said Snow White. Clearly she had been listening to every word.

"Oh yes we can!" said Rudger. "You're not *our* pinchess!"

"Oh, aren't I?" said Snow White. "All the rock and

dirt you live in is part of The Kingdom. And one day I'll be queen, so that makes you my subjects!"

"Piffy-pebbles!" said Rudger. "Dwarves lived in these lands thousands of years before you pitiful humans ever existed. If anything, you're *our* subject!"

Snow White's pale cheeks flushed. She placed her hands on her hips and rose to her full height, which was not as tall as most humans, but she still towered over the crew. "And what if I take you *all* by the beard? Will I be your princess then?"

The entire crew gasped. Amethina screamed, and curled up into a ball on the ground, keeping her head firmly tucked, even though she didn't have a beard to be taken. "Tyrant!" she shouted. "All of you humans are tyrants!"

"We'll bear no tyrants!" shouted Rudger. "And we'll suffer no fools! Let's drive them both out, the pin-chess and the Seventh!" He lifted his ax like he wanted to strike us down. Snow White flinched. At the same time, my beard yanked me to jump in front of Snow White to protect her.

"Stop, Rudger!" said Garnesha. "We'll not be driving out the Seventh. He'll have to remain with us. The princess, too."

Rudger paused with his ax in the air. "Have you lost your garnets, Garnesha? She just threatened to take us all by the beard! And the Seventh's responsible."

"Yes, but think," said Garnesha. "Remember that we're on The Surface, and our tunnels have collapsed completely. We have no way of getting to the council at all, not until we can dig our way back. If we let the human go, she could tell more humans where we are, and we'd be in even more danger, especially now that we're trapped on The Surface. We could be ambushed by an army of humans!"

"I'll take 'em," said Rudger, swinging his ax again. "I'll cut them off at their knobby knees!"

"Until one of them takes you by the beard," said Herkimer.

"And like it or not, we need the Seventh," said Garnesha. "As he said, he knows the most about The Surface. We'll need him to help us survive until we can dig our way back."

"I'm not staying another minute on The Surface!" said Amethina, her hands over her eyes. "I'll start digging right here, and be back to the main tunnels by sundown!"

"But we don't know where to dig," said Garnesha. "With the collapse, we'll be digging in new territory. It could take weeks or months."

"Nonsense!" said Amethina. "I have my maps. I'll tell us exactly where we can di–"

Amethina paused. Keeping her eyes shut tight, she felt around her waist, then on the ground around her. She began to wail. "I dropped them! I dropped my maps during the collapse! Now we'll never get back!"

"Don't panic, Amethina," said Garnesha. "We'll set it to rights. We're not lost."

"Epidot, you can't possibly allow the Seventh and his *pet human* to stay!" said Rudger.

Epidot stroked his long beard, thinking. "I d-don't know," he stammered.

"Please," said Snow White, her voice now high and innocent. "Please, please, don't send me away. If the queen finds me, she'll kill me." Tears sprang to her eyes and rolled down her cheeks. The crew all watched the sad scene, unsure what to do. Dwarves were not used to wet tears or plights of life and death.

Finally Epidot spoke. "Well, crew, I think our beards are t-tied, either way. We'll have to let her stay. B-b-both of them."

Both of them. I was one of *them* now. No longer one of the crew. Already banished, even if I hadn't been brought before the First Foredwarf and the council.

No one argued—they just continued to stare, awestruck at the leaky princess before them. Snow White clapped her hands, which made everyone jump again. "Oh, thank you!" she said, wiping the tears from her face. "You won't be sorry. I promise I'll be no trouble at all. I'm sure we'll all be very good friends, and one day, when I'm queen, you shall all be rewarded!"

# CHAPTER NINETEEN

## Beebles and Bells

I knew we wouldn't have a moment of calm until we built a shelter, so that was our first order of business. It would take too long to dig a proper cavern underground, so I suggested we build a makeshift Surface dwelling, for cover and safety.

Rudger and Amethina argued against this plan with vehemence, but they caved once they heard my description of rain, and once a strong gust of wind nearly knocked them off their feet.

I instructed everyone on how to build the dwelling according to the human fashion, with walls, a roof, and a chimney. I carved the plans into a flat boulder so the crew could understand how it would look.

"This is how humans live?" said Rudger. "What idiots. That thing will collapse in a week."

"Well, it's not like dwarf homes never collapse," I said.

"Human lover," he muttered.

Dwarves are generally fast workers, but the conditions on The Surface made everyone slow and clumsy. Rudger sneezed almost constantly, and Amethina insisted on walking around with a slab of stone on her head for shade. It wasn't very effective, and it slowed her usually speedy work considerably. We had barely built half the walls when the sun finally set. Darkness fell, which greatly relieved the crew but stalled our progress, as we had no glowfish or lanterns to light our work.

The crew were forced to sleep in the open air for the night, and despite everyone's exhaustion, no one slept very well. Between the cool breeze, the soft ground, and the starlight, no one could relax. Snow White's complaints of hunger and improper bedding didn't help.

As soon as the sky lightened the next morning, everyone hurried back to work. The crew were not eager to spend another night outside, so they all doubled their efforts. Epidot, Garnesha, and Herkimer finished the walls and chimney and began work on the roof. Amethina and Rudger searched the ruins of the collapse for some larger slabs of stone for sleeping, smaller stones for cooking and eating, and whatever adequate minerals they could scrounge up to make strolg. Gilpin and I used the fallen trees to make a table and stools. The crew were mesmerized by the wood and how easy it was to cut and carve, though Rudger said it wouldn't last a day.

Snow White was no help at all, but thought she was in

charge and questioned and criticized everything we did. She went around telling the crew how to place the stones, where the door ought to hang, that they should make it bigger, as she was taller than us, that we should paint it blue, since that was her favorite color. The crew were too nervous around Snow White to argue with her. Epidot couldn't string three words together without stuttering. Amethina's behavior was nonsensical and erratic, while Garnesha was timid and clumsy, not at all her usual self. All the males made a habit of clutching their beards and tucking them tightly into their shirts and belts.

When we had nearly finished putting up all the walls, Snow White pointed out that there wasn't a window.

"Dwarf caverns don't have windows," I told her.

"Well, we're not making a dwarf cavern, are we?" said Snow White. "We're making a safe shelter for *me*. I can't imagine living anywhere without a window. I'd feel like a prisoner."

"I wonder what that would feel like," I groused.

So we unstacked several layers of the wall and made a window, which Snow White said was too small, but she left it at that.

As the sun began to set behind The Mountain and the sky faded to the color of amethyst and amber, we finished the cottage. The crew all gathered inside. I shut the door and barred it with a thick slab of wood.

"Oh, that's better," said Amethina, collapsing in exhaustion onto one of the rough stone slabs.

"It's a bit dark, isn't it?" said Snow White. And then: "Someone needs to light a fire. And what's for supper? I'm simply starving. I haven't had a proper meal since yesterday morning."

"Me too," said Rudger. "Thanks to you."

I was surprised he would even speak to Snow White, but then I saw he was looking at me. I figured I didn't have much room to argue. It *was* my fault.

I built a fire out of wood, something the crew found fascinating, as dwarves always burned coal. Garnesha prepared some strolg in a rough stone pot she'd carved. When it was bubbling, she poured the strolg into some crude stone bowls.

When all was ready, Epidot sat at the head of the table. The rest of the crew sat on either side in order of their rank, which left Gilpin and me to sit next to the princess.

"Well, this isn't so bad, is it?" Epidot's stutter had gone away now that we were no longer so exposed to The Surface, but he was still nervous around Snow White. He clutched his beard as he picked up his bowl of strolg. He was about to take his first sip when Snow White coughed.

Epidot looked up at Snow White in surprise, but then understood. He set down his bowl. Inconceivably, he was deferring to her.

Snow White sniffed at the bowl of strolg in front of her. "Gruel is more fit for peasants than royalty, but I won't complain. I'm sure it's the best you can do, and I am grateful."

She took a sip and then spit it out right in my face. Globs of hot strolg dripped down my nose and beard.

Rudger muffled a laugh. "You have to admit, the human has impeccable aim."

"Ugh! What is this? It tastes like dirt!" Snow White gagged and spit some more.

"It's strolg," said Garnesha, clearly affronted by the princess's lack of appreciation for her cooking. "It's made of minerals."

"So it *is* dirt," she said. "That can't be good for you."

"It's good for dwarves," said Garnesha tartly.

Herkimer dug into the pouch at his waist. "I have some quartz. It's raw, but pretty good." He held a piece out toward the princess.

"Rocks!" said Snow White. "Dwarves eat dirt and rocks?"

"They make us strong and powerful," said Rudger. "Not flimsy, like you humans."

"We're not *flimsy*," said Snow White. "We're delicate and sensitive. A princess is especially sensitive and cannot eat rocks."

"What do you eat?" asked Herkimer, taking a bite of his quartz. Snow White flinched as he crunched.

"We eat *food*," she said. "Normal things like ham and cheese and bread and fruit. Apples are my favorite."

"What the blixes is *ap-please*?" Rudger asked.

Snow White looked shocked. "You've never had apples? Oh, you poor creatures! I suppose you don't get much fresh food, living underground. That's why you eat dirt, isn't it? How barbaric. But once you try an apple, you'll never go back to dirt again. They're the most delicious fruit. Sweet and juicy!"

"Trust me, they're disgusting," I whispered to Rudger, next to me.

"You've tried one?" he asked, sounding impressed. I nodded, feeling important.

"I'm afraid we don't have any of those things here," said Garnesha.

"Well, I can't eat dirt," said Snow White. "Without proper food, I'll surely perish!"

"Wouldn't that be a tragedy," I mumbled.

Snow White gasped. "No one has ever spoken to me that way in all my life!"

"Now, now. Don't be rude, Seventh," said Epidot. "Is that any way to speak to our guest?"

I blanched. She was our guest now?

"Don't mind him, Pin-chess," said Rudger. "The Seventh has always been a bit grumpy. But he'll find food for you. He has to protect you. Grump, your pet pin-chess is hungry and needs feeding. Otherwise, she'll die!"

My beard twitched. I glared at everyone, especially Rudger, then stood and moved to the door. My body ached from all the work we'd done, and I was exhausted. The last thing I wanted to do was gather food for a bratty princess.

"Bring a ham," said Snow White, "and some fresh bread and cheese, a few vegetables, and, of course, apples. You must not forget those. Nice red ones, if you can find them, though I shan't be picky."

"Spoiled brat," I muttered as I opened the door.

"Now, human princess," I heard Herkimer say, "can you tell us what *rain* is exactly and where it comes from? The Seventh said it's like water that falls from the ceiling, but I think he must be mistaken. . . ."

As soon as I was outside, Leaf crawled out of my shirt and flew off into the trees. The moon was out, and it was almost full dark. I needed to hurry.

I was fairly certain I would not find any apples for the princess, nor ham or bread or cheese. I wouldn't find any of those things unless I went to a human colony or the queen's castle, and I wasn't going to go there for all the rubies under earth.

I came upon a deer eating grass. Grass was a vegetable, I thought, so I gathered a few bunches of that. I found some fluffy-looking flowers that reminded me of yellow gypsum, which was sort of the color of cheese, so I got two handfuls of those. I found some white mushrooms that looked a bit like bread. I also found some red berries that probably tasted a lot like apples. I scooped up some beetles and worms from under a log, and on the way back to the cottage, I happened upon a dead rat. That was as good as a ham. What was the difference? The princess could be nothing but pleased with my savvy substitutes.

When I returned to the cottage, I was greeted by a curious sight. The crew were all gathered at the end of the table, looking intently up at Snow White, who was dramatically telling the story of her encounter with the huntsman in The Woods.

"And then he came after me, pointing his knife right at my heart!" She mimed bringing down a knife to her chest as Amethina let out a small yelp. "But I was faster than a jackrabbit, and I ran away. He chased after me, shooting arrows, but I ran and ran until I found a little hole in the ground, and I thought, *Aha!* The huntsman is too big. He won't be able to follow me in there! So I climbed through, and now here I am, safe with all of you dear little dwarves."

Amazing how quickly I had been erased from this story. Amazing how quickly the crew had wrapped themselves around Snow White's pale little fingers and forgotten that not only had she taken *me* by the beard, she'd threatened to take them by their beards as well.

"It was very smart of you to think to go underground," said Amethina. "There is no safer place in the world."

"A princess is taught to think quickly in difficult situations," said Snow White. "Royals are in constant danger. You never know what might befall you next. At any moment we could be attacked by— Apples!" She spotted me with my load. "Are those my apples?"

I laid my gatherings on the table. The crew leaned in to see what curious things I'd brought. Snow White sat down eagerly to eat, but her face fell as she gazed upon the meal.

"Haven't you brought me anything to eat?" Snow White asked.

My shoulders slumped. "Can't you eat these things?"

"Perhaps if I was a deer or squirrel! Where's the ham? The cheese? And where are my apples? That was my one firm request."

"I wanted to try one, too!" whined Rudger.

"I couldn't find any," I said. "And we don't have ham and cheese whenever you want them. This is not the royal palace."

"Really? I hadn't noticed," said Snow White. She sifted through the food I'd brought that apparently wasn't food.

"I detest mushrooms," she said, setting them aside. "Worms?! What do you take me for, a troll?"

I wanted to tell her that I could never mistake her for a troll. Trolls were nicer and smarter, but she didn't give me the chance.

"These berries look all right, but there aren't enough to feed a squirrel." She plopped a few in her mouth and immediately spit them out. Slimy red globs splattered across the table. "They're sour!" She gagged and pawed at her tongue.

Finally Snow White got to the bottom of the pile. She picked up the rat by its tail, screamed, and flung it so it smacked against the wall. The rat fell to the floor with a thud. Snow White started crying again.

Gilpin scooted a little closer and inspected the princess's face. He reached out and swiped one of her tears onto his finger and sniffed it. He frowned, as though he could smell the sorrow on the tear.

Gilpin walked over to the dead rat, picked it up, and gently placed it in front of Snow White. She shrank back from it, her face twisted in disgust, but then she dried her tears and set her jaw. "I shall not starve!" she declared. "I will not let Stepmother get the better of me!"

And with that, she took the rat by the tail and tossed it onto the smoldering coals of the wood fire. It smelled awful, but Snow White roasted the rat until it was black and charred, and ate it right down to the bone and tail. When she finished, she emitted a little belch and quickly covered her mouth. "Oh! Excuse me. That's not at all princess-like."

Rudger let out his own loud belch. "But very dwarf-like!" he said, and everyone laughed.

The crew were quite intrigued by the other things I'd brought. Amethina sampled some of the grass, but quickly spit it out. Herkimer squeezed a berry between his fingers and it squirted Gilpin right in the eye.

"Ooh, what are these?" said Rudger, pointing to some plump black bugs crawling on the table.

"Beetles," said Snow White. "They're not edible."

Rudger lowered his face close to one of the beetles crawling along the wood. "They look like obsidian nougats. Obsidian is one of my favorites. May I try a beeble, Pin-chess?"

"I don't recommend it," said Snow White. "They might make you ill."

"Oh, pishy-pyrite!" said Rudger. "Dwarves have strong stomachs." He picked up the beetle and popped it into his mouth. He crunched a few times and swallowed. The crew leaned in, waiting for his reaction.

"Hey! Beebles aren't so bad!" Rudger took another from the table and popped it into his mouth. "They taste like amethysts. Only, they're a little squishy after the crunch." He ate a few more. "Try them, Pin-chess! They're scrumptious."

"I am still a bit hungry," said Snow White, and she snatched one of the beetles skittering across the table and popped it into her mouth. She chewed and considered. "You're right. They're not so bad."

Rudger and Snow White ate beetles until their teeth were blue.

The rest of the crew sipped on strolg while pestering Snow White with questions. Were all humans so tall? Did they really *wear* gems? (She showed them her ruby ring, and they all ogled it.) What did bears look like? And just how much water could an *ocean* hold?

Suddenly there was a loud gurgling sound. Everyone paused. Rudger looked down at his stomach. "Blixers," he said. "Not sure my belly took too kindly to the beebles." His stomach emitted a deep groan, much like the sound before a tunnel collapses. He went a little cross-eyed and ran out of the cottage, but not before we heard what sounded like a small explosion.

"No more beetles for Rudger, I think," said Snow White.

The crew roared with laughter, but the laughter was interrupted by a sudden cacophony of clangs, like a gong, but higher, and several at once. Rudger came rushing back inside, hitching his pants up.

"Wh-what's that?" Epidot asked.

"The bells," said Snow White. "Usually they don't all ring unless there's a royal birth or a death. I remember them when my father died. I wonder who it could be."

Minutes later, a gravelly voice sounded through the window. It was a gnome. "Message! Message for all inhabitants of The Kingdom! The Princess Snow White is dead! She was killed by wild beasts in The Woods! There will be a mourning procession tomorrow at sunrise! Message! Message for all inhabitants of The Kingdom!"

The gnome moved on, his voice fading into the distance. Silence fell in the cottage.

"Well," said Snow White after a long pause. "I suppose it could be worse. I really *could* be dead."

"That's the spirit," said Garnesha. "Dwarves always say to look on the dark side and don't let anybody bring you up."

"Up? You mean, don't let anybody bring you down, don't you?" said Snow White.

"Oh no," said Amethina. "Down is good! The lower the better. It's the high places that get you into trouble."

"Up or down, I feel quite safe here with you sweet dwarves," said Snow White, and then she yawned. "Goodness, I'm tired. It's been a long, busy day. I think I'll go to bed now. Good night!"

She stretched herself across all our beds, using her cloak as a pillow. A moment later, she was snoring with her mouth hanging open.

The crew stared at her in amazement.

"Where are *we* supposed to sleep?" said Amethina.

"A human can't sleep in our beds," said Rudger. "Make her get off, Grump!"

"How?" I asked. "She's huge. It will take the entire crew to move her."

"I'm too tired to pick up anything else today," said Garnesha. "I couldn't move a pebble if I tried."

"Leave her be," said Epidot. "We can sleep just as well on the floor."

"But the ground is so soft," whined Amethina. "I get headaches if my bed isn't hard enough."

"We can make do for one night," said Epidot. "It's been a long day."

The crew started to claim spaces for sleep on the floor. I tried to make a bed against the wall, next to Amethina. "This spot's for Herkimer," she said.

I moved to the other side. "Don't even think about it," said Rudger.

Epidot and Garnesha took up the remaining floor space beneath the window, and Gilpin took the space in front of the fire.

"She is a curious thing, isn't she?" said Garnesha, glancing over at the princess.

Epidot nodded. "I never could quite admit it, but I've always wanted to see a human. They're stranger than I ever imagined. The long limbs! The tiny teeth! So funny."

"And scary," said Amethina. "You never know what she's going to do next."

"We males will have to be very careful," said Rudger. "She could take us all by the beard, and then we'd be no better than Grump."

I stretched myself out in front of the door, far away from everyone else. I reached for Leaf, then remembered he'd already flown off for the night. I felt cold and lonely, and I couldn't sleep.

Something shifted beside me, and a moment later I felt a weight on my chest. A flat stone to help press me to sleep. Whoever placed it there made a little whistle.

"Thanks, Gil," I whispered.

He lay down next to me, and I didn't feel so alone anymore, but just when I was almost pressed to sleep, Gilpin started snoring.

It had been a long day. It was going to be a longer night.

# CHAPTER TWENTY

## Grump and Brat

The crew woke stiff and cranky the next morning, moaning at the bright light now shining through the little window.

"Oh, that horrid light!" whined Amethina. "My poor head is pounding already."

"Ouch! My back!" groaned Rudger. "It feels like I slept in a strolg barrel."

Snow White woke with a groan. When she sat up, her long black hair stuck out like branches on a tree. Her eyes were still swollen from crying, and part of her face was indented where she'd slept against the rough stones. She looked monstrous. She stretched and yawned and—ew—let out a gust of foul breath worthy of a troll.

"I don't know how you dwarves sleep on such horribly hard, bumpy beds," she said. "I didn't sleep at all well."

"Great," I said. "We'll take the beds, and you can sleep on the floor."

"A princess sleep on the floor?" said Snow White. "Unfathomable! It wouldn't be proper. It's not proper that I'm living in these conditions at all."

"You're free to leave at any time," I said.

"Don't be ridiculous," said Snow White. "You know I can't go anywhere. The huntsman might be waiting right outside to kill me."

"Will he kill us all, do you think?" cried Amethina.

"No," said Snow White with great solemnity. "It's me the queen wants dead. Of course, she would be very angry if she knew you were protecting me, but don't worry. I won't let any harm come to you."

Amethina sighed in relief. "Thank you, Princess."

"You're welcome," said Snow White. "As your princess, I have a duty to protect you."

I snorted.

"Well, crew, shall we start digging?" said Epidot.

"I've already started!" said a muffled voice. We turned to find Garnesha digging furiously by the back wall. She was already a dwarf-length down, tossing out dirt so fast, it was piling up on the table and sprinkling on our heads.

Everyone gathered their axes and moved to join in, but when I lined up, Epidot held up his hand. "Not you, Seventh," he said.

"What do you mean?"

"What do you mean, what does he mean?" sneered

Rudger. "Someone's got to get rid of all the rubble. That's your job, Grump."

"And you need to stay with the princess," Epidot said in a low voice. "You are bound to protect her, after all."

My beard twitched. I didn't need a reminder.

"Stay safe, Princess," said Herkimer. "Don't let any other humans inside. Or bears!"

"And if that huntsman comes," said Amethina, "put your hands over your heart and scream and get down as low into the earth as you can!"

"Don't worry about me," said Snow White. "I'm a lot stronger than I look."

By now, Garnesha had dug a hole deep and wide enough for everyone to fit inside and work. Everyone except me. They dug and dug, flinging the dirt and rocks in all directions inside the cottage. I worked to move it all outside as well as I could, though it was difficult to keep up. I didn't have a wheelbarrow or even a shovel. I had to use the strolg pot as a bucket and my bare hands to scoop up the rocks and dirt.

"Here, let me help," said Snow White. She tried to take the pot to empty it, but it was too heavy for her. She dropped it and spilled all the dirt.

"Sorry," said Snow White. I bent down to pick up the pot. At the same time, Snow White tried to scoop the dirt back into the pot, but instead dropped it right over my head.

"I'm so sorry!" Snow White reached to brushed all the dirt off me, but I jumped back.

"Leave it!" I shouted. "Just get away from me!"

"I was only trying to help," said Snow White.

"Then stay out of my way," I said between clenched teeth. I scooped the dirt back into the pot. As I dumped it out the window, Leaf came flying inside. He flew right over my head and landed on the table in front of Snow White.

"Oh!" she cried.

"Leaf, come here," I said. I needed to get him inside my shirt before Snow White started screaming and breaking everything in the cottage.

"Hello, little fellow. Are you hungry?" Snow White held out one of the sour berries. Leaf nibbled it right from her hand and squeaked with delight, moving a little closer. Snow White smiled. "Aren't you sweet!" She reached out a finger as though to pet him, but I snatched him up.

"He doesn't like humans," I said. "You frighten him."

"Oh, I'm sorry," said Snow White. "He seemed friendly."

"Well, he's not. Not to you, anyway." I wrapped Leaf's wings around him and shoved him inside my shirt. He squeaked in protest for a moment, then settled in to sleep.

I went back to work, scooping up the rubble and dumping it out the window. Snow White sat at the table and watched. Occasionally she opened her mouth to say something, probably to tell me how I was doing it wrong or boss me around, but one look from me and she kept quiet.

Finally, I had gotten most of the dirt out. The crew had dug deep enough that the dirt and rubble came less often. I slumped onto a stool, exhausted.

Snow White cleared her throat a little. I turned to her and raised one eyebrow, wondering what she would dare say to me at this point.

"What should we do now?" she asked.

"We?" I said. "*You* can do whatever you want. I'm going outside." There was no way I would be stuck in this cottage all day with the princess.

"Perfect! I'll go with you." Snow White jumped up from the table.

"You can't go outside," I said. "What if someone sees you?"

"Who will see me? Everyone thinks I'm dead. We're deep in The Woods, and no one is looking for me. Besides, I can search for my own food. I need to eat something besides rats and beetles."

"I doubt you can find much better," I said.

"Oh, can't I?" She marched to the door and left without so much as a backward glance. I sat at the table and tossed pebbles out the window. In ten minutes she'd probably come back to me crying and hungry, begging me to find her food.

Ten minutes passed, and she didn't return. Another ten, and nothing. After an hour, I started to imagine what could have happened to her. She'd probably gotten lost. She was probably curled up beneath a tree, crying and trembling with fright. A bear might be lurking in The Woods, ready to eat her. With that thought, my beard tugged me to go find her. As much as I enjoyed the quiet, I couldn't let her be out there alone.

It didn't take long to find her. Snow White was neither lost nor frightened. She was kneeling by the stream with a whole pile of food, much to my chagrin. She'd found wild carrots and onions and a few other roots and things I didn't recognize. She scrubbed all the dirt off in the stream, humming while she worked. She even managed to catch a few fish with her bare hands, which impressed me, though I tried hard not to show it. I stood back from the stream, half-hidden behind a shrub. I didn't think she knew I was there until a splash of cold water hit me in the face and took my breath away. Snow White laughed as she dried off her hands. Then she saw me scowling.

"Oh, I'm sorry," she said, still laughing a little. "I was just trying to play."

I stomped back toward the cottage, dripping wet, beard twitching. I hoped a bear *did* come and eat her!

As I drew nearer the cottage, I was struck by how starkly it stood out through the trees. Anyone passing within fifty feet would notice it, and that put the whole colony at risk. I wondered if there was some way to disguise it. Perhaps I could pile up the dirt from the tunnel to make it look like a hill instead of a cottage. That would be a good way to keep busy and away from Snow White.

So I set to work gathering the dirt, piling it up around the cottage, and making a slope that would blend with the roof.

"What are you doing?" Snow White asked, carrying her pile of food in her skirt. She was sopping wet, like she'd given herself a bath in the stream.

"Covering up the cottage," I said. "Someone could see it and wonder who lives here. If they see you, they could report it to the queen."

"You're doing all this to protect me?"

"And the crew," I said. I didn't want her to think I cared all that much about her. "I don't want the queen to know we're here, either."

Snow White set down her bundle of food by the door and put her hands on her hips, surveying my work with a critical eye. "It might help if you add some bigger rocks beneath all the dirt. Otherwise, when it rains, it will all just wash away."

I gritted my teeth. "What do *you* know about dirt or rocks?"

Snow White looked startled. "Not nearly so much as dwarves, I'm sure. I'm only trying to be helpful."

"If you want to be helpful, just go inside. Eat your food."

Snow White looked hurt for a brief moment, but then she smoothed her face. "Fine," she said. "I'll leave you to it." She picked up her food and went back into the cottage.

When the crew returned from the tunnel that evening, they were carrying a long rectangle of stone.

"We made you a bed, Princess!" said Epidot.

"It was my idea!" said Garnesha proudly. "I cut out the big stone."

They set the bed beneath the window. The top was smooth and dipped ever so slightly to cradle Snow White's body. The sides were ornately carved with all kinds of things from The Surface, or at least the things I'd brought into the cottage—leaves and grass, berries and mushrooms, and something that sort of looked like a rat.

"And see here?" Rudger pointed. "I carved some beebles!"

Snow White clapped her hands in delight. "Oh, it is beautiful! I've never had such a lovely bed, even if it is quite hard—but you are all such dear little dwarves!" And she kissed each of them on the head. Some of them shrank from her touch, but bore it with patience. Gilpin seemed to enjoy it. The tips of his ears turned blue. I kept well out of the way.

Epidot reported that they had dug nearly fifty feet but still had no sense of where the main tunnels were. "But we found some good deposits of limestone and quartz! So we'll have a hearty supper tonight."

Snow White sat at the head of the table, and the crew all gathered around her, eager to hear what she had done that day and curious about the food she'd gathered.

"My father used to take me for walks through The Woods, and he taught me all about the plants and things so I could survive if I needed to. Wasn't that smart?"

She let them taste her food if they wished, which all did except Rudger. He was a little hesitant after his experience with beetles.

"It's so squishy," said Herkimer, chewing on the fish.

Garnesha sampled a carrot. She probably thought

since it was orange, it might taste something like citrine. "It's so soft," she said. "I feel like my teeth are melting!"

After supper, the crew all gathered around Snow White's new bed. She told human stories from The Surface, ones where humans went on quests for magic and fought dragons and demons. The crew listened with rapt attention.

In the middle of a silly story about talking birds and bunnies, Leaf crawled out of my shirt. He perched on my shoulder for a minute. He seemed to be listening, too. After Snow White said, "The end," Leaf flew off my shoulder and landed on Snow White's head. He crawled down her hair and squeaked in her ear. I expected Snow White to scream and slap him away. Instead, she laughed and pet his head. "Oh, you want another story, do you?"

"I do, too!" said Rudger. "Human stories are fastynating."

"Leaf, get off her," I said. "She doesn't want you there."

"Oh, he's all right," said Snow White.

But I wasn't going to have it. I reached for Leaf, but he screeched at me and hid himself in Snow White's hair.

"Aw, let him stay there for now," said Snow White. "I don't mind."

"Traitor," I muttered under my breath.

"Once upon a time," said Snow White, "there was a princess who was much beloved by her kingdom. . . ."

She went on to tell one of the most absurd tales I'd ever heard. The princess was blessed by eleven fairies but cursed by an evil fairy and was doomed to prick her finger on a spinning wheel and die. Years later, the princess did prick her finger on a spinning wheel and fell as though dead. I thought that was the end of the story, but it went on.

"The princess slept in a tower for a hundred years," said Snow White, "until a prince came along. He knew the princess was his true love, so he kissed her awake and they lived happily ever after. The end."

I snorted. "That's ridiculous."

"It's not ridiculous at all," said Snow White. "True love's kiss is the most magical thing in this world."

"But you said she'd been sleeping for a hundred years."

"So?"

"So the prince wasn't a hundred years old. He was born while she was asleep. How could it be true love if he never even met her?"

"It was love at first sight."

"But the princess couldn't *see* him. She was asleep! So how could it be love at first sight?"

"Well, I . . . it . . . I don't have to *explain* it!" said Snow White. "It's *magic.* Don't dwarves believe in magic?"

"We do indeed, Princess," said Epidot. "In fact, it's thanks to dwarves that humans know of magic. We taught it to them, in the beginning."

"Though your kind is rather clumsy with magical power," said Garnesha, "if you'll forgive my saying so."

"And we can all agree that there's no such thing as a magical kiss," I said.

"I don't believe you," said Snow White, her little nose sticking up in the air. "I'll bet true love's kiss could break *your* curse!"

"What curse? You mean the curse of having to put up with a bratty princess?"

"No. I mean the one you were born with. You're cursed with . . . with grumpiness!"

The entire crew erupted with laughter, encouraging Snow White to go on.

"You're such a grump, in The Kingdom it would be your name!"

The crew laughed all the harder. Rudger was wiping tears away. "Very good, Pin-chess!" he said. "I often call him Grump, too!" Herkimer clutched at his stomach, and Gilpin's ears twitched as though they were having silent fits of laughter.

"Well, then your name should be Spoiled Brat!" I shouted, but they were all laughing too hard to hear me, or they didn't care.

I stalked outside and slammed the door. I paced back and forth in front of the cottage. I pressed my hands over my ears, trying to block the sounds of laughter and merriment. After a minute, the door opened and Gilpin appeared. He waved for me to come back inside.

"No," I said. "They don't want me around, and I don't want to be around them, either."

He tugged on my sleeve with a pleading look. I yanked my arm free.

"Just leave me alone!"

Gilpin frowned. His ears flopped down as he shut the door.

I crouched against the cottage and watched the last

light fade from the sky. Through the window, I heard Epidot announce that it was time for sleep.

"But I want to hear more human stories," said Amethina.

"I'll help tuck you in," said Snow White. "And then I'll sing you a lullaby."

"Oh, humans sing, do they?" asked Herkimer. "We dwarves are very fond of singing. Music has a magic all its own."

"I quite agree," said Snow White. "Now get into bed. You have to close your eyes as though you're going to sleep."

I heard the grind and scrape of shifting stones as the crew readied for bed. "Will you slam this rock on top of my head, Princess?" asked Amethina.

"But won't that hurt you?" Snow White asked.

"Oh no! It calms me down. I never sleep well without a good head-crushing, especially here on The Surface." There was a thump. "Aaaah. That's better. Thank you."

Once the crew were all settled, Snow White began to sing. The song was almost as silly as her stories.

*Twinkle, twinkle, little star*
*How I wonder what you are*
*Up above the world so high*
*Like a diamond in the sky*

"Diamonds!" Rudger burst in. "I love diamonds. They're my favorite."

Soon the entire crew were singing the song along with Snow White, Gilpin whistling the tune. I felt a little chip in my chest. How was it that in just two days a human could be more part of the crew than I ever was?

One by one, the crew nodded off to sleep until the cottage was silent. I rested my head against the wall. My eyes grew heavy, and I was starting to fall asleep myself when suddenly I sensed a presence and snapped awake.

Snow White was standing right above me. "I'm sorry we quarreled," she said.

I shrugged.

"It was rude of me to poke fun at you. You've been kind to me. You saved my life."

"It was nothing," I grumbled. It wasn't like I had a choice in the matter.

"Maybe nothing to you," said Snow White. "But it's everything to me, and I want to show you my gratitude. This isn't much, but it's all I have that would be of any worth to you." She held something out to me. It was her ruby ring. The ruby was small, but very fine indeed. The pungent smell was intoxicating.

"I don't want it," I said, turning away. Rubies were what the queen had used to manipulate me into liking her, trusting her. I wouldn't be so foolish now.

"Why not?" said Snow White. "Gilpin told me they're your favorite."

"How? Gilpin can't talk," I said.

"He talks in his own way," she said. "And he's very fond of you. Please. Take it." Snow White pried the gold prongs open around the ruby and it fell out of the ring.

My hand shot out reflexively, and I caught the ruby in the center of my palm.

"There, it's yours now," said Snow White. She waited. "Aren't you going to eat it?"

"I told you, I don't want it." I held it back up to her.

"I don't want it, either," said Snow White.

"Fine. Neither of us wants it." I hurled the ruby into the dark night.

"Oh!" Snow White let out a tiny yelp. There was silence for a moment, and then Snow White said, "That ruby belonged to my mother!"

"You said you didn't want it."

"It was a gift, a peace offering, and you just threw it away like it was nothing!"

"I don't want your peace offering," I hissed. "I know what you're trying to do. I know what you're doing to the rest of the crew! All you humans are the same. You only care about other creatures as far as they can benefit you. Well, I'm no fool, and you can't bribe me!"

Snow White stiffened and backed away. "Fine," she said in a cool voice. "If that's the way you feel about it. Good night, *Grump*!" She slipped back inside and slammed the door shut.

"Spoiled Brat," I muttered.

I stayed outside all night and shivered all through my sleep. I preferred to freeze to death than be anywhere near those rubble-headed fools, especially Snow White.

# CHAPTER TWENTY-ONE

## Princess Rescue

I woke to raindrops splashing on my nose and cheeks. I grumbled as I stood and stretched. My neck was horribly stiff and my limbs sore from sleeping sitting up all night in the cold. The rain started to pour down.

When I went inside the cottage, the crew were all gathered around the window, watching with fascination as the drops fell from the sky. A few of them reached out their hands to feel it.

"Fascinating," said Herkimer.

"All right, crew," said Epidot. "Let's get to work! Time to dig! Maybe we'll sense a tunnel today."

After the crew left, I looked longingly outside. The rain continued to pour. It pounded against the roof. I thought of Leaf. Was he caught in the rain?

"Leaf?" I called out the window.

"He's all right," said Snow White. "He's asleep in my

cloak, see?" She pointed to her bed. Leaf was curled up inside her cloak like a bird in a nest. I picked him up. He squeaked a little but went back to sleep when I put him inside my shirt.

"He's a sweet little fellow," said Snow White as she busied herself tidying up the cottage. She stacked all the dishes, then swept the dust off the table and floor. She even scooped up some of the dirt and rubble from the tunnel and tossed it outside. I just sat at the table and glared at her while I sipped cold strolg. When there was nothing left to do, Snow White sat at the table across from me and rested her chin in her hands.

"I'm bored. Aren't you?"

I pretended not to hear her. I just sipped my strolg and looked out the window. It had to stop raining eventually.

"Want to play a game?" Snow White asked.

"No," I said.

"Oh. I guess dwarves don't play games. You must be too busy digging all the time."

"We play lots of games," I said.

"Oh good, let's play Princess and Ogre." Snow White stood from the table. "You can be the ogre."

"What's an ogre?" I asked.

"A horrible, ugly creature that wants to eat princesses. They growl and drool and walk like this." She hung her arms and hunched over, dragging her feet as she walked.

"You're very convincing. I think you should be the ogre."

"But I'm already a *princess,*" she said. "A princess can't be an ogre."

I begged to differ.

"Fine. Why don't we play a dwarf game, then?" she suggested.

"Huh!" I laughed. "Humans could never play dwarf games. Your limbs are too long and your brains are too small."

Snow White raised her eyebrows. "Why don't you try me?"

I decided it would be entertaining to watch her try. So I gathered some round pebbles and flat stones for a game of Spitzeroff and started to teach Snow White how to play. The game was played by lining up five towers of five flat stones. You tossed a pebble and tried to knock over all the stones in the first tower, and then the second, and so on. If you knocked over the whole tower with one throw, you got to go again. If you knocked down all five towers in a row, you got double points. If you missed knocking a tower down, your turn was over. After each round, you'd shift the towers farther apart and farther away from the player to increase the difficulty. It wasn't a complicated game to learn, but it took good aim. With her long, skinny limbs, I doubted Snow White would be any good, but on her first try, she pinged the tower right in the center and it toppled to the floor.

"Beginner's luck," said Snow White with a little smile, but then she knocked down the next four in a row, and when I shifted the stones farther away, she toppled each of the towers *again.* I was awestruck. I couldn't let a human beat me at a dwarf game! Especially not a bratty princess. I set my aim and toppled the first tower, then the next four, but when I shifted the towers back, I only toppled half of the third tower.

"That's all right," said Snow White, as though she were the one teaching me. "You got most of them."

Snow White beat me on her very first game. I crushed a rock in my fist.

"That's fun!" said Snow White brightly. "Want to play again?"

We played again. I lost again. We played again, and tied.

"I can't wait to teach this game to Florian," said Snow White.

We played all morning. I won by the skin of my teeth a few times, but Snow White won more times than I cared to count. It took every bit of my self-control to keep from throwing all the rocks in her smug little face.

"Oh, look," said Snow White after she'd won yet again. "It stopped raining."

Indeed, the rain had stopped, and the sun was shining through the little window.

"Let's go for a walk, shall we? My arm is a little sore from all that throwing, and I need to stretch my legs."

I was glad for an excuse to stop the humiliation. I followed Snow White outside but split away from her as she started to sing silly songs and pick flowers and talk to birds as if they could understand her. I walked around the cottage and frowned. The rain had dissolved the piles of dirt I'd stacked against the walls and had turned it all into a swampy mess.

"Oh no," said Snow White. "All your hard work, wasted."

"I can fix it," I said. "It's not that hard."

"I'll help you," she said. "We can do it faster if we work together. Perhaps we should add some bigger rocks or some branches this time, as I suggested before. . . . Shall we start now?"

"No," I said, feeling annoyed.

"Okay, later, then," said Snow White.

I walked away from her, farther from the cottage. A sparkle of red caught my eye. I bent down to find Snow White's ruby in a patch of grass. I picked it up and held it in my palm. It sparkled in the sunlight, and its fragrance wafted up to me, sweet and inviting. I was tempted to eat it right then. Snow White would never know. But I stopped myself. I did not want any reason to feel indebted to her, even if she didn't know. I also remembered how Snow White had said the ruby had belonged to her mother, and the hurt on her face when I'd thrown it. I should give it back. I turned toward the cottage, but Snow White wasn't there. I looked all around, and then spotted her a hundred feet up The Mountain. I put the ruby in my pocket and ran after her. By the time I caught up, the terrain had become increasingly rocky and steep. Snow White continued to climb upward until we reached the base of a cliff that rose at a near vertical incline. I thought Snow White would stop and turn around then, but she simply hitched up her skirt and started to climb.

"I don't think that's a good idea," I said. "What if you fall?"

"I won't. I'm a good climber." She grasped on to a ledge above her and put her foot into a crevice to hoist herself up.

I folded my arms and waited for her to fall. I'd have to try to catch her to save her and then she'd probably crush me. But she didn't fall, and soon she peeked her head out from above a ledge and said, "Come up! It's beautiful here!"

Reluctantly, I climbed after her until I reached her on a narrow ledge carved into the cliff face. I was winded from the exercise, but my breath left me completely when I turned around. The land and sky stretched out before us as far as the eye could see. The Kingdom sat below us like a small maze of square stones, patches of golden fields, rolling hills, and winding rivers and streams that sparkled like silver in the sunlight. Cool wind whipped at our faces and clothes. Snow White stood with her face tilted upward, breathing in the sunshine and fresh air. "I love to be up high," she said.

"Me too," I said.

"It makes you feel free, doesn't it? Like nothing can pull you down and no one can hold you back."

I didn't want to admit that I felt the same, but I couldn't help but nod in agreement.

Snow White gazed over the land, her focus pausing on the castle. "I don't know if I'll ever be able to go home," she said. Her voice was suddenly a little wobbly. I tried to steel myself, block out any feelings of empathy, but I couldn't stop them from trickling in.

"I may never see my home again, either," I said, and I

was suddenly filled with sadness. Despite all those years I had longed to escape, home still had strings attached to my heart, and they pulled at me now.

"Nothing has been the same since Father died," said Snow White. "He understood me, you see. Everyone thinks being a princess means dressing up and sitting straight and smiling and nodding, but Father understood that I can't just sit and watch everyone else take action. He understood that I need to *do* things, too. He never meant for me to be a decoration. He taught me all about ruling a kingdom and let me help him make decisions. He wanted me to be prepared for the day I became queen. But when he died . . ." She choked on her words. A tear trickled down her cheek.

I stared at her, wondering if this was somehow her way of manipulating me, trying to get me to be on her side so she could use me for her own purposes, like Queen Elfrieda. Somehow it didn't feel the same, though.

The sun began to lower, and shadow overtook the cliff. I shivered as the wind blew.

"We should get back," I said. "It will be dark soon."

I had turned around to climb down the cliff when the edge of the ledge crumbled beneath my feet. I slipped and began to fall. My hands scrabbled at the ledge, struggling to find a grip, but there was nothing to hold on to. The rocks slipped from beneath my hands, and I slid down. I was going to fall! I was going to die!

Suddenly I jolted to a stop. "I've got you! Hold on!" Snow White was clinging to my wrist with both her little hands. She gritted her teeth, straining to pull me up. I struggled to find a foothold or anything to grab on to, but there was only smooth, flat stone. Snow White's face was now red with the effort of holding me. She began to slide forward, too, closer and closer to the edge. If she didn't let go, she would fall, too. My beard twisted.

"You have to let go!" I said.

"We can do it!" she cried. "Just hang on!"

She slid farther forward still. Rocks tumbled down. "Snow–"

"No, I won't let go!" she said.

I scraped my feet against the cliff, struggling in vain to find a toehold. I scraped my free hand against the rock, trying to dig into the cliff, and then it hit me.

*Your ax, you idiot, you have an ax!*

I pulled out my ax and swung it as hard as I could with one hand, wedging the blade into a crevice in the rock. It held, and I was able to brace my foot against the ax to keep from slipping. Snow White yanked with all her might while I pushed with my leg, and the force gave me just enough momentum to gain hold of the ledge and boost myself to safety.

I fell flat on my stomach, gasping for breath against the dirt and stone. I sat up and skittered back against the wall of the cliff.

"Whew!" said Snow White, breathing hard. "That was a close one!"

"You saved me," I said, still panting. "You could have died. Why . . . ?" My voice trailed off as I tried to take in more air.

"Why wouldn't I?" she said. "You saved *me*."

I wanted to say that it wasn't the same. I had to save her because she took me by the beard. She didn't have to save me. It made my rescuing feel pitiful. No matter how many times I saved her, it would never be a selfless, heroic gesture, like hers.

We sat on the ledge until we caught our breath.

"Shall we try again?" said Snow White.

"What?" For a moment I thought she was referring to us. Start over. Try to be friends.

"The cliff." She pointed. "Do you think you can climb down now?"

"Oh. Yes. Let's try again."

Snow White went first this time. "If you fall, I'll catch you," she said. "I'm a lot stronger than I look."

But I was very careful this time and used my ax the entire way down. When we reached the bottom, we walked back to the cottage in silence. And when we were nearly to the door, I remembered the ruby. I retrieved the gem from my pocket, and held it out to Snow White. "I found this," I said. "I'm sorry I threw it away."

Snow White looked down at the ruby. Relief seemed to wash over her. "Will you keep it safe for me?" she asked.

"Why?"

She gave a little shrug. "I don't know. You *are* pretty grumpy, but I think that's maybe why I like you."

"You like me? Because I'm grumpy?"

She nodded. "You don't pretend to be anything but what you are, so I trust you more than I do other people. This world is full of pretenders. To find a friend who is genuine and trustworthy is rarer than rubies." She smiled a little. "So don't ever change, Grump."

She went inside the cottage, leaving me gaping with the ruby in my palm. She liked me? She liked me not in spite of my grumpiness, but . . . *because* I was grumpy? She didn't want me to change. She didn't think I needed to.

I put the ruby in my pocket, suddenly feeling much lighter.

# CHAPTER TWENTY-TWO

## Lost Prince

For the next several days, Snow White and I worked together to hide the cottage. We gathered larger sticks and stones and stacked them against the walls before pouring the dirt on top. Snow White worked as hard as any dwarf on a crew and even had some top-notch ideas. She suggested we dig up some shrubs and smaller trees and plant them around the cottage and in some of the mounds to make it truly look like just a little hill.

The days passed much more pleasantly now that Snow White and I were . . . friends? At least I think we were friends. She helped me clear the rubble from the cottage every day and even attempted to make the inside more colorful and homey. She picked bouquets of flowers to put all over the cottage, but they made Rudger sneeze so much, we had to get rid of them. So we focused on other home improvements. We found plenty of borlen around the cottage, and made some better dishes. I made some little shelves out of wood so we could neatly stack the dishes after meals.

When we were finished with our chores, we played games. Snow White continued to beat me at Spitzeroff most of the time, but she also taught me some of her human games besides Princess and Ogre. I didn't like Tag, You're It! so much. I was always It because Snow White's legs were four times as long as mine. I was pretty good at Hide and Seek, though. I always found Snow White because she'd usually start giggling at some point, but Snow White usually had to forfeit because she could never find me. I was good at hiding.

Leaf couldn't get enough of Snow White. He stayed inside at night a little longer and came home a little earlier just to have the pleasure of her adoration. He split his time between sleeping in my shirt and in the hood of Snow White's cloak. I didn't mind. There was enough friendship to go around.

The crew was also much more tolerable now that Snow White and I were friends. One morning Rudger greeted me with his usual nasty grin and said, "Good morning, Grump!"

"Now, now," said Snow White. "Only I get to call him that. Isn't that right, Grump?"

I smiled. "That's right, Spoiled Brat."

Rudger looked a little confused but then shrugged and let it go. He didn't tease me anymore after that. No one wanted to displease Snow White.

I felt so content, I barely noticed the passing of the

days and weeks until the air started to grow chilly. The colors on The Surface changed, too. Leaves turned from emerald green to yellow beryl, amber, and citrine.

"Winter is coming," said Snow White. "Soon there will be snow."

"I've never seen snow," I said. "What does it look like?"

"It falls from the sky, a little like rain, only instead of water drops, it's delicate, fluffy flakes. It covers the earth in the brightest white. It was snowing on the day I was born. That's what I was named for."

"I was named for a kind of dirt," I said. "Borlen is very dark and dense."

"Dirt and Snow," said the princess. "What a pair we make!"

One day, Snow White and I went for a walk, searching for her food. I didn't search so much as just keep Snow company. She'd grown pretty savvy about finding her own food, and had even started stockpiling lots of it in the cavern, drying the meats and berries. She said food was always scarce in the winter.

Snow White found a berry bush and sang as she picked berries and put them in a basket she'd woven herself out of sticks and grass.

*I'm waiting for my true love*
*My true love, my true love*

*I'm waiting for my true love*
*He'll be here any day*

"Do you even know who your true love is?" I asked.

"I think I'll know it when he comes," she said.

"When will he come?" I asked.

I wondered if she thought he would appear out of nowhere and magically fall in love with her at first sight, like in the tale of the sleeping princess.

Snow White shrugged. "When the time is right, he'll come."

"How do you know?"

"I just do."

I picked at some leaves on a bush. "And when he comes, you'll go away?"

Snow White opened her mouth, but before she could speak, there was a rustle in the branches nearby. We both stilled. The steady clip-clop of hooves made me fear the presence of a human. A flash of white and sapphire blue confirmed my suspicions.

"Hide!" I whispered to Snow White. "It could be the huntsman—or the queen!"

Snow White set her jaw. She began to tremble, not with fear but with anger. "I'll face them," she said too loudly. "I'll throw rocks at them!" She picked up a large stone and wound her arm back.

I leapt up and grabbed the stone out of her hand. "Don't be ridiculous! You can't risk being seen. Go back to the cottage. I'll scare them away and make sure you're not found."

"But—"

"Go!" I whispered as fiercely as I could.

Snow White huffed, but she turned around and stomped back toward the cottage. I watched her go, then turned my attention to the intruder. He—or she—was very near. I could see a figure on a horse, and whoever it was seemed to be searching for something. I caught a whiff of diamonds and sapphires. Could it be the queen?

I hid behind a tree and squeezed the stone in my hand.

*Clip-clop. Clip-clop.* The horse stopped. It snuffed and blew. The rider clicked their tongue and whistled, then said to the horse, "What's the matter?"

I peered around the tree. It was a young man, about Snow White's age, and I recognized him as the boy she'd been dancing with at the ball that fateful night. Florian, I think his name was. He passed by me and headed right in the direction of the cottage. I couldn't allow him to find it! If anyone knew Snow White still lived—even a friend—word would surely get back to the queen.

I threw the stone at the horse's hindquarters. It whinnied in terror and reared up on its hind legs, throwing the boy. Florian flipped backward out of the saddle, and the horse tore off into the trees, thankfully in the opposite direction of the cottage.

The boy was on the ground, tangled up in his blue cloak. I aimed another stone at him, but when he finally freed himself, I saw that he was so frightened, he could scarcely breathe.

"Horse?" he called in barely more than a whisper.

"Come back!" He turned all about, searching frantically. "Horse!" Then his eyes found me.

"A gnome!" he said. "Yes, I'll send a gnome to the castle, and they'll come and find me and rescue me. . . ." He made as if to snatch me up, and I brandished my stone, but then the boy staggered back a step, clutching at his curly hair. "Oh, but what will they think of me then? The soldiers will laugh at me again. Queen Elfrieda will write to Father again and tell him I'm a coward and then he'll make me stay away for another year! Be brave, Prince Florian! Be a man! A hero! Go find your horse!" He puffed up his chest and strode in the direction his horse had gone, until a bird shot up from the ground, flapping wildly. The prince shrieked and stumbled back, falling flat on his bottom. He let out a pitiful little sob. I shook my head. This prince was nothing like the heroic figures in Snow White's stories.

"I wish Snow White was here," he said. "She always made me feel brave. And court life is very boring without her. Oh, why did you have to be devoured, Snow! Why did you go into The Woods by yourself? I should have been there to save you!"

My heart softened at this. To think that Snow White was mere feet from where he sat! I had half a mind to lead him to her, or her to him, but it was too dangerous, especially if he was still a guest at Queen Elfrieda's court. I had to be rid of him.

I followed the scent of iron and silver until I found the prince's big white horse grazing serenely a little way up

The Mountain. I got behind him and threw the rock at his hindquarters again. He whinnied and galloped toward his sulky master. A few moments later, I heard the prince shout for joy at the sight of his faithful steed. "Come on, horse, let's go back to the castle. I've had enough bravery for one day."

He mounted and turned toward The Kingdom. He trotted down the mountainside and disappeared through the trees. I felt a slight tingle in my beard and wondered if I'd done wrong in keeping him from Snow White. But what choice did I have?

On my way back to the cottage, Leaf emerged from my shirt and perched on my shoulder. He stretched his wings.

"You would never leave me, would you, Leaf?" In answer, Leaf slapped my cheeks with his wings, like he was trying to wake me up. Of course he would leave me. He couldn't live forever. Bats didn't live half as long as humans. He flew off into the trees in search of his breakfast.

A dark feeling gathered in my stomach. I had a mounting fear that someday soon, I'd be alone again.

When I returned to the cottage, Snow White asked me who it was that I'd seen. "Was it my stepmother? Was it Horst?"

"No," I said. "Just some rider. I scared him away." I'm not sure why I didn't tell her. Maybe I was afraid that if she saw her old friend, her new one wouldn't be so important to her anymore.

Snow White nodded, but seemed almost disappointed that the excitement was over. I could tell she was growing restless in hiding.

That night, the crew returned very excited. Epidot could finally sense the direction of the main tunnels. "Clearly, the collapse was extensive," he said. "But we should be able to break through within a week!"

"Less, if I have anything to do with it!" declared Garnesha, lifting her strong arms and puffing out her chest.

There were shouts of joy from the crew.

"As soon as we get home, I'm going to slam my head into my bedrocks and sleep for a month straight!" said Amethina.

"And I'm going to eat a cartload of diamonds," said Rudger.

"You won't be able to lift an ax for a month straight if you do that," said Garnesha.

"Exactly," said Rudger, smiling dreamily.

I didn't say a word as the crew discussed all the things they would do once they got home. I wasn't sure it was my home anymore.

Snow White was also quiet.

"What about the princess?" asked Herkimer. "What will happen to her once we reach the colony?"

"Oh, you've all done so much for me already," said Snow White. "I can't ask for more."

"But we can't just leave you behind," said Rudger.

"If only I'd been born a dwarf and not a princess," she said, smiling with sad eyes.

"You'd have made a fine dwarf!" said Rudger, and

everyone chuckled, but the laughter went out as quickly as a flame doused with salt and was replaced by an awkward silence. It was fine to joke about Snow White living in the colony, but it would never be allowed. The fact that we were living with her on The Surface was bad enough.

"Perhaps the Seventh can see her safely to someplace?" said Garnesha. "Is there another Surface colony you know of, Princess, that would be safe for you?"

"There could be," said Snow White, "but it would still be a risk. My stepmother could find out I was still alive, and *then* what would happen? She might try to kill me all over again and succeed. Or worse, she could start a war! I couldn't bear for others to lose their lives over me."

"We'd fight for you, Princess!" said Amethina. "Wouldn't we, crew?"

"Yes!" said Epidot. "We wouldn't let anyone harm you."

"I'd take 'em out at the knees!" said Rudger, and the crew raised their axes and pledged to protect Snow White, all without being taken by the beard.

My own beard prickled. Was this not proof of Snow White's goodness? Did this not truly make her the fairest in the land?

Tears sprang to Snow White's eyes. "You're all such dear, sweet dwarves!"

The crew celebrated the news. They feasted on what was left of their emergency reserves—diamonds and sapphires and emeralds. They sang and danced, and Snow

White clapped along with them from her bed. Herkimer and Rudger got just a little diamond drunk and started dancing on top of the table, until it cracked and they both fell.

"Shilly tree tables!" said Rudger. "So flimsy!"

The next morning, the crew rose early to go dig, but Snow White didn't wake like usual. When at last she rose, she seemed a bit withdrawn. She didn't eat any breakfast. I asked if she wanted to play Spitzeroff, but she said she didn't feel like it.

"How about a walk?" I said. "It's cold, but the sun is bright."

"Not today," she said. "I'm just a little tired." She stared out the window for the rest of the morning, wrapped in her cloak, then slept all afternoon. She barely ate anything for supper and went to bed early, without a song or story.

"Is she all right?" Garnesha asked.

"She said she's just tired," I said.

But the next day, it was clear there was something very wrong with Snow White. She didn't get out of bed at all. She wouldn't eat or drink, even when I brought the food right to her lips. She shivered with cold, though her skin was lava hot. When the crew returned, they were in a fit of worry over her.

"Would a jade paste cure her, do you think?" Amethina asked. "I have a few bits in my emergency pouch."

"No, no," said Garnesha. "Remember, humans can't eat rocks. Our medicines won't help."

"Well, she needs something," said Amethina. "Seventh, do you know about human medicine?"

I knew nothing of human medicine.

"What if she's dying?" said Rudger.

"Humans have such fragile lives," said Epidot. "I doubt there's much we can do."

I pulled away from Snow White and the crew and quietly slipped outside into the brisk air. I could see my breath curling out of my mouth like smoke. I watched the sun set, and then I watched the stars appear, glittering diamonds in the tanzanite blue sky. I started to sing Snow White's silly song, hoping it would make me feel better.

*Twinkle, twinkle, little star*
*How I wonder what you are . . .*

It didn't help. I needed something more than a song now. I needed to help Snow White. But how?

I shoved my hands into my pockets and felt Snow White's ruby and my Fate Stone. The ruby would do nothing for her, but my Fate Stone . . . I had barely thought of it these past weeks, but perhaps it could help. I could ask it to show me something to make Snow White better.

I pulled out my mirror and looked at it, concentrating on what I needed. *I need to help Snow White.*

The mirror swirled. An image began to form, starting as a haze and then growing clearer.

My heart stopped.

I didn't know what I had expected to see, but it was not this. This was the last thing above or under earth that would help Snow White.

In the mirror was Queen Elfrieda.

# CHAPTER TWENTY-THREE

## Cracked

I gawked at Queen Elfrieda. She looked different somehow. Maybe it was her lips, painted a deep crimson, or her eyelids, lined heavily with black so her eyes glowed like blue flames between coals. She wore more jewels than ever, gobs of diamonds, sapphires, and rubies all around her neck, as if to taunt and entice me. I felt nothing but revulsion. I could practically see poison flowing in her veins.

"Dwarf!" said Queen Elfrieda. "I've been gazing into this mirror for weeks trying to find you. Why haven't you returned to me?"

I had not thought this through. I had not thought about the risk of seeing the queen in my Fate Stone. Of all the things that might help Snow White, this was the last.

I swallowed, trying to find words. "I . . . I got lost."

"Lost?" said the queen.

I nodded, trying to look pitiful. "I've been wandering in The Woods for weeks. The food is terrible." That much was true.

"Oh, poor dwarf," she said, pouting her lips. "Why didn't you look for me in your magic mirror? I could have helped you, you know!"

"I did!" I lied. "But it wasn't working, for some reason. I think there's some kind of magical interference here in all these trees. Hard to get a clear buzz of magic."

Queen Elfrieda's eyes narrowed. She was suspicious. "Well, it's no matter. But I *have* missed you. There's no one to play our game. Shall we play it now? Mirror, mirror, on the wall, who is the fairest of them all?"

"I . . . you . . . I . . ." I couldn't get the words out.

The queen's eyes narrowed even more. "Tell me the truth, Dwarf. Don't be shy."

I felt my beard twitch. The longer I waited, the harder it twisted and pulled. When I could stand the pain no longer, I blurted, "Snow White is the fairest!" I let out the breath I'd been holding.

"Impossible!" shrieked Queen Elfrieda. "Snow White is dead. See this?" She held up the silver box encrusted with gems. "Inside this box is Snow White's tiny, pitiful, beat-less heart. The huntsman brought it to me, still warm from the killing. Unless . . ."

The queen drew closer in the mirror. Her eyes became glowing blue slits. "You were supposed to witness her death. You did, didn't you?"

I shook my head. I bit my tongue, held my breath until I felt myself turn blue, but the words burst out of me of their own accord. "The huntsman didn't kill Snow White! She ran away and hid."

The queen looked down at the box in her hands. "And the heart?"

"A boar's," I said. "I saw the huntsman kill it."

The queen turned red, purple, and, finally, green. She started to shake. She slammed down the box, and her image rippled. "The huntsman deceived me," she snarled. "I'll make him eat his own heart!"

A shiver ran down my spine. "Well, then, I guess I'll be going now. Good ni–"

"Wait!" said the queen. "We're not finished here, Dwarf. Did you see where Snow hid? Do you know where she is?"

I took a breath, relieved. She hadn't commanded me. "No," I lied. "I tried to run after her, but she was too fast."

"Hmmm," the queen mused. "Well, that's no matter. You can ask the mirror to show us, can't you?"

I shook my head. "It might not work. She might be too far away to see."

"Well, we can try. Go on, Dwarf. Ask it to show us where Snow White is hiding!"

I began to tremble. I clutched the mirror. I wanted to break it. "Mirror," I said in a tremulous voice. "Where is Snow White hiding?"

The mirror fogged. I silently pleaded for it to show nothing, but then the mirror showed trees. The Woods. The stream. The mirror's view moved along the stream until it came to the cottage buried beneath a mound of dirt, its little window aglow. The mirror looked through the window, and there was Snow White, lying on her bed, surrounded by the crew.

A scuffling noise startled me, and I dropped my Fate Stone. I looked around to see Gilpin. He was carrying a torch through the trees. His eyes lit up at the sight of me, then traveled down to my Fate Stone, lying on the ground. His expression grew serious, his brows lifted. The image of Snow White was still there.

I snatched it up and slid it into my pocket. "It's nothing," I said. "Just my Fate Stone."

Gilpin's right ear folded down, and the left perked straight up in suspicion.

"Come on," I said, irritated.

I walked back to the cottage, Gilpin trailing behind me. I could almost hear his thoughts, his questions, but my own were louder. Had the queen seen Snow White? Would she know where to find her from that brief image? I wished on all the stars that she wouldn't.

The crew were still gathered around Snow White when I returned. Garnesha was trying to spoon some strolg into her mouth. Amethina placed some of her healing crystals around her head—tanzanite, jade, opal.

But none of that would help her, and there was the queen to consider. I had to get Snow away from here, someplace safe. But where? And how? She was so ill, the travel alone could kill her. I could go to Prince Florian, ask him to take Snow White to his own kingdom on his horse. But Florian was still a guest at the queen's court. What if I ran into the queen while I was there, or worse, what if the queen came here while I was away?

Gilpin stood beside me, both ears perked up in concern, but he wasn't looking at Snow White. He was looking at me. For a split second, I wanted to tell him everything. Tell everyone. All about the queen and my beard. But what good would it do? Queen Elfrieda could just as easily take the rest of the crew by the beard (excepting Garnesha and Amethina). I knew she would love a crew of faithful dwarf servants. And then she might invade our tunnels, take more dwarves by the beard, enslave our entire colony, as she had the trolls! No, it was no use to tell them. The best hope for the crew was to reach the main tunnels as soon as possible. The best hope for Snow White was to get her well and then get her away from here, far from the queen. For myself I had no hope.

My beard buzzed all night, and I woke to it tightening in gradual twists.

The crew were eager to get to work—they hoped to break through to the colony today or tomorrow—but they were reluctant to leave Snow White in her delicate condition.

"Keep the crystals around her head," said Amethina. "And see if she'll at least let the jade rest on her mouth, or even her tongue. It might help her heal a little faster."

"But don't let her choke!" said Rudger.

"I'm bound to protect her, remember?" I said.

Gilpin looked back at me one last time, his brow knitted and his ears bent, before he disappeared into the tunnel.

My beard buzzed and itched all morning. I jumped at

every little sound—birds, wind, snapping twigs—wondering if it was the queen or the huntsman or an army.

"What's wrong, Grump?" Snow White asked in a croaky voice. "You seem worried."

"Nothing," I lied. "You're perfectly safe. I'll protect you."

"I know you will," said Snow White. "You're like my knight in shining armor, only a little smaller than I imagined. And a lot grumpier."

A smile tugged at my mouth, despite the sharp rocks I felt in my throat. "Let me get you some food," I said. "You need to eat."

I prepared Snow White some of her food and made her eat. She didn't seem to notice. By afternoon, she was sitting up and humming as she looked out the window. She seemed a little recovered. When would she be well enough to travel?

I jumped at a flapping sound outside. "It's only a bird," said Snow White. "Help me up, will you? I need to stretch." I stood by her bed and let her place a hand on my head to help her stand. She walked only a couple of turns around the cottage before she needed to sit down again. This did not help my anxiety.

"Oh, cheer up, Grump!" she said. "I'm not going to die. Well, actually, I *might* die of boredom. Play a game with me—I'll bet I can still beat you at Spitzeroff!"

For the first time, I wished Snow would beat me at Spitzeroff, but she was so weak, she could barely throw her pebbles at all. Not that I did any better. I was so distracted, my aim was completely off. On the third round, I tossed a pebble and hit Snow White right on the nose.

"Hey!" said Snow White, rubbing at her nose. The pebble was small enough that it couldn't have hurt too much.

"Double points for hitting a princess?" I said.

She frowned but then tossed her whole pile of pebbles so they rained down on my head. "Triple for the grumpy dwarf!" She laughed and then fell off her chair. I fell down laughing, too. We were still on the floor, laughing uncontrollably, when a shadow darkened the window.

"Oh!" said Snow. She stood up quickly and teetered on her weak legs.

My heart stopped beating for a moment. A face appeared in the window; it wasn't the queen's, but a haggard woman's. How relieved I was to see her wrinkled face, the wart on her nose, her straggly gray hair.

But then the woman looked at me with one big pale blue eye. It narrowed in recognition, and I knew it was Queen Elfrieda in disguise. My beard confirmed this with a tight, wrenching twist.

# CHAPTER TWENTY-FOUR

## Beard in a Bunch

If the queen was surprised to see me, she didn't show it. She smiled, revealing crooked, blackened, broken teeth.

"Good day, dearies," said the hag-queen. "Would you care for an apple?" She lifted up a basket of shiny red apples and rested it on the windowsill. Snow White forgot her alarm and her weakness. She leapt to the window.

"Oh, yes!" said Snow White. "I've been craving apples for ages!" She reached for one, but my beard wrenched. I surged forward and shoved the basket out the window. Apples tumbled in all directions.

"Grump!" shouted Snow White.

"Oh, my apples! My apples!" The hag hobbled all around, trying to retrieve her apples.

Snow White turned to me, glaring. "Why would you do such a mean thing to a poor old woman?" She didn't wait for me to respond. She marched to the door, unbarred it, and went outside.

"Wait!" I ran after her.

Snow White chased after the apples rolling all over and helped the old lady put them in the basket. "I'm so sorry," she said. "He didn't mean to do it."

"Oh, my beautiful apples! They're all ruined."

"Oh dear, and I've been craving apples for such a long time," said Snow White. "This one's not so bad. Only a few bruises." She held up an apple and was ready to take a bite, but the queen snatched it out of her hands.

"Oh no," said the queen, "I can't let such a pretty, sweet thing like you have a bruised apple. You must have the most delicious apple! Here." She reached inside her robes and pulled out another apple, one that hadn't been inside the basket. She held it by the stem so it spun in a circle. One side was pure white, the other bright red, and the stem was coal black.

"What kind of apple is that?" asked Snow White. "It seems . . . unusual."

"It's a very special apple," said the queen. "I've been saving it for someone deserving of such a treat. Someone kind and so *fair*, just like you." She held it out to Snow White. I caught its scent as it was passed over my head—sickly sweet, tinged with a putrid undertone. Snow White took it in her hands.

"Don't eat it!" I shouted. "It's poisoned!"

Snow White recoiled. The queen snarled at me. "Poisoned? My beautiful apple? I grew that apple right in my own yard and picked it with my own hands! Keep quiet, Dwarf!"

My tongue became wood in my mouth.

"There, there, dearie," the queen cooed to Snow White. "Don't let the dwarf frighten you so."

"He's only worried," said Snow White. "I've had attempts made on my life before."

"A sweet little dove like you?" said the queen.

"Yes, and the dwarf is bound to protect me, you see, so you'll forgive him if he's a little cautious."

"I see," said the queen. She gazed at me for a moment and smiled wickedly through her rotting teeth. "Dwarves are powerful creatures, very cunning. You are lucky to have such protection. And he himself can prove to you that the apple is safe! Here, Dwarf. Take a bite of the apple." The queen held the apple out to me, the white side of it.

I shook my head and opened my mouth to object, but of course I couldn't speak. Instead, I took a bite of the apple.

"Chew and swallow," said the queen.

I nearly choked on the sickly sweetness, but I swallowed.

"There's a good dwarf. See? No poison here!"

"I suppose it's safe, then," said Snow White. "He's the most faithful friend, I know he would never allow any harm to come to me."

"I have no doubt," said the queen. "Now you can take a bite of the other half." She held out the apple.

I stepped forward. I didn't need to speak. I would

wrench the apple from Snow White's hands and throw it down The Mountain. I wouldn't let her eat it.

The queen seemed to anticipate my plans.

"Here, Dwarf, since the pretty girl trusts you so, why don't you give her the apple. Make sure she takes a bite." Her command seized upon me. My hand reached out. I took the apple. I strained against the order. I tried to throw the apple to the ground, but my hand would only go in one direction. I lifted the apple toward Snow White.

"Thank you," she said as she reached for the apple.

I kept my fingers wrapped around it. I wouldn't let her have it! My fingers released the apple. Snow White lifted it toward her mouth.

She had to take a bite.

She couldn't take a bite.

I had to do as the queen commanded.

I must protect Snow White.

My beard ached, split in two directions. In a moment, *I* would be split in two.

I felt in my pockets. In one was my Fate Stone, in the other, the ruby.

Snow White brought the apple to her mouth, ready to take a bite.

I grasped the ruby with my fingers. I set my aim. I could not fail this time. I would knock that apple out of Snow White's hands and send it flying down The Mountain.

I wound up and threw the ruby as hard as I could. It shot through the air and sparkled as it caught a ray of sun.

Snow White opened her little mouth as wide as it would go. The ruby hit the apple, but instead of knocking it aside, it sank into the flesh just as Snow White bit down.

Snow White closed her eyes and chewed. "It's delicious."

*No!*

"Yes!" said the queen, watching the princess intently. "Good!"

"It has the most curious flavor," said Snow White. "Like . . ." Snow White stopped talking. She stopped chewing. Her eyes opened wide. She looked right at me. And then she fell to the ground.

Queen Elfrieda let out a cackle, harsh and shrill. "See, Dwarf? Now I'm the fairest!"

I ran to Snow White and fell to her side.

"I'm the fairest! I'm the fairest of them all!" The queen hobble-danced all around the princess and me. "Say it, Dwarf! Tell me I'm the fairest of them all!"

My tongue was loosed. I opened my mouth to scream at her, to shout that she was not the fairest, that she was a horrid old tyrant! But the only words I could utter were: "You're the fairest of them all!" And the queen cackled some more.

I shook Snow by the shoulders. "Snow White? Princess?"

She didn't move.

I heard voices, shouts coming from the cottage.

"Where are they?" someone shouted. "Princess!

Grump! We're through! We're through to the main tunnels!"

"What is that?" asked the queen.

I thought quickly. I could not put the crew at risk. She'd take them all by the beard.

"It's an army," I said.

"An army?"

"From the Northern Kingdom. They found out Snow White was alive and came to rescue her. They'll be very angry if they find out what you've done."

The queen grew alarmed, but then she smiled. "But they won't know what I've done," she said. "I command you not to tell anyone. In fact, if anyone asks, I command you to tell them *you* killed her! Ha! Farewell, Dwarf. I'll see you in the mirror." And like a wisp of smoke, she disappeared into the trees.

A head poked out of the window. Gilpin. He saw me hunched over Snow White's lifeless form on the ground. His ears rose in alarm. He turned back and whistled.

"Gilpin's found 'em!" called Herkimer.

I shook Snow White again. "Please wake up."

She did not move. Her chest did not rise and fall. Her heart did not beat.

The door to the cottage opened. The crew were coming. My heart raced. I looked around. I couldn't let them find me like this. They'd think I'd killed Snow White. And I'd have to tell them I had. I had, hadn't I? I told the queen she was alive. My mirror showed Queen Elfrieda where Snow White was hiding. I gave her the apple.

I was not the hero of this story. I was the villain.

"I'm sorry," I said to Snow White. "I'm so sorry I didn't protect you."

I picked up the poison apple. As I stood, the rest of the crew came out of the cottage.

"There they are!" shouted Rudger. "I see them! But what's wrong with the pin-chess?"

I fled through the trees. I ran in the only direction I knew the crew would not follow—up. I climbed and climbed, up the steep mountainside, up the cliff where Snow White had saved me. I climbed until I was at the peak of The Mountain, on top of the world with my heart in the deepest depths of despair.

# CHAPTER TWENTY-FIVE

## Banished

Cold wind sliced at my face and ripped at my beard. Gray clouds rolled in like silent boulders. Tiny flakes began to float all around me, fluffy and pure white. I held my hand out and caught a few. They melted quickly on my palm. Snow. More and more snowflakes floated down from the sky, landing on my nose and cheeks, catching in my beard. It was a torturous reminder that Snow White was gone. Dead. Because of me.

The poison apple was still clutched in my hand. I squeezed it to the core. The juice ran over my fingers and down my arm, and quickly froze in the frigid air. I threw the apple as hard as I could. It spiraled in the sky and disappeared in the misty white. Only after it was gone did I think I might have made a mistake. What if an animal ate it? Or worse, what if the seeds grew into more poison-apple trees?

I stayed on the mountaintop for hours, until the world was cloaked in white and I was nearly frozen solid from the icy wind. Before I lost all feeling in my limbs, I walked down the rocky mountainside and found refuge in a small, shallow cavern. It was damp and cold, a perfectly grim place for a grumpy dwarf. I'd stay here, alone, for the next thousand years, or however long I lived, until I died and turned to rubble.

I pulled out my Fate Stone, willing it to show Snow White. The fog in the mirror cleared to reveal six somber dwarves surrounding the still form of the princess. Pale and fragile, she lay on her stone bed. Gilpin stood at her head, shaking with cold or grief or both. Everyone's eyes were clouded with dust. They each placed a stone on Snow White, an ancient funeral ritual to usher a dwarf from flesh and bone to stone and gem. Snow White, being human, would never turn to diamond. She'd turn to dust and dirt. It didn't matter, though. This was the only way the crew knew how to show their love for the princess.

The crew lifted up a delicate clear cover and placed it over Snow White. This was something I hadn't seen before. "To protect the p-princess," stammered Epidot, "even in death. We carved this crystal coffin to preserve the goodness of her memory and kindness as long as p-possible."

Gilpin placed a hand on the crystal case. His ears flopped down and his shoulders shook. Dust trickled down his cheeks.

I wiped at my own eyes, but then heard Rudger whisper to Herkimer, "Nearly cracked the Sixth to hear of the Seventh's treachery."

"It weighs heavy on all of us," said Herkimer.

"Not me," said Rudger. "I always knew he was a sorry excuse for a dwarf. He deserves to be banished! I only feel bad for his parents. What a shame to have such a son!"

My parents! Oh, how miserable they must be! The first news they would hear of me in months was a story of deceit and betrayal.

"Yes," said Herkimer. "His parents both cried rivers of dust when they heard."

That was not a scene I desired to see, but I would have preferred it over what I saw next. I was about to put my Fate Stone away when Queen Elfrieda appeared in the mirror.

My anguish turned to rage. It burned in my stomach and chest. It grew so hot, I thought it would burn a hole right through me. I glared at the murderous queen. Her disguise had not completely worn off. She still had missing teeth and streaks of gray in her hair.

"Mirror, mirror, on the wall, who's the fairest of them all?"

I said nothing.

"Hello? Are you there?" She lowered her voice to a whisper. "This is when you tell me that I'm the fairest. Go on! Say it now!"

My beard twitched with her command, and I wondered why I hadn't found some way to disobey the queen. I should have eaten the whole apple myself rather than let Snow White take a bite. I should have ripped off my beard and warned her.

"You are the fairest, Your Majesty," I said dispassionately, a tinge of disgust in my voice.

"Don't be droll, Dwarf," said the queen. "This is a celebratory affair. Say it with conviction!"

I sighed. I thought of my rage and forced it into enthusiasm. "Over the land, as far as I see, thou art the fairest of all, O Queen."

Queen Elfrieda squealed with delight. "Say it again!"

I had to tell her at least ten times in ten different ways—with pride, joy, triumph, persuasion, elation, and admiration. The queen dissolved in a fit of exultant giggles.

With all the force I possessed, I hurled my Fate Stone against the rocks. It clinked and landed upright against the rocks, unbroken, not even a scratch on it.

"What am I to do now, mirror?" I shouted at it. "You're supposed to show me wisdom and guidance, so show me!"

My own reflection remained, as though it were mocking me. I picked up my Fate Stone and threw it again, but this time I threw it off the mountaintop, where it disappeared into the falling snow. There. It couldn't roll back to me now, and I didn't care who found it.

I fell into a fitful sleep. When I woke the next morning, my stomach emitted a deep growl, reminding me that I hadn't eaten anything since yesterday morning. I wasn't willing to go in search of decent food, and in all this snow, I didn't think I'd be able to find much anyhow.

I gnawed on common rocks in the cavern. They were stale and chalky, but I doubted a pile of rubies would taste much better now.

I gazed out at the white world. It was so quiet and still. It was as if all the earth had died or gone to sleep, everyone and everything in mourning over Snow White's death. I, too, remained perfectly still and quiet. I thought I would remain in that state forever—blank, frozen—but then I noticed a black speck in the white sky. It got bigger and bigger, until I could see its wings flapping and I heard it squeak.

"Leaf!" I reached for him, desperate. He landed on my shoulder and immediately crawled down into my shirt. He wrapped his wings tight around himself and trembled with cold.

"It's okay, Leaf," I said. "I'll take care of you."

I cared nothing for myself. I would have stayed in the cold cavern until I turned to stone, but Leaf didn't deserve that. He needed warmth and food. I ventured out into the snow and found enough dry wood to make a fire. I dug into the frozen earth until I found some beetles and worms. When I had the fire going and the cavern heated up, Leaf finally stopped trembling and slept.

It was Leaf that kept me going in the days and weeks that followed. I remained in the cold mountainside cavern, just surviving. Not really living. But I would get up each morning to see that Leaf was fed, and this reminded me to feed myself. Eventually, he went back to his routine. During the days, he curled up inside my shirt, and in the evenings, he flew off to hunt. His absence made me anxious, and I didn't sleep well. I had recurring nightmares of Snow White and the queen and the poison apple. Over and over again, Snow took a bite of the apple. Each time, I was powerless to stop it. And then I'd see the crew, their angry faces, Rudger shouting, "You did this! You killed the pin-chess!" And then I'd see my parents, crying clouds of dust, knowing they'd never see me again.

Leaf was a comfort, but not great company. I shouldn't have minded the solitude. All alone, I couldn't harm anyone and no one could take me by the beard. But I found at least a thousand times a day I wished to see another face—my parents, Gilpin, the crew, even Rudger.

At my lowest point, I was lonely enough to wish to see the queen. Anyone to talk to.

After months of snow, the icy stillness of winter began to crack. The air finally warmed, and the icicles hanging from my cave began to drip and fall. The green grass began to push through the patches of melting snow, and little buds formed on the branches of bushes and trees. Birds began to chirp, and other creatures began to stir and move about.

Eventually, I ventured out of the cavern to search for some decent food. My diet had been terrible, and I was starting to feel the effects. Without any nutritious gems, my energy lagged and my mind was muddled. But there were no gems on The Surface, of course, only limestone and granite. I found a few bits of quartz in a nearby stream, and that gave me a little more energy, but still I was severely malnourished.

One morning, as I was searching in the stream, I saw

a glimmer through the grass. I hopped through the water and, to my utter astonishment, found a small nugget of amber. I popped it into my mouth and savored the bright, tart flavor. My energy perked up immediately, as did my mood. I assumed it was just a lucky find until the next week, at the exact same spot, I found a small yellow diamond. I looked around. This could not have been a coincidence. Someone had to be watching me, leaving the gems for me to find. I pocketed the diamond and saved it for my supper.

The next week, I found a sapphire, then an amethyst, a topaz, pink crystals, and a black tourmaline. I started lingering by the river for hours, hoping to spot my secret friend, but I never saw any sign of them. Still, it was nice to know that someone was looking out for me.

One evening, as I boiled some minerals for strolg, a pungent odor filled the air, followed by the sounds of grunts and snorts. I peered over the edge of my cavern and saw the source of the noise and smell below.

Trolls.

"I smell magic," said one troll. "It's near here somewhere."

"It's powerful," said the other troll. "We'll have to be careful."

I didn't bother to hide from them. Eventually, one of the trolls looked upward and saw me.

"I found it," said the troll. "It's the queen's dwarf."

Though trolls looked mostly alike to me, I was fairly certain this was the same one I'd met with Queen Elfrieda. The one who had smelled the magic of my Fate Stone.

"Did the queen send you?" I asked. I was ready to throw rocks at them if she had.

"No," said the first troll. "We ran away! We're free trolls now."

"Oh," I said, feeling a little jealous. I had run away, too, but I certainly wasn't free. "Care to join me for supper?"

Smelly though they were, I was overjoyed to have company, and as they ascended to my little cave, I made an effort to sweep away loose rubble and build up the fire. I wished I had chairs for each of them, but once they arrived, it became clear that they both preferred the ground anyway and certainly cared nothing for neatness or manners.

The first troll's name was Bork and the second's was Gub. I asked them how they had escaped the queen. Apparently, Bork had threatened to eat their taskmaster and incited a rebellion among his fellow trolls.

"We're revolting," said Gub. "We're going to free all the trolls and search The Kingdom for magical objects so we can keep them safe from humans."

"And that's how you found me?" I asked.

"We found this first," said Bork, taking something from his sack. He held it out to me. It was my Fate Stone.

I recoiled. "I don't want it."

Bork sniffed deeply at the mirror. "Powerful magic. It's bonded to you," he said.

“Then maybe you should take me as well. Hide me from the humans. Magic can cause trouble, as you said.”

Bork snorted and sniffed at me some more. “Told you not to let her take you by the beard,” he said.

“I didn’t *let* her,” I said angrily. “She just took it.”

“That’s a human for you,” said Gub. “Always taking whatever they want, trampling over any creature to get it.”

I didn’t care to dwell on this fact. It wouldn’t do me any good now. “Would you like something to eat?” I asked, hoping to change the subject.

“Yes!” said Bork. “I’m so hungry, I could eat rocks!” Both trolls snort-laughed heartily at that.

# CHAPTER TWENTY-SIX

## K.I.S.S.

Bork and Gub were delighted to share my pot of strolg, though they called it *sludge* and added some of Leaf's worms and beetles to their cups before slurping it down. Not long after, I was forced to pull my shirt over my nose. Rudger's beetle incident was nothing compared to this.

Odors aside, the trolls were fine company, good humored and simpleminded. Not that they weren't intelligent, they just weren't bothered by details or complexities. When they were hungry, they ate. When they were tired, they slept. They didn't worry about shelter or luxury or cleanliness.

They told me more about their time as slaves to the queen, how she'd forced them to sniff out magic and bring it to her. They'd collected thousands of spells, enchantments, magic trinkets and objects, and instead of hiding or disposing of them, as was their instinct, they were forced by the queen to turn everything over to her. If she wasn't satisfied, she'd whip them. If they tried to run away, she'd use that same whip to bind them.

"I found that whip myself!" cried Bork. "I knew what its magic was for. I thought surely the queen would destroy it when I told her. It never occurred to me that she would be so cruel as to *use* it!" Brown, muddy tears leaked out of his yellow eyes.

"And I'm the one who told her how to turn humans into weasels and rats," said Gub. "I thought it would be a nice spell, you know? A nice change for humans, who lead such complicated lives. But I guess humans don't like it, because now there are weasels and rats running around everywhere begging to be changed back to humans, but I have no idea how!" He cried so hard, gobs of snot ran down his nose and chin.

"Your mistakes are nothing, friend," I said. "I'm afraid I have aided the queen in far worse crimes." The trolls calmed their sobs, wiped snot on their hairy arms, and listened to my tale. I started with my arrival to The Surface, how I met the queen, how I thought she was my friend, how I helped her imprison dozens of young maidens and even a baby. I ended with the tragedy of Snow White's death.

"Snow White?" said Gub. "The princess? She's not dead."

"Yes, she is," I said. "I saw her with my own eyes."

"We saw her with our own eyes, too," said Gub. "And she's alive."

"Well, *alive* is not quite the word to describe her," said

Bork. "But she's not really dead, either. She's more like dead asleep."

"I don't understand," I said.

"Let me explain," said Bork. "Before we escaped the queen, our taskmaster took us up this mountain to search for more magic. We caught a scent and followed it. That's when we found the princess, asleep in a crystal coffin. Everyone had heard the princess was dead, but we all thought she'd been devoured by wild beasts, so we were surprised to find her at all. We knew at once she wasn't really dead. She was in a deep, enchanted sleep."

My heart began to pound all of a sudden. "And what did you do? Did you wake her up?"

"No," said Gub. "We couldn't even lift the crystal lid before a crazy dwarf with enormous ears suddenly came out of nowhere and attacked us with an ax. I nearly lost my nose!"

I pictured Gilpin, lying in wait, guarding Snow White, even though he believed she was dead. Or did he? Perhaps with his magic ears he could sense the life still in her. . . .

"So we returned to the queen," continued Gub, "and the taskmaster told her what we'd found and how we trolls believed the princess was still alive."

"And what did the queen do?" I asked.

"She seemed shocked," said Bork. "She could hardly speak for a full minute, and then she wanted to know if the princess would ever wake up."

"And will she?" I asked, my heart now pounding so hard, I thought it might crack open.

"No clue," said Bork, taking another sip of his strolg.

"Impossible to say," said Gub. "We told the queen we'd need to know more about the magic that put Snow White to sleep before we could say if she'd wake up. All we know is that she isn't really dead and nothing can harm her while she's under the enchantment."

"But you do know what enchanted her," I said. "It was the apple! A poison apple from the seed that *you* gave the queen!"

"The apples . . . ," mused Bork. "But those apples were deadly poisonous. They should have killed her straight away."

"Unless," said Gub, "there's some other magic at play, another enchantment that counteracted the poison apple. . . ."

I stroked my beard, thinking. . . .

"Would you mind passing me a few more grubs?" Bork asked. I passed him Leaf's dish of beetles and worms. He took a handful and plopped them into his cup of strolg.

My mind was still reeling with the information about Snow White. It was like a ton of rocks had been lifted off me. Snow White wasn't dead. She was in an enchanted sleep. It pulled at something in my memory, but I wasn't sure what, exactly.

"Ah! Look at the moon!" said Gub.

I gazed up. The moon was a silver sliver hanging in the obsidian sky.

"A new moon means a new beginning," said Bork. "A fresh start. We trolls are starting fresh. You should, too."

"I'm not sure it's as simple as that," I said. "Not for me, anyway."

"Sure it is," said Gub. "K.I.S.S. is the motto of the trolls!"

"What?"

"K.I.S.S. Keep it simple and sloppy."

K.I.S.S. Kiss. My brain came full circle. That was it! Snow White's story! The princess in an enchanted sleep, the prince who kissed her awake . . .

"Is there such a thing as true love's kiss?" I asked.

"Sure," said Bork. "If the love is true and you kiss, then it's true love's kiss, isn't it?"

"I never understood why a kiss was any sign of love," said Gub. "If I really loved someone, I'd give her a handful of worms, the fattest, juiciest ones I could find."

"I'd take a big stinky pile of mud and smear it in her face!" said Bork.

"But a kiss? What good is that?"

"To some creatures—or, to humans, at least—it's a sign of true love," I said. "Could true love have some kind of magical powers? Could it wake someone from an enchanted sleep?"

Bork and Gub snorted violently. It made me jump with fright, but then I realized they were laughing. "I've heard human stories of such things," said Gub, "but I've never seen it."

My heart sank.

"But even trolls don't know everything about magic," said Bork. "It works in mysterious ways. Just because we haven't seen true love's kiss doesn't mean it isn't real. It might just be very rare."

"True," said Gub. "Some magic we can't capture or

bottle up. Some magic just happens. That's usually the best kind. The kind that comes from the deepest center of the soul. Most creatures—especially humans—don't know how to reach that kind of magic, though."

"It's like your magic mirror," said Bork. He held my Fate Stone out to me.

I flinched and shook my head. "I don't want it. You should keep it, bury it somewhere so it doesn't cause any more trouble than it already has."

Bork grunted. "This isn't the same as the whip or the apple seed. It's that good kind of magic like Gub talked about. Raw and deep. It may have gotten you into some trouble, but it can also set things right if you use it well."

"Could it free me from the queen?"

"Maybe," said Gub. "Beard magic is powerful, but so is mirror magic. The reflection is the key."

His words took me back to the time I first found my Fate Stone and what the First Foredwarf had told me: *Life is one big mirror. That which we put out into the world will always come back to us.* So far, what I'd put out into the world was a whole lot of trouble and mess. And trouble had certainly come back to me in cartloads. But what could I do about it now?

Bork stretched and yawned. "Thanks for the sludge," he said. "Good night." He lay down right where he was, shifted, grunted, and immediately began snoring so loud, its echoes shook the cavern walls.

"Same," said Gub. He stretched himself out on the ground right next to Bork, emitted a last round of smelly explosions, and instantly fell asleep. Leaf squeaked in disgust and promptly flew off. I didn't blame him. I wouldn't have minded flying off myself. I certainly wouldn't get any sleep with this symphony of smells and snores. But with all the thoughts swirling in my brain, I needed the time to think, anyway.

I gazed at the moon. It pulled at me all night. New beginnings. Reflections . . . I chanced a look in my mirror, just for a brief moment, to see Snow White. Alive. Asleep. Enchanted. True love's kiss. What could be simpler (and sloppier) than that?

When dawn arrived, I had a plan fully formed. By the time Bork and Gub snorted awake, I had already made another pot of strolg and gathered more worms and beetles for them.

"Beetles always make the best breakfast," said Bork, dropping a handful into his cup.

"How hospitable," said Gub, slurping down a worm.

Of course, I regretted my hospitality five minutes later.

"Well, we'd better go, Gub," said Bork. "We've got more trolls to free, more humans to convince we're going to eat them."

"Where will you go?" I asked.

"Down The Mountain," said Bork. "There's another band of trolls near the castle. The queen likes to keep them close to her."

"Might I travel with you?" I asked. I knew what I had

to do, but I also knew the terrible risks I'd be facing. I would feel safer if I could travel with the trolls for part of the way.

"Of course!" said Bork. "We'd be glad to have your company, wouldn't we, Gub?"

"Yes," said Gub with a deep belch.

I filled my pouch with as much limestone as I could fit. Leaf returned from his nighttime hunt, and I promptly tucked him inside my shirt. "We're going for a little journey," I told him.

My beard tingled a little as the trolls and I descended from the cave and set our course toward the castle. I was going to find Prince Florian. I hoped he was Snow White's true love. I doubly hoped true love's kiss was a true thing.

# CHAPTER TWENTY-SEVEN

## Royal Persuasion

As we descended The Mountain, Bork and Gub discussed their plans to free their fellow trolls.

"You tell the taskmaster you're going to eat his hands, and I'll say I'm going to eat his feet," said Bork.

"Yes!" said Gub. "And then we'll fight over the eyeballs, but I'll surrender and entreat you for the entrails. Does that sound awful enough?" he asked me.

"Horrible," I said. "But make sure you show your teeth and growl."

"Like this?" Bork grimaced, showing his yellow fangs. He let out a low growl.

"A bit louder," I said. "And show your tongue."

They both growled and stuck out their long gray tongues.

"Perfect," I said. "The taskmaster will run for his life."

When the land began to level out, Bork and Gub

tried to sniff their way to the trolls by picking up on the scent of magic, but they kept circling around to me, catching the scent of my mirror. "It's just so strong," said Gub.

It was I who picked up on the trail as I began to smell the stench of troll ever increasingly as we got nearer the castle. It was coming from the direction of a manor at the bottom of the hill.

"Are you ready, Bork?"

"Ready, Gub!"

"Let's go free our fellow trolls!"

"Good luck," I said. "Don't forget to growl and stick out your tongues!"

They both wagged their tongues and growled as they ran through the trees toward the manor. "I'm going to eat your eyeballs!" shouted Bork.

"And I'll crunch on your toes!" cried Gub.

There were some shouts and screams, grunts and snorts, but it all left me feeling confident that the trolls would be victorious.

By late afternoon, I arrived at the castle. At first, I circled around the grounds several times, hoping I would see Prince Florian on his horse or something, but I didn't spot him. Reluctantly, I resigned myself to searching inside the castle. I shivered. I really didn't want to cross paths with the queen, and I had no idea where

Prince Florian might be. I almost abandoned my plan, deeming it hopeless, but then I thought of Snow White. This was her only hope. For her I would take the risk.

Using my ax, I scaled the castle wall to a window and entered an empty chamber. The moment I exited, I was accosted by a girl in the corridor. "Oh, gnome! Oh, gnome! I have a message!" She reached out for whatever she could get hold of and, of course, caught me by the beard.

I was brought face to face with a girl about the same age as Snow White. She had brown hair, set in big curls, and a giant purple bow on top of her head. "Deliver this message to Prince Florian right away," she said in a bossy voice, and instantly I felt the command tighten around me.

*Dear Prince Florian,*

*Would you care to take a walk with me this evening? Perhaps we could dance in the moonlight and wish on a star together. You can hold my hand if you want. I'll be waiting by the willow tree, which is my favorite romantic place.*

*Forever yours,*
*Lady Violet of Beyond*

She released me, and I crashed to the floor. I glared up at the girl.

"Well?" she said. "What are you waiting for, you silly gnome? Go and deliver the message to the prince!"

I wanted to chop off her foot with my ax, but my beard yanked at me to follow her command. "Message for Prince

Florian!" I chanted. I probably should've been grateful she thought I was a gnome. I should've been grateful the message was for Prince Florian. But I hated to deliver such a ridiculous message in such a humiliating way.

"Message for Prince Florian!" I chanted as I waddled down a corridor.

It was still quite a journey to reach the prince. I was shoved and kicked in all directions so that I began to feel sorry for gnomes. *He went that way! This way! He's in the fencing room! The dining hall! He's in the bath!* After many circles and turns and shoves and kicks, I finally found him in the castle library.

The library reminded me of the colony's records room, but instead of stone tablets, its shelves were full of flimsily bound papers. *Books.* For a moment I stood and gawked, thinking of everything I could learn by reading human records. But then my beard gave a little tug and I remembered my task.

Prince Florian was reading in a corner of the library. I approached him quietly. "Message for Prince Florian," I chanted.

He looked up. He seemed a little wary of me. Or of the message. "Who is the message from?" he asked.

"Lady Violet of Beyond."

He groaned. "Not her again. Go away."

I desperately did not want to repeat the message, but the need to get it out was torturous. The words bubbled and burned in my mouth until the message finally burst out of me and unraveled in all its ridiculousness. With each word, I felt more and more foolish. When I finished,

Prince Florian sighed. "Well, I suppose it's better than the time she asked me to sing ballads at sunrise."

I sighed, too. My beard loosened. I was free from Lady Violet's command.

"You may go," said Prince Florian. "I'm not going to send any reply to Lady Violet."

"Actually, I have another message," I said.

"From whom?"

"From the Princess Snow White."

Prince Florian snapped his book shut. "Snow White is dead. She was killed by wild beasts in the forest."

I shook my head. "That's what her stepmother told everyone. Snow White is alive, but she needs your help."

Prince Florian observed me with a mixture of curiosity and suspicion. And then his eyes widened with recognition. "I remember you. You're the dwarf who serves Queen Elfrieda. Why should I trust you? The queen never liked Snow White."

"Because *I* like Snow White," I said. "The queen ordered her huntsman to kill the princess, but Snow got away. She lived with seven dwarves in a cottage in The Woods until the queen found her and gave her a poison apple to kill her, except that didn't kill her, either. The princess is in an enchanted sleep, or at least that's what the trolls say, and you can probably save her with true love's kiss. Come on!" I tugged on Prince Florian's hand, but he didn't move.

"Are all dwarves this crazy?" he said, then opened his book and started reading again.

Fizznugget, this was going to be harder than I thought.

I stood in front of Prince Florian. He kept his face covered with his book. I read the title: *Secrets of a Hero: How to Be Strong, Courageous, Valiant, and Admirable.* Aha! Now I knew how to persuade him.

"That's fine," I said. "I understand if you're afraid. The journey is treacherous, the quest fraught with danger. The one who saves Snow White will have to be very *strong. Courageous. Valiant and admirable.* In short, she needs nothing less than a hero. Well, I suppose I'll have to go find someone who possesses those particular qualities, a knight or a soldier. . . ."

Prince Florian peered over the edge of his book. "Why would you come to me if you need a hero?" he asked.

"Oh," I gushed, "only because Snow White spoke so highly of you. She talked about you very often."

"She did?"

Perhaps that was a bit of an exaggeration, but I nodded enthusiastically. "And when she talked about you, she always sang songs about true love. It wasn't difficult to read between the lines."

Prince Florian's cheeks turned pink, but he sat up a little taller. "Snow White had a very pretty voice, I remember."

"She did," I said. "She *does.*"

"When Lady Violet sings, she sounds like a fish inside a parrot," said Florian, more to himself than to me. "To think my father wants me to spend the rest of my life with that . . ."

"Then you'll come?" I asked hopefully.

Prince Florian set his book down. "What do I have to do? Fight a dragon? Climb a tower?"

"Maybe," I said. "The important thing is that you kiss her awake."

Prince Florian made a face. "*Kiss* her?"

"Yes! True love's kiss! Don't you know about true love's kiss?"

"But what makes you think I'm Snow White's true love?"

"Who else could it be?"

Prince Florian shrugged.

"Please come to her," I pleaded. "Maybe you aren't her true love. Maybe there's no such thing as true love's kiss, but what harm is there in trying?"

Prince Florian thought for a moment, his fingers drumming on his book. "I'll go," he said, and I let out a deep sigh of relief. But then he added, "But do I really have to kiss her? On the lips?"

"We'll discuss that later." I grabbed his arm and practically dragged him out the door. "Let's go!"

# CHAPTER TWENTY-EIGHT

## To the Rescue

Persuading Prince Florian to come with me turned out to be the easy part. Getting him out the door and on the journey was a quest in and of itself. Though he wasn't wild about the idea of kissing Snow White awake, he was quite fond of the idea of playing the hero, and he wanted to make sure he was adequately prepared with the right clothing.

"Do you think I should bring the gray coat or the blue? Or both?" Prince Florian had torn apart his entire wardrobe and couldn't decide which jacket to bring. "How long will we be gone, do you think?"

"Not long. A day or two, at most. Hurry!"

But after the jackets, there was the matter of the shirts and collars and cuffs and undergarments. After an hour, I was ready to throw the entire contents of his wardrobe out the window, and him after them.

"Now for the food," he said. "I have some sandwiches ready here. I wonder if I can get the cook to prepare a roast for the road. . . ."

I rolled my eyes. "You can catch your own food on the way. Let's go!" I shoved him toward the door.

"We'll have to get out without anyone noticing," said Florian. "I'm not supposed to leave without a guard ever since I got lost riding on my own."

"Well, you're pretty noticeable right now," I said. He was sagging beneath the weight of two bulging satchels.

"What should we do?"

I looked at the window. "Give me your bags," I said. He dropped them to the floor. I heaved them up to the edge of the window and pushed them over. Then I lifted myself to the window. "Now go down and meet me outside," I said.

Five minutes later, we were on the castle grounds together. "I'll need my horse," said Prince Florian.

I let my head fall back. "How long will that take?"

"It depends," said Florian, "on whether or not we can distract the stable boy."

"How do we do that?"

Prince Florian shrugged. "I don't know. Snow White was always the one with the good ideas."

"Well, she's not here now," I said. "That's the whole point of this journey." But Florian clearly had no ideas, so I started racking my brains. "I suppose I could throw rocks—I have very good aim."

"No," said Prince Florian. "That won't work. Stable boys deal with much worse."

We thought some more. I saw the girl, Lady Violet, come out of the castle and head in the opposite direction. "I think I know what to do," I said, even though the idea forming in my head made me cringe. It was a testament to my friendship with Snow that I was willing. I whispered the plan in Florian's ear.

Florian smiled. "Brilliant!" he said. "Do it now!"

I ran inside the stable.

"Message . . . message," I blathered, and tried to look as blank as possible. This was so humiliating, to play a gnome twice in one day! "Message for the stable boy."

The stable boy looked to be no older than the prince but wore ragged, dirty clothes and carried a pitchfork.

"All right, I'm the stable boy," he said. "Out with it, then."

I delivered the message in a gravelly, monotone voice.

*Dear Stable Boy,*

*I've been admiring you from my window and wondered if you might join me for a stroll in the garden? Perhaps we could sing some ballads or dance around the fountain. You can hold my hand if you wish. Meet me without delay in the garden, beneath the willow tree, which is my favorite romantic place.*

*Forever yours,*
*Lady Violet of Beyond*

At the end of the message, I blinked and stared blankly at the boy. The stable boy stared right back at me, his mouth gaping. He still held his pitchfork up in the air. He seemed to be in a state of shock. Finally, he stood up straight and smiled dreamily. He assessed his filthy, patched clothes and ran dirty fingers through his greasy hair. "Send a reply to Lady Violet. Tell her I am at her service!" He tossed his pitchfork aside, ran to a bucket of water, and started splashing himself all over, scrubbing at the dirt on his face and neck.

I ran out, chanting "Message for Lady Violet!" until I came around to the other side of the stables to where Prince Florian was shaking with silent laughter.

Moments later, the stable boy ran out in eager haste.

"Well done," said Prince Florian as he went to his white horse. It was clear he was not used to preparing his own horse. At first, he put the saddle on backward. After he got it on the right way, it took him several minutes to buckle it and make it tight enough. I looked around anxiously, fearing that the stable boy might return, or someone else.

Finally, Prince Florian mounted and held his hand out to me. "Coming?" he asked.

I took his hand, and he pulled me up onto the horse to sit behind him. Moments later, we were galloping out the gates of the castle.

We rode as far and as fast as we could until the sun set and the horse grew tired. We were in The Woods now, but I was having a hard time recognizing anything. Had the trolls taken me down that ledge? Had the trees ever been so thick? Did we turn right here? Left there?

"Are we nearly there?" Florian asked.

"I think so," I said, though, truthfully, I was beginning to fear that we were lost. My sense of direction was failing me. I had no idea where we were or how close we might be to Snow White. I wasn't even sure we were traveling on the right mountain. Where was the stream?

A rustling of leaves and a snap. A dark shadow passed between the trees.

"What was that?" Prince Florian slowed his horse. He looked all around, tense.

"Nothing," I said. "Just an animal. There are lots of animals in these woods, but we'll be safe."

We continued to ride, but I felt a little more on edge after that. I seemed to see shadows everywhere. I thought I heard footsteps. I couldn't shake the feeling that we were being watched and followed.

It grew too dark to travel. Leaf crawled out of my shirt and flew up to the trees. I felt cold and exposed without him.

"Let's set up camp for the night," I said. "It shouldn't be much farther."

Prince Florian stopped the horse and dismounted gracefully. I dismounted not so gracefully.

"I'll go gather some wood," I said.

"I'll . . . wait here," said Florian.

The wind rustled eerily through the dark trees. An owl hooted. Creatures skittered over the ground. Branches creaked. Footsteps. Something big was lurking in the trees. I gathered a few more sticks and hurried back to Florian. Again I felt eyes on my back, something following me.

When I returned, Florian was shivering with cold, wearing both his blue and his gray jackets. I struck stone against stone and got the fire started. Once it was lit and cast a warm glow on our surroundings, we both relaxed and ate our supper. Florian had carefully wrapped sandwiches and a little crystal bowl of fruit. He took small, dainty bites. I didn't eat. I had plenty of limestone in my pouch, but I was too anxious to be hungry.

"Tell me again about Snow White," said Florian. "A little slower this time."

So I told him the whole story, how the queen feared the princess would try to take her crown, how the queen ordered the huntsman to kill Snow, and how Snow had come to live with seven dwarves in a tiny cottage in The Woods.

"Snow always loved The Woods," said Florian. "I'll bet she enjoyed living there."

"Sometimes," I said. "When Snow White first lived with us, we didn't have any food for her. She was so hungry, she ate a rat."

"She ate a rat?" said Prince Florian. "Ha! I would have loved to see the expression on her face."

I imitated the look of horror Snow White had on her face when I presented her the rat. Florian burst out laughing. "We always had fun together, Snow White and I."

"We did, too," I said. "We didn't get along at first, but then we became friends." I thought of how she saved my life on the cliff that day. I so desperately wished to return the rescue.

"I was heartbroken when I heard she had died," said Florian.

"You were?"

He nodded. "I even cried."

"You did?"

"Don't tell anyone. It's not very princely."

"I won't," I promised, but it gave me hope that perhaps he really was Snow White's true love, and that true love's kiss was truly magic.

*CRACK! Snap!*

Florian and I both jumped. "What was that?" he whispered, and reached for his sword with trembling hands. Something was moving in the dark. I could see the black shape of it prowling in the trees. A bear? A wolf? The queen? The horse whinnied and pounded its hooves. The thing was coming toward us, closer and closer. I was just about to scream "Run for it!" when I noticed the ears of the creature—large, round, floppy.

"Gilpin?"

He came into the light of the fire, smiled, and waved an ear.

"What under earth are you doing here?"

His ears sagged. He looked uncertain.

"Not that I'm not glad to see you," I said. "I am! I just . . . Does the crew know where you are?"

He shook his head vigorously, then dug into his pouch and held out his hands. I gasped. He had a small feast cupped in his palms—diamonds, sapphires, amber, amethysts, jasper, and jade.

"Beryl's beard, Gilpin . . ." I licked my lips. My stomach made crunching noises.

"A friend?" Florian asked.

"Yes," I said, "a very good friend," and Gilpin smiled. He sat down with us at the fire. Through Gilpin's ear flapping and hand gestures, I gathered that he had been keeping an eye (and both ears) on me for quite some time. The crew believed that I had caused Snow White's death, but Gilpin was adamant that I had not. Apparently, he'd heard the queen all the way down in the tunnels, but no one would listen to him (or watch him, rather), so he had been sneaking to The Surface to check on me and make sure I was okay.

"It was you who left me the gems!" I said.

He nodded.

"That was very kind of you, Gil. I don't think I could have survived without them."

He waved me away to say it was nothing, then continued his story. He had come to bring me more gems when the trolls appeared. He'd heard our conversation, and when I left with the trolls to go get Florian, he decided to follow me, leaving quartz markers along the way so he would know how to get back.

"Gilpin, you genius! We were completely lost, and now you've saved us!"

"We were lost?" Florian asked. "You didn't tell me we were lost!"

"It doesn't matter now, does it? Gilpin's here, and all is well."

The tips of Gilpin's ears blushed blue. We shared the beautiful feast he'd brought, and I started to feel my strength and senses being restored. The amber and citrine helped my eyesight grow sharper, the sapphires cleared my head for proper thinking, the diamonds gave me a surge of strength, and the amethysts calmed my anxious heart. Everything was going to be okay.

We rose at first light and continued on our journey. Florian rode his horse, but Gilpin and I, full of strength and energy, chose to walk and run alongside him. With Gilpin's help and his quartz markers, we were able to travel with speed and accuracy. By late morning, we found the stream. We followed it for several miles, until at last our surroundings started to look familiar. Those rocks. That fallen tree. Those berry bushes.

"I think I see something!" said Prince Florian.

The glass coffin lay in a small clearing. Grass and shrubs and flowers had grown up around the sides, so only the crystal covering could be seen. Prince Florian dismounted the horse and ran to Snow White. He pressed his nose against the crystal case. "I can't see her very well," he said. "Oh, there are cobwebs around her face. I'll bet she doesn't like that."

"Let's take this lid off," I said. Gilpin and I took one end, and Florian took the other. We lifted the crystal covering and set it on the ground. Gently, Florian dusted the cobwebs away.

Snow White lay perfectly still, her skin white as snow, hair black as onyx, and lips red as rubies. With both ears pressed down, Gilpin touched the stone he had laid on her arm.

"So . . . what do we do now?" asked Florian.

"Wake her up with true love's kiss," I said. "That's what we came for."

"Right. Okay," said Florian. He walked around to the other side of Snow White. He knelt down, then stood. He wiped his mouth on his sleeve and squished his lips between his fingers in preparation.

"What are you doing?" I asked.

"Nothing," said Prince Florian. "I just . . . I've never kissed anyone."

"Well, here's your chance. First time for everything."

"It feels a little strange, kissing her while she's asleep," said Florian.

"Yes, but you're doing it to save her life," I said.

"Right."

Gilpin suddenly held up a hand. His ears were perked to high alert. He held his ax in front of him as he stared intently into the trees. Something rustled. Gilpin jumped a little, and then lifted his ax.

"It's nothing, Gil," I said. "There are lots of animals moving around in those trees." He lowered his ax a little, but his ears remained on full alert. I felt an uneasiness start to rise in me, though I couldn't say why, exactly.

"Kiss her, Florian," I said. "Wake her up now."

He knelt down again and leaned in toward Snow White. I leaned in from the other side. Would it work? It had to work! His lips were almost touching hers, and then Florian looked up at me, frowning. "Are you going to kiss her, too?"

"What? No!"

"Then back away, please. You're making me uncomfortable."

I jumped back. "Just kiss her, already!"

"All right, I will!" Prince Florian leaned down, closed his eyes, and kissed Snow White. I held my breath and waited.

# CHAPTER TWENTY-NINE

## Revivals and Rivals

I watched Snow White closely, looking for any stirrings of life—a twitch, a breath—but she didn't move.

Florian scratched his head. "Now what?"

"Maybe try again?" I said. "With a little more . . . true love?"

"Okay." Prince Florian kissed Snow White again, longer, but I wasn't sure it held more true love. Again, nothing happened. Her eyes remained closed. Her limbs didn't so much as twitch. My hopes started to crumble.

"I guess you're not her true love," I said. "Or maybe true love's kiss doesn't really work."

"Or maybe she just needs a little extra help waking up," said Florian. "Snow White has always been a deep sleeper. Once, when she came to visit me at my castle, it took three servants and a bucket of cold water to wake her up. Oh, she was furious! She's not a morning person."

"Yes, I know," I said.

Florian prodded Snow White a little. "Hey," he said. "Snow White, wake up!" He shouted in her ear and shook her. Nothing.

Gilpin came forward, leaned over Snow White, and slapped her cheek a few times, but it had no effect. Her skin didn't even change color. It remained pale as snow.

"Maybe we should try the cold water method," I said, nodding to the stream.

"Good idea," said Florian. "Let's give her a little splash. I'll carry her."

Prince Florian began to pick up Snow White but struggled beneath her deadweight.

"You get the front end," I said. "Gil and I will take the legs." We tried to rearrange the princess, but it was all very awkward, with her dress getting tangled and her limbs flopping all over. Prince Florian got a mouthful of her hair, and Gilpin shoved her foot in my face. I turned my head to avoid it but then froze in place as I caught sight of the cottage. Someone's head was poking out the window. Rudger. He saw me and Florian holding Snow White. He couldn't see Gilpin because Snow White's skirt had flopped over his head.

"They're stealing the pin-chess!" Rudger shouted. He disappeared from the window. A moment later, he burst out of the cottage and ran toward us. After him came Herkimer, Amethina, Garnesha, and, finally, Epidot, all running as fast as they could with axes poised over their heads.

"What in the world?" said Prince Florian.

"Release her, you pin-chess stealer!" shouted Rudger.

"Stop!" shouted the prince. "I'm Snow White's true love!"

They didn't stop.

"Let's go!" I said. "We have to move!" But I didn't specify what direction, so Gilpin and I bumped into each other, crossing Snow White's legs, while Florian twisted Snow White's upper body in the opposite direction.

"Other way!" I shouted, which was no better. Gilpin and I went in the opposite direction again, and Florian stepped backward and tripped over the crystal coffin. Snow White rolled right over Florian and landed with a solid thunk on the ground. Something red and shiny shot out of her mouth and disappeared in the grass.

The crew stopped running and shouting. They froze with their axes in midair.

And then the magical miracle happened.

Snow White moved! She blinked her eyes open. She gasped and her chest expanded with air.

"She's alive!" Herkimer called. "Snow White is all right!"

Alive! Awake! I wanted to run to her, hug her, dance and sing!

But Prince Florian was there first. He rushed to her side and knelt next to her like a proper prince, a hero. "Snow!"

"Florian?" Snow White's voice was dry and groggy.

"You're awake! It worked!" said Prince Florian.

"What worked?"

"The kiss! I just kissed you." He beamed.

"You did?" Snow White touched her lips and looked at her fingers as if she were trying to see the kiss.

"Yes, and you woke up because I'm your true love." He puffed out his chest.

"You are?"

"Yes, and we're going to live happily ever after." He held his hand out to her.

She looked at it, flummoxed. "We will?"

Prince Florian dropped his hand. He rubbed the back of his neck, looking confused. "Aren't you happy about this?"

Snow White lifted herself up on her elbows. "Think, Florian! I've been asleep for . . ." She looked around, confused. "How long have I been sleeping?"

"Many months," I said. "Half a year."

Snow White's eyes widened. The sleepiness was knocked right out of them. "I've been asleep for half a year! Which means I haven't eaten in half a year! You know how cross I get when I'm hungry, and now you're telling me you just woke me up with true love's kiss, which is something I've been dreaming of for my entire life, but I never dreamed it would be *you*, and I can't even remember the kiss! This is all horribly unfair!"

Prince Florian glanced at me like he was looking for directions on what to do next.

I shrugged, smiling. "Remember, she's not a morning person."

Snow White looked at me and scowled. "Well, at least I'm pleasant the rest of the time, which is more than I can say for you, Your Grumpiness!"

My smile fell, but Prince Florian grinned from ear to ear and then burst into a laugh. "I've really missed you, Snow."

Snow White tried to keep a straight face, but then her face split into a grin. "I've missed you, too, Florian."

Florian held out his hand again to Snow White. She took it and stood, but then teetered and nearly toppled over. Prince Florian caught her in his arms.

"I'm okay," said Snow White, pushing him away. "You don't have to carry me." She stumbled a few more steps and caught herself on her crystal coffin. "There. I'm fine." She stood and brushed off her skirt, then pressed back her hair. "But I am very hungry. Did you bring me something to eat?"

"No . . . ," said Florian. "I hadn't thought . . ."

Snow White crossed her arms. "Florian, I don't want to seem ungrateful, but it seems like you could have planned a little better before you dashed off to be my hero."

Prince Florian sputtered and pointed at me. "It was all the dwarf's idea! I barely had time to pack my own food before he shoved me out the door."

"Oh, so is *he* my hero, not you?"

"No! I mean . . ." Florian was getting very red in the face.

"Now, now," said Epidot. "Everything will be all right. The Seventh can go and find something for Snow White to eat."

"Yes, but what if he tries to kill the princess again?"

"*You* tried to kill her?" asked Florian. "I thought you said it was the queen."

Gilpin suddenly jumped into the middle of the crowd and gestured wildly, miming the old hag-queen giving an apple to Snow White. He pointed at me and shook his head so vigorously, his ears slapped against his cheeks.

"Gilpin is right," said Snow White. "It was an old woman who gave me the apple, not Grump."

"It was the queen!" said Florian. "She was in disguise."

"I think maybe we should have believed Gilpin the first time," said Herkimer.

"It doesn't matter now," said Garnesha. "The princess is safe. We'll protect her."

"And we should celebrate!" said Amethina. "But inside the Surface dwelling. I can't stand the light. . . ."

"Don't forget the food, Grump!" said Rudger.

The crew surrounded Snow White and Florian and ushered them toward the cottage. Gilpin remained behind.

"Go on," I said. "I'll come as soon as I find some food for Snow. You know how cranky she gets when she's hungry."

Gilpin wiggled his ears and gestured, asking me if I wanted help.

"No thank you, Gil. You've helped me enough already. You go on ahead and help Snow White."

He nodded and turned toward the cottage, while I turned toward the trees, my heart a thousand times lighter. I found a berry bush and hummed as I gathered its fruit. Birds twittered in the trees and the sun filtered down through the branches. It was a perfect day. I felt as though all was right in the world.

But I was wrong.

A shadow fell on my path. I gasped and dropped all the berries. They spilled to the ground and rolled around a pair of purple slippers with diamonds on their toes. I looked up into the ice blue eyes of Queen Elfrieda.

# CHAPTER THIRTY

## Reflective Rat

I stood frozen to the ground. I wanted to run, but I couldn't.

"So, Dwarf, Snow White lives," said Queen Elfrieda. "Thanks to you and that sniveling prince."

I swallowed, and shifted nervously.

"Oh, don't be frightened," said the queen. "I understand. Snow White took you by the beard, too, didn't she? Tried to pit us against each other. You poor, sad little creature. Why didn't you come to me for help?"

"I . . . I . . ." I was stuttering worse than Epidot.

"It's no matter," said Queen Elfrieda. "I've already thought of a plan. You may have to protect Snow White, but you also have to do what I say, which means I can free you of that conniving little minx. I could command *you* to kill Snow White. Perhaps you could drown her in the river? Chop off her head with your ax? We'll think of something."

My beard twitched. I grabbed it and squeezed tight, pulling on it until the pain was so intense my vision blurred. "No!" I shouted.

"Pardon me?" Queen Elfrieda cocked her head and stared at me with those pale blue eyes, and I shrank back and began to tremble. "Poor little dwarf. So tortured by the princess's hold over you. Don't worry. Once she's dead, you'll be free and able to faithfully serve at my side once again. Let's go to her now. Together we will defeat our common enemy."

My feet started moving. We walked through the trees, up the hill. The cottage grew larger in my view, like some terrible monster ready to devour me.

We entered the cottage to a merry scene of laughing and dancing. Florian and Snow White held hands and twirled around the room, shrieking with laughter. Snow's shriek turned to a terrified scream when she saw Queen Elfrieda standing with me in the doorway. The merriment stopped. Prince Florian jumped in front of Snow White. He guarded her with his chin up and chest puffed out, no longer the reluctant prince but the valiant hero.

Snow White stepped outside his protection and locked her eyes on me. "Borlen?" she said. "What are you doing?"

I could not answer. I looked down at my feet in shame.

"He's my faithful servant," said the queen.

"He is not!" said Snow White. "He's my friend!"

"Dwarf, shut the door," said Queen Elfrieda. I tried

to resist. My beard pulled at me. It began to itch, and the itching moved down my neck, chest, and arms until it felt like I was being eaten alive. Finally, I shut the door. The itching stopped. The crew all stared at me in disbelief.

Prince Florian drew his sword, which he could barely hold up with both hands. "You shan't harm Snow White!" he shouted. "I won't let you!"

"Neither will we," said Epidot, stepping shakily in front of Snow White. The rest of the crew did the same. They lifted their axes, though they all trembled with fright. "We'll all protect Snow White."

"How sweet," said the queen with a smile. "Snow White protected by her prince and an army of dwarves." She drew out a cord—no, a whip. I knew that whip. I'd seen what it could do.

"Run!" I shouted. "Run for the caverns!"

Before anyone could take more than two steps, Queen Elfrieda flicked the whip so it coiled around everyone—Snow White, Florian, and the crew—binding them all together. Florian was forced to drop his sword, and most of the crew dropped their axes, except Rudger, who held firmly to his ax until it was bound up in the whip and pressed right against his own neck.

"Such a useful whip," said the queen. "My troll servants gave it to me. Lately, they've been rather unreliable, but I think I've found some new servants who will be much more . . . cooperative." Queen Elfrieda stroked Epidot's long white beard. He trembled violently.

"P-p-please!" he stuttered. "P-please d-don't!" he gasped as Queen Elfrieda grasped his beard.

"As long as I am queen, you will do as I command."

She grabbed Herkimer by the beard and said the same, then Rudger and Gilpin. "As long as I am queen, you will do as I command." Gilpin's ears shot upward so they were practically on top of his head.

When Queen Elfrieda came to Garnesha and Amethina, she paused. "No beards for you two?"

"Ha! No!" shouted Garnesha in her husky voice. "You can't control us!"

"We'll never do what you say!" said Amethina in her shrill one.

Queen Elfrieda smiled. "Oh, but we can think of other means of persuasion. I'm sure your fellow dwarves could help if I command them to chop off your fingers or toes or heads. . . ."

Amethina burst into a dust storm of tears. "Don't! Please! We'll do whatever you say. Just don't hurt us!"

The queen smiled cruelly, then turned her gaze on Snow White. Snow White did not shrink, but stood tall, even in her bound state. "And, Snow White . . . it has been quite some time, but you haven't changed much, have you? Pale and sickly as ever."

"What did I ever do to you?" said Snow White between gritted teeth.

"Oh my dear, don't you know?" said the queen. "You have conspired against me ever since your father died. You have been plotting to take my crown, which is a crime worthy of death."

"I never tried to take your crown!" said Snow White. "All I wanted to do was *help*!"

"But you *will* try to take my crown someday," said Queen Elfrieda. "It has been foretold by the dwarf himself. Through the magic mirror he holds."

The crew all gazed at me in horror. Snow White's eyes brimmed with tears that spilled down her cheeks. "Please. I won't try to take your crown. Just let me be."

"What? Let you go? To run off with your prince and raise an army against me? I don't think so. You have escaped justice twice now, but you won't a third time. What shall it be, Dwarf? Beheading? Drowning?"

"You won't get away with this!" said Prince Florian. "My father—"

Queen Elfrieda interrupted. "Will be devastated to learn that his son was killed and eaten by a pack of wild trolls, but don't fret, dear Prince. I will offer my condolences and even offer to bring the brutal murderers to justice. Now, where were we? Ah, yes. Who shall we kill first, Dwarf? Snow White or her prince? Or should I kill *you* first? After all, you're bound by your beard to protect Snow White, and that could get in the way of things. I know you wish to do all you can to help me succeed, even if it means giving up your own life."

I closed my eyes. *Think, Borlen.* I had to do whatever the queen said. I had to protect Snow White. I could not do both. Or could I? Could there be a way to satisfy both sides? As if in answer, my mirror seemed to pulse in my pocket.

I took out my Fate Stone and looked down at my reflection. My beard was split in two opposite directions, one side toward Snow White, the other toward the queen.

But it was me, Borlen, in the reflection, and it was my own actions that mattered now.

"Your Majesty," I said, "I think I have a better idea for how you can defeat the princess."

The queen raised an eyebrow. "Really? And what makes you think so?"

I glanced at Snow White. She looked hurt. Betrayed. She would feel even more so in a moment.

"You could kill me. And, sure, I wouldn't be able to protect Snow White anymore, but who knows how many more beards Snow White has taken, demanding their protection? Here are six dwarves who have been protecting Snow White for many months. Dwarves *hate* humans, you know. They wouldn't protect her unless they'd been forced to. *I* wouldn't have, only my loyalty to you was so fierce, even before you took me by the beard. But clearly these dwarves have been bewitched, forced to protect Snow White against their will."

I glanced at the crew. Herkimer seemed to catch on to the idea first. "That's right!" he said. "She took me by the beard. She made me promise to protect her."

"And I!" said Rudger. "The pin-chess grabbed me by the beard, too!"

"Me t-too," stammered Epidot.

"And I promised to protect her, even though I don't have a beard!" said Amethina. "She threatened to steal all my gems if I didn't!"

"Me too!" Garnesha added.

Gilpin wiggled his ears, joining in.

"Well, then, I suppose I'll just have to kill all of you,"

said the queen. "It's such a shame. I was looking forward to having you as my servants."

"But wait, Your Majesty!" I said. "Even if you kill all these dwarves, and me, you don't know what other dwarves Snow White has taken by the beard, what magical protection she forced them to bestow upon her. She's been in our caverns. She may have bewitched many more of us. A whole army of dwarves with magic and axes could come upon you at any moment!"

The queen suddenly looked behind her as if she expected to be attacked.

"But don't fret, Your Majesty," I continued. "My magic mirror has shown me a prophecy, a way you can defeat Snow White, free us dwarves of her curse, and keep us as your faithful servants."

The queen seemed intrigued. "Go on. . . ."

"You want to be the fairest in the land. Snow White wants to live. None of us can let you kill her while we're alive. We'll be in a constant battle between obeying you and protecting the princess."

"Yes, yes, I know all that. Get to the point, Dwarf!"

"What if, instead of killing Snow White, you simply make her the *un*fairest in the land? I don't have to protect her from that, only from death. And if she's not the fairest, it won't matter to you if she's alive. Didn't the trolls once give you a spell for this very thing? Something about rats . . ."

Queen Elfrieda's eyes lit up. She smiled, then tipped her head back and laughed. "Oh, Dwarf! You do have a sense of humor. Yes, that should do nicely. I can use it on the prince, too, and then we'll all live happily ever after."

"Borlen!" shouted Snow White. "You miserable Grump! How could you?"

"Oh, you worthless piece of rubble!" shouted Rudger. "We'll see you banished! I'll throw you in the lava rivers myself!"

I didn't look at Snow White or any of the crew. I kept my eyes fixed on Queen Elfrieda. She came closer to Snow White, who was now fighting against the whip's binding power harder than ever, but to no avail. "This won't hurt a bit, my dear," said Queen Elfrieda. "Or it might. I don't know."

Slowly, I moved behind the bound crew, Snow White, and Florian. Queen Elfrieda started to mutter the words of a spell.

*Fur and tail, claws and whiskers . . .*

She lifted her hands. My beard ached. The mirror pulsed in my hand. Foredwarf Realga's words seemed to echo in my mind.

*That which we put out into the world will always come back to us.*

*. . . will always come back to us.*

*. . . will always come back to us.*

My actions would come back to me. So would Snow White's, and the queen's. Life was one great big mirror.

*We all need to reflect on ourselves from time to time. . . .*

It was time for the queen to reflect a little.

I lifted the mirror just as the queen waved her hands and a jet of purple streamed toward Snow White. The reflection caught the spell. The purple stream split apart into several threads that shot back at the queen, wrapping around her like a net. She looked at me then, her eyes full of terror. She opened her mouth to say something, but all that came out was a squeak. The queen's forehead shrank. Her nose elongated, and whiskers poked out of her cheeks. She shrank and shriveled, then disappeared inside her dress, all the while squeaking. Her gown fell to the floor. A moment later, a rat crawled out of the dress. It ran circles around me, squeaking madly. I bent down and picked it up by the tail. The rat-queen squeaked and wriggled in my hand. She had exceptionally blue eyes. I wound back my arm and flung her out the window. She cartwheeled in the air until she disappeared.

As soon as I touched the whip, it loosened. Snow White, Florian, and the crew all sighed with relief as they were freed.

"How did you do that?" asked Rudger.

I held up my Fate Stone. "I just gave the queen a chance to reflect a little."

Snow White ran to the window. "Will she be a rat forever, do you think?"

"I think so," I said. "And I think she'll be happy, too."

"Happy? How so?" asked Snow White.

"Have you ever seen a fairer rat?"

Snow White tipped her head back and laughed. Florian and the crew looked perplexed but also laughed.

"Now then," said Snow White, "did you bring me anything to eat, Grump? I'm still famished!"

"Maybe we should have kept the rat," said Florian. "I hear that's your favorite dish."

Snow White gasped and then glared at me. "Grump! You told him about the rat?"

I shrugged. "I think he was impressed, to tell you the truth."

"I was," said Florian. "Not many princesses would eat a rat."

"I'm not a princess anymore," said Snow White, with an air of grandeur. "Now I am *Queen* Snow White."

"That's right," I said. "And the fairest in the land."

*Fairest.* One word, two meanings, and, pretty or not, Snow White truly embodied the meaning that mattered.

Hours later, after we had feasted and celebrated with singing and dancing, we said our goodbyes to Snow White and Florian. The crew all gathered around the princess-become-queen, and she kissed each of them on the head. When she came to me, she knelt down so we were eye to eye.

"You'll come visit me, won't you?"

I shrugged. "Perhaps, if you have some decent food for me."

"I'll have a heap of rubies waiting for you." She leaned in, and before I could get away, she kissed me on the forehead. I didn't mind so much.

"Goodbye, Grump."

"Farewell, Spoiled Brat."

Snow White stood, and Prince Florian gave her a leg up onto his horse.

"Thanks for the help," Florian whispered to me. "You make a fine hero, even if you are a bit small."

"Goodbye!" Snow White waved as they rode down the mountainside, toward The Kingdom—*her* kingdom. All the crew waited and waved goodbye, shouting their farewells. Gilpin had dust streaming down his cheeks.

"Don't cry, Gil," said Herkimer. "We might never see her again, but think of the stories we'll have to tell! And the stories they'll tell about us on The Surface!"

"Every human will always know us as the dwarves who helped the human pin-chess," said Rudger.

"They'll know our names and everything!" said Amethina.

"Aaa-*choo*!" Rudger sneezed. "Oh, let's get back underground quick. All these florixes are making me very dusty!"

"And the light is giving me a headache," said Amethina.

The crew trundled off underground. I stayed behind, not sure if I was welcome or not. Not sure where I belonged anymore.

As the sun set behind The Mountain, I caught a flash of red in the green grass. I walked over to inspect it, and picked up something red and shiny. A ruby. And not just any ruby. *My* ruby! The one Snow White had given me. The one I had thrown to try to knock the apple out of her hands but ended up in her mouth instead. She must have swallowed it! Its magic must have protected her from the poison and kept her in that enchanted sleep. But when she fell to the ground, the force of her fall must have knocked the ruby out of her, and that's when she woke up.

Snow White hadn't been saved by true love's kiss.

Snow White had been saved by me.

I gazed out over The Surface, taking in the trees and grass, the flowers and birds, the sun and sky. Such a volatile, fragile, perishable place. So dangerous and unstable. But I knew I couldn't leave it behind for good. Nor could I cut myself off from my roots—my parents, my crew, the colony. I would have to face them all. I would have to stand up and confess my crimes and reveal all my doings on The Surface and let the rocks fall where they may.

Gilpin poked his head aboveground and flapped his ears, inviting me to follow.

"I'm coming, Gil," I said, and I descended underground.

# EPILOGUE

## Always a Grump

I was not banished from the colony.

I was brought before the First Foredwarf and the council, and I confessed that I had escaped to The Surface. I told them of all my doings, about my interactions with the queen and Snow White, how they had each taken me by the beard. Though everyone agreed that my actions had endangered the safety of the colony, they also agreed that I had been a valuable resource when the crew was stuck on The Surface. And they agreed that my knowledge of The Surface would be a great benefit to the colony. With the support of all the crew, I was named the first-ever Dwarf Ambassador to The Surface. Mother and Father were so proud, though Mother was still nervous and for centuries to come would complain that I was "frightfully young" for such ventures, no matter my age.

For decades, I visited Snow White on The Surface, as

promised. She was crowned queen and decreed by all to be the fairest ruler The Kingdom had ever seen, in every sense of the word. She set free all the maidens the queen had imprisoned, outlawed the enslavement of trolls, and chopped down the queen's poison-apple tree with her own two hands. Florian tried to help, but Snow proved to be a bit wild with an ax.

Whenever I came, she always presented me with a ruby, not as a bribe but as a token of true friendship.

"How lovely to see you, Grump," she would say.

"Always a pleasure to be in your presence, Spoiled Brat."

A decade later, she and Prince Florian married and joined their two kingdoms. I visited them and their children for many years, until Snow White was wrinkled and her black hair had turned white. Within less than a century, she and Florian were gone—and most of their children, too. I mourned their passing and did not visit The Surface as often after that, but the humans continued to tell the story of Snow White and the evil queen and the dwarves who got mixed up in their feud. The humans changed many of the details, leaving out the most important parts, adding things that never happened, until we dwarves didn't even have real names. That was the way with humans. They always wanted to be the most important characters in the story. But I guessed dwarves weren't really so different, or even trolls or gnomes. We just had different ideas about what was important.

On my hundredth birthday, Mother made me a marble cake, frosted with silver, studded with sapphires, and crowned with a single ruby. "A century! I can hardly believe how fast you're growing. Can you, Rubald?"

"I think he grew a full inch in one decade," said Father. He placed a granite box before me. "A small present."

The box was very warm, almost hot. I heard a small squeak, a little scratching against the stone. I eagerly took the lid off the box and gasped as I looked inside. Curled up and puffing steam out of its nostrils was a baby dragon.

"Your mother thought she'd be a good companion for you, keep you underground a little more." He winked.

I reached inside and picked her up. Her wings trembled. It reminded me of the first time I'd found Leaf. He'd died decades ago. I hadn't had the heart to replace him, but now . . .

"I'll train her to like The Surface," I said. "She can scare all the humans away."

"Oh no, that wasn't at all the idea!" said Mother.

I got a few bits of coal from our cooking cavern, and the dragon snatched them out of my hand. Her belly glowed with heat.

"What will you call her?" Father asked.

I looked her over. Her wings were much like Leaf's, but a little more knotty and gnarled. "Twig," I said.

Mother and Father shrugged at each other. Nearly two millennia between them, yet they'd never once seen such a common thing as a twig.

Twig ate a few more bits of coal, curled up in my hands, and fell asleep. She purred with contentment.

Decades passed. I explored The Mountain, The Woods, Yonder and Beyond, and even farther than that. When Twig grew to full size, we often explored The Surface together, discovering new lands, new kingdoms and mountains, forests and deserts, islands and seas. I found sorcerers, magicians, and witches who all made a mess of magic in one way or another, turning children into frogs and birds and bewitching your boots to travel seven leagues with every step and also make you itch for seven years with every step. The trolls did their part to collect and hide as much magic as possible, but it was a never-ending task. There was always some fool getting tangled in some curse or another.

I mapped all my travels right on the walls of our home in the caverns and recorded my findings on tablets and plates to be preserved in the records room. I gained a reputation among the other dwarves for my knowledge of The Surface. This reputation spread throughout the colony, and even to The Surface, where the humans believed that all dwarves had great knowledge and magic. Unfortunately, rumor also spread among humans that if they caught a dwarf by the beard, we'd have to grant them our help. I was careful to stay away from the villages and kingdoms, but every century or so, someone would catch me unawares.

More than two centuries after the first time I'd come to The Surface, I was marching in The Woods, very near the place our cottage had stood, when a little girl not more than a decade old caught me by the beard.

"Oh, Dwarf," said the girl. "I take thee by the beard and—er—request your assistance on my journey."

The magic overcame me. My beard tightened. The little girl looked so smug and superior, I couldn't help myself. I took the flat end of my ax and thumped her on the fizzy-bone.

What can I say? I'll always be a little bit of a grump.

# A GUIDE TO PRECIOUS STONES AND THEIR MAGICAL PROPERTIES

**amber:** pain relief and protection
**amethyst:** peace and tranquility
**beryl:** knowledge and intelligence
**citrine:** strength, energy, and longevity
**crystal ball:** fortune-telling
**diamond:** strength and clarity
**emerald:** heightened intuition and awareness
**jade:** love and generosity
**jasper:** relaxation and relief of nausea
**marble:** creativity and productivity
**obsidian:** focus and concentration
**opal:** creativity and imagination
**peridot:** friendliness and compassion
**pink topaz:** everlasting hopefulness and optimism
**reflecting stone:** self-awareness
**rose quartz:** intuition
**ruby:** long life, enhanced powers, and protection from evil
**sapphire:** truth and wisdom
**tourmaline:** happiness and compassion

# ACKNOWLEDGMENTS

Though writing a book is largely a singular task, I'm always amazed when I reflect on the many people who contributed their time and talents throughout the book's development. A thousand thanks to my editor, Katherine Harrison. This makes four books we've created together! I have loved every moment. May there be many more to come.

To my agent, Claire Anderson-Wheeler, thank you for always being there to talk through my craziness and assure me that I'm *not* crazy, even though I probably am.

To Katrina Damkoehler, Kevin Keele, and Jacey for a brilliant and hilarious cover. It still gives me a chuckle every time I look at it.

Thank you to the wonderful team of copy editors and proofreaders—Artie Bennett, Janet Wygal, Marianne Cohen, and Amy Schroeder—who must wade through my swamp of magic and complete nonsense and try to make it all "correct." You are all wizards! Any remaining mistakes are mine alone, in which case I made them on purpose!

To my critique partners and writing friends—Peggy Eddleman, Kate Hannigan, Brianna DuMont, Janet Lefley, Susan Tarcov, Erin Cleary, and Tabitha Olson—thank you for reading my first attempts and very rough drafts, sharing your wisdom, and offering encouragement and support along the way. And a special thanks to Franny Billingsley. I dropped by the bookstore often, supposedly to buy more books, and always came away with gold nuggets of writing advice. A bargain! Thank you for helping me figure out this story when I felt completely stuck.

To my sweet kids, Whitney, Ty, Topher, and our new little guy, Freddy. Thanks for being the best kids in the world. You make me a proud mama. And, Scott, thanks for . . . we don't have that much space. I love you a gazillion! Let's stay together for infinity.

And last but not least, it would be ungrateful of me if I didn't acknowledge the many teachers, librarians, book bloggers, and fans who have read, loved, and shared my books with their friends. You are the ones that breathe life into books. Rubies all around!

Red is not afraid of the big bad wolf.
She's not afraid of witches or pixies
or deep, dark caves,
or even enchanted beasts.
No, Red is not afraid of anything, except *magic*.
And there's magic at every turn in this tale!

**READ ON FOR A SNEAK PEEK!**

Published in the United States by Alfred A. Knopf, an imprint of Random House Children's Books,
a division of Penguin Random House LLC, New York.

# CHAPTER ONE

## Magical Mistakes

The first time I tried my hand at magic, I grew roses out of my nose. This was not my intention. I meant to grow flowers out of the *ground*, like any normal person would. But I've never been normal, and magic is unpredictable, finicky, and dangerous, especially in the wrong hands.

Granny had taught me magic from the cradle. Some grandmothers shower their grandbabies with cuddles and kisses and gumdrops. I got enchantments and spells and potions. Granny knew spells to conjure rain and wind, charms to make things grow or shrink, and enchantments of disguise and trickery. She could brew a potion to clear your mind or clear your stuffy nose. She had elixirs for toothaches, bellyaches, and heartaches, and a special balm for bottom itch. There was no end to the wonders of magic.

There was also no end to the troubles.

When I was five years old, I wanted to grow red roses for Granny's birthday. Roses, because her name is Rose, and red, because my name is Red. They would be the perfect gift. I knew I could do it. I had seen Granny grow fat orange pumpkins and juicy red berries straight out of the ground with just a wave of her hands and a few words.

I chose my own words with care.

**Red Rose Charm**

*Sprout and blossom, red, red rose*
*Let your fragrance fill my nose*

I felt the tingle of the magic in my fingertips. I gave a flourish of the arm, a flick of the hand, just as Granny did, but nothing happened. I tried again. I spoke louder, flourished grander, and . . .

A red rose exploded out of my right nostril.

I tried to rub the rose off, but that only made me sneeze, and another rose shot out of my left nostril.

Granny could not stop laughing. You might even say she cackled.

"Granny! Do some-ding!" I sobbed through the roses. I expected her to wave her hands and make the roses disappear. Instead, she ripped them right out of my nose.

"Aaaaouch!" I screamed.

"Thank you for the roses," said Granny, placing them in a vase on her table. "We can call them booger blossoms."

"*Achoo!*" I replied.

Granny laughed for a full five minutes.

I sneezed for five hours.

I'll admit, it was sort of funny, even if it did hurt worse than pixie bites. But I worried that this might be an omen—that the magic was somehow wrong inside me.

After the booger blossoms, I decided to stick to practical magic, such as a drying spell. I'd seen Granny do this countless times: just a snap of her fingers and she'd have dripping laundry dry in minutes.

But when I snapped my fingers, no wind came. Just fire. Yes, *fire*, as in flames. Flaming skirts and blouses and undergarments. In less than a minute, they were cinders and ash.

"Well, they're certainly dry," said Granny.

When I was six, I had a friend named Gertie. We were only allowed to play at her house with constant supervision from her mother, Helga. Helga was always worried. She worried Gertie would fall in a well or off a cliff. She worried Gertie would choke on her morning mush. She worried trolls would come in the night and carry Gertie away for their supper. This worrying became problematic when I wanted to take Gertie into The Woods to play.

"Mother says I'll be eaten by wolves," Gertie said.

"You won't," I said. "I've never been eaten by wolves, and I play in The Woods all the time."

"Don't you ever get lost? Mother is always afraid I'll lose my way."

"I'm never lost. I have a magic path." Gertie's eyes got as big as apples. Magic was rare, and my path was something special. It only appeared when I wanted it to, and it led me wherever I wanted to go in The Woods. Surely this would entice Gertie to come with me, but it didn't. She stepped away from me. Her eyes grew wary.

"Mother says magic is dangerous."

"My path isn't dangerous," I said with indignation. "Granny made it to keep me safe. She made it grow right out of the ground after a bear attacked me and I almost died." I thought this would impress her. The possibility of death was always exciting, and being able to defy it with magic was even better.

"Mother says your granny is a witch," said Gertie.

Of course Granny was a witch. I knew that, but Gertie said it like it was a bad thing. Desperation took hold of me. I *really* wanted to play with Gertie in The Woods. So I did the only sensible thing I could think of. I cast the Worrywart Spell on Gertie's mother.

**Worrywart Spell**

*Worry's a wart upon your chin*
*It spreads and grows from deep within*
*Make the wart shrink day by day*
*Send your worries far away*

Unfortunately, the spell did nothing to cure Helga's worries. Instead, she grew a wart on her chin. The wart grew steadily bigger, day by day, until Granny was summoned to remedy my mistake. Needless to say, I wasn't allowed to play with Gertie anymore—or anyone else—for, in addition to being a worrywart, Helga was also the village gossip. The news spread all over The Mountain.

"She's a witch," Helga told the villagers, "just like her grandmother." She seemed to forget it was Granny who had cured her.

Gertie stopped talking to me, and no one else would even look at me. The magic in me grew hot and sticky. It coated my throat. It stung my eyes. I wished I could swallow it down and make it disappear.

"Don't worry, Red," Granny told me. "We all make mistakes. When I was your age, I tried to summon a rabbit to be my pet, and instead I called a bear to the door!"

"No!" I cried. "How did you survive?"

"The bear was actually quite nice. My sister married him."

"She married a *bear*?"

"Oh, don't be ridiculous. He wasn't really a bear. He was a prince under a spell."

This did nothing to alleviate my concerns. I didn't want to marry a bear *or* a prince.

"All the magic I do is bad," I said.

"Nonsense, child," said Granny. "They're only mistakes. It takes a hundred miles of mistakes before you arrive at your own true magic."

"But what if my mistakes are too big?"

"No such thing, dear," said Granny.

But she was wrong. I went on trying spells and charms and potions, and I went on making mistakes. Big ones. Small ones. Deadly ones.

My last mistake was worse than warts, fire, or roses out the nose.

I was seven years old, and Granny and I were in The

Woods. It was early spring, so the trees were just budding. Granny thought I could help them grow.

**Growing Charm**
*Root in the earth*
*Sprout above ground*
*Swell in the sun*
*Spread all around*

"What if I burn down The Woods?" I asked, trembling. Fire seemed to be the only magic I had a knack for.

"Don't be afraid, Red," said Granny. She pointed to a tree branch above us, a large one that dipped low enough that I could see the little branches and buds shooting out of it. "Focus on that branch. Feel its energy and the energy inside you. They are connected. See if you can make its leaves grow. Growing is the best kind of magic."

Yes, I loved it when Granny made things grow. She could grow juicy strawberries and fat pumpkins, spicy herbs and fragrant blossoms. Roses. Granny was particularly good with roses.

I focused on the magic inside me. I felt it swirling in my belly, like a bubbling pot of soup ready to spill over. I felt it flow through my arms and to the edges of my fingertips. Then I let the magic pour out of me and flow toward the tree. The buds on the branch swelled and started to unfurl. Nothing exploded. Nothing caught fire.

"I'm doing it!" I said.

"Good!" said Granny. "Keep going!"

Buds kept swelling, leaves unfurling, until the branch

was full of green and pink. Then the branch itself started to grow. It got thicker and longer.

"Slow it down now," said Granny. "Pull that magic back inside."

But I couldn't. The magic bubbled and spilled out of me faster than I could control it. The branch swelled and extended, too big and heavy for the tree. It sagged and creaked.

Everything happened at once.

The branch snapped. Granny pushed me out of the way. As I tumbled to the ground, so did the branch. There was a scream and a crash. When I looked up, Granny was on the ground, trapped under the branch.

Her eyes were closed and she was still.

"Granny?" I raced to her. I shook her shoulder, but she didn't wake. There was blood on her face, a trickle of red that seeped into the lines on her cheek. My heart pounded in my chest. I tried to pull the branch off her, but it was too big and I was too small.

I ran out of The Woods, tears blurring my vision so I could barely see my path. When I reached home, I burst through the door, sobbing.

"She's dead! I killed her! I killed Granny!"

Papa ran into The Woods. Mama held me in her arms as I curled into a ball and trembled like a sapling in a thunderstorm. I cried and cried. In my mind, I could see Granny, eyes closed, still as stone, and the blood on her face bright red. It was a message.

*You did this, Red. You killed your granny.*

Mama could not calm me.

When Papa returned, he got down low and whispered to me. "She's all right, Red. Just a few scratches and a hurt foot. She's just fine." I started crying anew, flooded with relief and sorrow. She was alive, but still I had hurt her. It was my fault.

Granny's foot never quite healed after that. She had to use a cane, and she hobbled like an old lady—like a witch. I hated to see it, but it reminded me every day of what I had done, what I was. Granny may have been a witch, but she was a good witch. Her magic made things live and grow. My magic made them bleed and die. It didn't matter if this was mile ninety-nine of my hundred miles of mistakes, I couldn't journey one step farther.

I would never do magic again.

You might think you know all about giants and beanstalks and that foolish boy who traded his family's cow for some magic beans. But you don't know JACK!

READ ON FOR A SNEAK PEEK!

Published in the United States by Alfred A. Knopf, an imprint of Random House Children's Books,
a division of Penguin Random House LLC, New York.

Jack was brisk and of a ready, lively wit, so that nobody or nothing could worst him.

—*Jack the Giant Killer*

# CHAPTER ONE

## A Sprinkling of Dirt

When I was born, Papa named me after my great-great-great-great-great-great-GREAT-grandfather, who, legend had it, conquered nine giants and married the daughter of a duke. Mama said this was all hogwash. Firstly, there was no such thing as giants. Wouldn't we see such large creatures if they really existed? And secondly, we had no relation to any duke—if we did, we'd be rich and living on a grand estate. Instead, we were poor as dirt and lived in a tiny house on a small farm in a little village. Nothing great or giant about it.

But Papa wasn't concerned with the details. He

believed there was greatness in that name, and if he gave it to me, somehow the greatness would sink into my bones.

"We'll name him Jack," Papa said. "He'll be great."

"If you say so," said Mama. She was a practical woman and not particular with names. All she needed was a word to call me to supper, or deliver a scolding. I got my first scolding before my first supper, just after birth, for as soon as Papa pronounced my name, I sprang a sharp tooth, and bit my mother.

"Ouch!" Mama cried. "You naughty boy!" It was something she would call me more often than Jack.

Papa had the nerve to laugh. "Oh, Alice, he's just a baby. He doesn't know any better."

But Mama believed I *did* know better. To her, that bite was a little omen of what was to come, like a sprinkle before the downpour, a buzz before the sting, or the onset of an itch before you realize you're covered in poison ivy.

Maybe I was born to be great, but great at what?

At five months old, I learned to crawl. I was fast as a cockroach, Papa said. One minute I was by Mama's skirts, and the next I was in the pigsty, rolling around in the muck and slops. Mama said she had to bathe me twice a day just to keep me from turning into a real pig.

I learned to walk before my first year, and by my second I took to climbing. I climbed chairs and tables, the woodpile, trees. Once Mama found me on the roof, and snatched me up before I slid down the chimney into a blazing fire.

"Such a naughty boy," said Mama.

"He's just a boy," said Papa.

But I didn't want to be "just a boy." I wanted to be great.

At night, Papa would tell stories of Grandpa Jack: how he'd chop off giants' heads and steal all their treasure and rescue the innocents. I knew if I was going to be great, I'd have to go on a noble quest and conquer a giant—or nine—just like my seven-greats-grandpa Jack.

There was only one problem. I'd never seen a giant in all my twelve years.

In a magical kingdom where your name is your destiny, twelve-year-old Rump is the butt of everyone's joke, until an old spinning wheel changes everything. . . .

**READ ON FOR A SNEAK PEEK!**

Published in the United States by Alfred A. Knopf, an imprint of Random House Children's Books,
a division of Penguin Random House LLC, New York.

# CHAPTER ONE

## Your Name Is Your Destiny

My mother named me after a cow's rear end. It's the favorite village joke, and probably the only one, but it's not really true. At least I don't think it's true, and neither does Gran. Really, my mother had another name for me, a wonderful name, but no one ever heard it. They only heard the first part. The worst part.

Mother had been very ill when I was born. Gran said she was fevered and coughing and I came before I was supposed to. Still, my mother held me close and whispered my name in my ear. No one heard it but me.

"His name?" Gran asked. "Tell me his name."

"His name is Rump . . . *haaa-cough-cough-cough* . . ." Gran gave Mother something warm to drink and pried me from her arms.

"Tell me his name, Anna. All of it."

But Mother never did. She took a breath and then let out all the air and didn't take any more in. Ever.

Gran said that I cried then, but I never hear that in my imagination. All I hear is silence. Not a move or a breath. The fire doesn't crack and even the pixies are still.

Finally, Gran holds me up and says, "Rump. His name is Rump."

The next morning, the village bell chimed and gnomes ran all over The Mountain crying, "Rump! Rump! The new boy's name is Rump!"

My name couldn't be changed or taken back, because in The Kingdom your name isn't just what people call you. Your name is full of meaning and power. Your name is your destiny.

My destiny really stinks.

I stopped growing when I was eight and I was small to begin with. The midwife, Gertrude, says I'm small because I had only the milk of a weak goat instead of a strong mother, but I know that really it's because of my name. You can't grow all the way if you don't have a whole name.

I tried not to think about my destiny too much, but on my birthday I always did. On my twelfth birthday I thought of nothing else. I sat in the mine, swirling mud around in a pan, searching for gold. We needed gold, gold, gold, but all I saw was mud, mud, mud.

The pickaxes beat out a rhythm that rang all over The Mountain. It filled the air with thumps and bumps. In my head The Mountain was chanting, *Thump, thump, thump. Bump, bump, bump. Rump, Rump, Rump.* At least it was a good rhyme.

*Thump, thump, thump*
*Bump, bump, bump*
*Rump, Rump, Rump*

"Butt! Hey, Butt!"

I groaned as Frederick and his brother Bruno approached with menacing grins on their faces. Frederick and Bruno were the miller's sons. They were close to my age, but so big, twice my size and ugly as trolls.

"Happy birthday, Butt! We have a present just for you." Frederick threw a clod of dirt at me. My stubby hands tried to block it, but it smashed right in my face and I gagged at the smell. The clod of dirt was not dirt.

"Now that's a gift worthy of your name!" said Bruno.

Other children howled with laughter.

"Leave him alone," said a girl named Red. She glared at Frederick and Bruno, holding her shovel over her shoulder like a weapon. The other children stopped laughing.

"Oh," said Frederick. "Do you love Butt?"

"That's not his name," growled Red.

"Then what is it? Why doesn't he tell us?"

"Rump!" I said without thinking. "My name is Rump!" They burst out laughing. I had done just what they wanted. "But that's not my real name!" I said desperately.

"It isn't?" asked Frederick.

"What do you think his real name is?" asked Bruno.

Frederick pretended to think very hard. "Something unusual. Something special . . . Cow Rump."

"Baby Rump," said Bruno.

"Rump Roast!"

Everyone laughed. Frederick and Bruno fell over each other, holding their stomachs while tears streamed down their faces. They rolled in the dirt and squealed like pigs.

Just for a moment I envied them. They looked like they were having such fun, rolling in the dirt and laughing. Why couldn't I do that? Why couldn't I join them?

Then I remembered why they were laughing.

Red swung her shovel down hard so it stuck in the ground right between the boys' heads. Frederick and Bruno stopped laughing. "Go away," she said.

Bruno swallowed, staring cross-eyed at the shovel that was just inches from his nose. Frederick stood and grinned at Red. "Sure. You two want to be alone." The brothers walked away, snorting and falling over each other.

I could feel Red looking at me, but I stared down at my pan. I picked out some of Frederick and Bruno's present. I did not want to look at Red.

"You'd better find some gold today, Rump," said Red.

I glared at her. "I know. I'm not *stupid*."

She raised her eyebrows. Some people did think I was stupid because of my name. And sometimes I thought they were probably right. Maybe if you have only half a name, you have only half a brain.

I kept my eyes on my pan of mud, hoping Red would go away, but she stood over me with her shovel, like she was inspecting me.

"The rations are tightening," said Red. "The king—"

"I *know,* Red."

Red glared at me. "Fine. Then good luck to you." She stomped off, and I felt worse than when Frederick and Bruno threw poop in my face.

Red wasn't my friend exactly, but she was the closest I had to a friend. She never made fun of me. Sometimes she stood up for me, and I understood why. Her name wasn't all that great, either. Just as people laugh at a name like *Rump,* they fear a name like *Red. Red* is not a name. It's a color, an *evil* color. What kind of destiny does that bring?

I swirled mud in my pan, searching for a glimmer. Our village lives off The Mountain's gold—what little there is to find. The royal tax collector gathers it and takes it to the king. King Barf. If King Barf is pleased with our gold, he sends us extra food for rations. If he's not pleased, we are extra hungry.

King Barf isn't actually named King Barf. His real name is King Bartholomew Archibald Reginald Fife, a fine, kingly name—a name with a great destiny, of course. But I don't care how handsome or powerful that name makes you. It's a mouthful. So for short I call him King Barf, though I'd never say it out loud.

A pixie flew in my face, a blur of pink hair and translucent wings. I held still as she landed on my arm and explored. I tried to gently shake her off, but she only fluttered her wings and continued her search. She was looking for gold, just like me.

Pixies are obsessed with gold. Once, they had been very helpful in the mines since they can sense large veins of gold from a mile away and deep in the earth. Whenever a swarm of pixies would hover around a particular spot of rock, the miners knew precisely where they should dig.

But there hasn't been much gold in The Mountain for many years. We find only small pebbles and specks. The pixies don't dance and chirp the way they used to. Now they're just pests, pesky thieves trying to steal what little gold we find. And they'll bite you to get it. Pixies are no bigger than a finger and they look sweet and delicate and harmless with their sparkly wings and colorful hair, but their bites hurt worse than bee stings and squirrel bites and poison ivy combined—and I've had them all.

The pixie on my arm finally decided I had no gold and flew away. I scooped more mud from the sluice and swirled it around in my pan. No gold. Only mud, mud, mud.

*Thump, thump, thump*
*Bump, bump, bump*
*Rump, Rump, Rump*

I didn't find any gold. We worked until the sun was low and a gnome came running through the mines shouting, "The day is done! The day is done!" in a voice so bright and cheery I had the urge to kick the gnome and send it flying down The Mountain. But I was relieved. Now I could go home, and maybe Gran had cooked a chicken. Maybe she would tell me a story that would help me stop thinking about my birth and name and destiny.

I set my tools aside and walked alone down The

Mountain and through The Village. Red walked alone too, a little ahead of me. The rest of the villagers traveled in clusters, some children together, others with their parents. Some carried leather purses full of gold. Those who found good amounts of gold got extra rations. If they found a great deal, they could keep some to trade in the markets. I had never found enough gold even for extra rations.

Pixies fluttered in front of my face and chirped in my ears, and I swatted at them. If only the pixies would show me a mound of gold in the earth, then maybe it wouldn't matter that I was small. If I found lots of gold, then maybe no one would laugh at me or make fun of my name. Gold would make me worth something.

# ONE MAGICAL KINGDOM. FOUR FAMOUS CHARACTERS.

**READ ALL THE (FAIRLY) TRUE TALES!**

**"Lighthearted and inventive." —Brandon Mull, #1 *New York Times* bestselling author of *Fablehaven***

**"Liesl Shurtliff has the uncanny ability to make magical worlds feel utterly real." —Tim Federle, author of *Better Nate Than Ever***

**"*Red* is the most wonder-filled fairy tale of them all!" —Chris Grabenstein, *New York Times* bestselling author of *Escape from Mr. Lemoncello's Library***

**"Shurtliff excels at turning familiar worlds on their heads." —*The New York Times Book Review***

Photo: Erin Lake

# LIESL SHURTLIFF

grew up in Salt Lake City, Utah, and just as Snow White had seven dwarves, Liesl had seven siblings to keep her company! Before she became a writer, Liesl graduated from Brigham Young University with a degree in music, dance, and theater. Her first three books—*Rump, Jack,* and *Red*—are all *New York Times* bestsellers, and *Rump* was named to over two dozen state award lists and won an ILA Children's Book Award. She lives in Chicago with her family, where she continues to spin fairy tales.

LieslShurtliff.com